Secrets at the Ambrose Café

ALSO BY CARRYL CHURCH

STANDALONES
The Forgotten Life of Connie Harris
Secrets at the Ambrose Café

SECRETS
at the
AMBROSE
CAFÉ

CARRYL CHURCH

Choc Lit

A JOFFE BOOKS COMPANY

Choc Lit, London
A Joffe Books company
www.choc-lit.com

First published in Great Britain in 2025

Cover art by Jarmila Takač

ISBN: 978-1781898857

For John and Darren.

CHAPTER 1

Exeter, 1925

Della stepped back to assess the birthday cake. The first cake Hastings trusted her to decorate without guidance. Three tiers of sponge encased in fondant icing stood regal on a glass stand. Embossed gold-leaf frescos circled the base, edible pearls tumbled over the layers and the top was crowned with wishes to the birthday girl in swirls of chocolate ganache. Twenty-one silver candles finished the decadent masterpiece.

Mrs Hastings came to her side, flour-dusted hands resting on generous hips. Della felt the weight of the Ambrose's reputation heavy on her shoulders as her boss studied the cake, searching out imperfections.

Eventually she threw Della a smile. 'You've the steadiest hand, Della Wilde. That lettering is flawless.'

William crashed through the double doors to the kitchen, leaving them swinging back and forth long after his arrival. He weaved his tray aloft and dumped it on the washing trolley. 'It's getting a bit rowdy in there.' He cocked his head at the ballroom beyond the servery doors, where a birthday party was in full swing.

1

Anthony was next, spinning his empty tray like an acrobat. 'Della, they're ready for the cake.' He stopped to inspect her work. 'Blimey. It's beautiful.' He met her gaze, eyes wide with admiration.

A cheer from the other side of the doors snatched their attention. Anthony lit a match and set the candles ablaze.

'Ready?' He moved to take the trolley.

'I'll take it.' William stepped in his path, leaving Anthony little choice but to acquiesce.

Della followed her cake on its journey to the servery doors, hoping it lived up to the occasion. She opened one side — Anthony took the other. As William entered the party, more cheering erupted. It was a rare opportunity to hear guests take pleasure in her work. She lingered to see the clientele in their finery. The birthday girl stood on the top table, adorned in a crimson bias-cut dress twinkling with sequins. Long necklaces of jet beads fell in layers across her taut body. A feather boa trailed her sinewy arms, and a headband sat regally on dark blonde hair cut in the daring Eton crop. A single artfully sculpted curl escaped from behind her ear, which dripped with diamanté earrings. She turned, exposing a smooth, bare back. Della followed the contours of her spine to the base.

Anthony shared in her voyeuristic activity. 'I've never seen the like.'

'Who is she?' Della couldn't drag her gaze from the spectacle. Silk stockings and silver heels pranced among the café's finest china and cut-glass coupes. The birthday girl held one aloft while she threw her head back in laughter, exposing the tight ribbing of her neck. A cigarette smouldered at the end of a silver holder in her free bejewelled hand. A tuxedoed man looked on with proprietorial eyes.

'Alice Winters,' Anthony replied.

Della shrugged.

'You know, the MP Robert Winters. She's his daughter — and a handful by the looks of things.' He checked his watch and disappeared to collect more glasses.

Della returned her attention to the gathered party of about one hundred guests who were similarly adorned. How did rich people occupy the world with such ease and grace? Born to it, Della supposed. She remained where she was long enough for the birthday girl to crouch to cut the cake, offering a flash of garter. William stepped back, melting into the shadows, trained to anticipate his clients' every whim while remaining inconspicuous. An Ambrose waiter to the core.

Alice's tuxedoed companion gripped her arm as she sunk the large, silver knife into the layers of sponge. She straightened and the knife slid to the table with a clatter. Alice looked directly at Della and for a brief second her smile faltered, leaving her unmasked. Della broke her gaze and turned away, aware she'd crossed a line. Her job was done, time to go home.

* * *

The following morning, while night was still in command and rain misted her face, Della hurried past the baroque entrance of the Ambrose to the yard at the back. A squally wind sent debris skittering at her feet. Despite the February gloom, the sight of the building never failed to lift her spirits. It was easily the grandest in Exeter if you didn't count the cathedral, which wasn't for the likes of her.

On her way to the kitchen, where the ovens would see off the chill of the night, Della couldn't resist a peek at the abandoned ballroom before the other café staff arrived. With its sprung floor, marble columns and ceiling at a giddying height, it was one of the most glamorous rooms the Ambrose could offer.

The scene of the previous evening's birthday party remained vivid in her mind as she pushed her way through the double doors. Stale smoke, alcohol and sweat lingered in the fetid air. Della threw open a couple of windows and the noise of the awakening city spilled into the room. A tram rattled past, a bicycle bell. She weaved between tables, the parquet tacky beneath her feet, picking up discarded streamers, burst balloons and paper hats. A black tie dangled from one of the chandeliers. The distant hum of a hoover told her the cleaners would be here soon and none too pleased over the mess that awaited them.

Della pulled up short at the top table where the birthday girl had pranced the previous evening, her gaze met with wanton destruction, her painstakingly decorated cake smeared over every surface. Clumps stuck to the columns, the table, the chairs. The candles were scattered, and cake footprints made a mess of the floor. *Bloody gentry.* All her hard work and they'd used her handicraft for a food fight. She looked at the trolley, still housing the elegant glass stand on which the remnants of the cake lay crushed, an indistinguishable heap of crumbs and icing. It wasn't as if such a thing were destined for her stomach, but she liked to imagine it all the same. That first bite, the crunch of the sweet icing contrasting with the sponge melting on her tongue.

A soft groan emitted from beneath the stained tablecloth. Della crouched, moving the starched linen to one side. There in a heap lay the birthday girl, heavy eye make-up smudged, a blonde curl stuck to her cheek, rouged lips parted and chapped. Della dropped the cloth and took a step back. She'd broken the Ambrose rule, pulled aside the invisible veil. If this girl was an MP's daughter as Anthony said, she wouldn't take kindly to being humiliated in front of a subordinate. Della was about to move away when manicured fingers closed around her ankle.

'Oi!' She startled despite herself and lifted the cloth again to find those kohled, bloodshot blue eyes staring back at her.

'Help me,' the birthday girl whispered.

Della cast around the room in the vain hope she might be addressing someone else before crouching at her side. 'You alright, Miss?'

'No.' It was an abrupt but honest answer. 'Where's Toby?'

'I dunno who you're referring to, Miss, but there ain't no one here but us.'

4

The large eyes dilated. 'You've got to get me out of here.' The woman gripped her ankle again for emphasis.

William walked in and began loading a tray with empty glasses. Della dropped the tablecloth, finding her ankle released.

'Blimey, Del, you scared me half to death. Shouldn't you be in the kitchens?'

She made to move but her ankle had once again been accosted, this time with a light squeeze. Sensing her new friend didn't want William to know about her existence, Della searched for a distraction. 'Can you tell Mrs Hastings I'm on my way.' She gestured to the debris. 'Look at this mess.'

'The cleaners will see to that.' William ceased his work and took a step closer. The hand slid back under the table. He leaned against the column, the very column where she'd let him kiss her at the staff Christmas party after one too many glasses of punch. It wasn't an experience she intended to repeat, but William hadn't disguised the fact he'd been looking for another opportunity ever since. He studied her face. A stupid grin spread across his lips, suggesting he was thinking about it too. His eyes sparked with curiosity. 'What are you hiding?'

Denial was futile; she'd never achieved a convincing poker face. She'd have to pass off the truth as fiction. Della met his probing gaze. 'You got me. The birthday girl is under this table, she wants me to sneak her out.'

He smirked. 'Funny. As if Alice Winters would spend the night on the floor. Alright, I'll tell Hastings her protégé is on her way. She won't like it though.'

Alice, that was her name. Della fussed with the cake until William finished loading his tray and disappeared through the doors.

'Gosh.' Alice emerged from beneath the cloth with a speed that belied her state. 'You like to play it close.'

'Says the lady passed out drunk under the table.' Della sucked in a breath, cursing her lack of deference.

Alice's smudged lips twitched into a smile. 'How are you going to smuggle me out?'

5

Casting around the room, her gaze settled on the cake trolley. It was big enough to fit someone of Alice's size underneath. She lifted the cloth.

Alice folded herself in.

Della gripped the handle. 'Hold on tight.'

She heaved the trolley through the double doors and almost collided with Mrs Hastings, a rare look of irritation across her face.

'You're late.'

'Sorry, Mrs Hastings, I got distracted. Look what they done to my cake.'

Hastings surveyed the mess on the trolley, her expression softened. 'Ah, Della, you poor love. The gentry can be an inconsiderate bunch of spoiled brats.'

Della wondered what Alice was making of Hastings' assessment of her class from under the trolley. 'They really can,' she added, rather enjoying herself.

'Take it downstairs to the servery, they'll get rid of it.'

'Right away.'

William was leaning against the tradesman's lift, drawing on a cigarette, when she emerged from the kitchen. 'Are you following me?'

'Don't flatter yourself, I'm taking the cake downstairs.'

He rested his hand over hers on the trolley handle. Threads of dark hair protruded from the crisp white cuff of his shirt. She forced her eyes to meet his.

That smirk again. 'You *are* hiding something.'

'I ain't.' His hand was clammy and she wriggled free.

'Alright, I'll take it down.' He crushed his cigarette and called the lift. 'Anything for my favourite girl.'

Della didn't want to be his favourite girl. 'It's my cake.'

He sighed. 'Fine, take your precious cake. I've got better things to do with my time.'

The lift creaked, announcing its arrival. William pulled the gate open and gestured for her to go through. He closed it behind her and put his face to the bars. 'I'm onto you, Della

Wilde.' He winked as she pressed the button for the basement and the lift carried her away.

A giggle erupted from the trolley. Della crouched and shifted the cloth to one side. Those large kohled eyes blinked back at her, filled with mirth. 'He's a charmer.'

'I can handle his sort.'

'I could do with a dose of your courage.'

'Says the woman who was dancing on the tables last night.'

Alice's smile faltered as if she, like Della, was remembering the brief look they'd exchanged. 'I can act the fool. Trouble is, sometimes I'm not sure I'm acting.'

Della had no idea how to respond, but the lift ground to a halt, providing distraction. 'Here we are.' She dropped the cloth, snatching her view of Alice's troubled expression, and heaved the gate aside. They hurried through the basement servery, where rows upon rows of glasses, teacups, plates and polished silver gleamed in the weak morning light. The air was perfumed with the scent of bacon and eggs waiting under domed serving dishes. Trays of toast, pots of butter and jam.

Della's stomach rumbled as she pushed the trolley, unnoticed among the hubbub, through a storeroom before arriving at the back entrance. 'You can come out now.'

Alice emerged and unfolded her long body. She was a head taller than Della and all limbs. 'Thanks for the ride.'

'You're welcome, Miss.'

'Alice.'

Della gestured to the door. 'Follow the alleyway out of the yard and you'll be on Bedford Street.'

Alice remained rooted to the spot, staring at the remnants of cake. Perhaps she hadn't heard or was going to apologise for the mess her thoughtless friends made. Della prepared to be gracious, but instead, Alice scooped a chunk of icing and took a bite.

Della rocked back and forth on her pumps, aware they might be caught any moment. Icing dusted Alice's lips, which spread into a grin. She licked them then made for the open door, disappearing through it like a mirage, feather boa trailing behind.

At the corner of the yard, she turned and blew Della a kiss.

She might not have apologised for wrecking the cake, but somehow it didn't matter anymore.

CHAPTER 2

Alice pulled the bell at the Winters residence — the *winter*
house, as she thought of her home, thanks to the chill which
ran from its very foundations to the last of its elegant chim-
neys. It was also the colour of snow. A Georgian stucco man-
sion nestled among its similarly elaborate neighbours in one
of Exeter's most desired addresses.

The echo of Gillespie's tread on the polished parquet
floor thundered in her head until the door drew open. 'Miss
Alice.' He nodded in greeting. His inscrutable expression gave
nothing away. If she told Gillespie his hair was on fire, he
wouldn't react. Were all Scots as dour as him? She caught sight
of her ravaged visage in the gilt-framed hall mirror, slipped off
her heels and hauled herself up the stairs. At the top, she threw
the butler a wave as he hovered at the bottom — a nod in
deference and the tiniest hint of irritation in the curl of his lip
before he retreated to the kitchen. He had opinions after all.

Despite her night on the ballroom floor, the hour was
not yet sufficient for her nocturnal absence to be noticed.
Mummy seldom rose before midday and Father would have
been ensconced in his study since dawn, if he'd left it at all.

In her bedroom, Alice unfurled the feather boa and slung
it across the chair. Toby said it was gauche. She supposed

9

it was, but that's what attracted her to it. She suspected he thought her rather gauche too. She checked her arm, still irritated by his clamping fingers when she'd cut the cake. 'Steady on there, girl,' he'd whispered, a tautness to his jaw. His concern for her propriety hadn't stretched to seeing her home.

Tobias Roland. She liked the way his name rolled off her tongue. His family were something big in banking. Alice met him at one of her mother's interminable fundraising dinner parties. It hadn't escaped her attention they'd been thrown together — a young woman from a good family and an eligible man of a marriageable age. Alice had determined to be thoroughly uncommunicative all evening, but Toby disarmed her with his wry observations about the other guests, and much to her irritation she'd found herself charmed.

Weeks later he'd cornered her in her parents' drawing room, eyes sparking with intrigue. 'You need taming, Alice Winters.' She'd taken it as a backhanded compliment, liked the idea of herself as this wild, unruly thing, but what he'd meant was she needed him to give her credibility. Everyone knew her parents' marriage was as chilly as their name. They were a raging cliché wrapped up in a package of thinly veiled respectability. Alice's only escape was Toby. Her mother was convinced it was just a matter of time until a diamond ring was put on her finger. She could see it all. Toby's confident expression as he entered her father's study seeking permission. The satisfied smiles from the men as they emerged, puffing cigars, pleased with the trade-off. Alice's eviction from the winter house would be secured. But what would she be escaping to?

The question troubled her as Alice slid out of her dress and pulled on her pyjamas. She filled the sink, peeled the eyelashes from her arid lids and ran a flannel over her face. The crimson and black of her make-up swirled down the plug hole. The apparition of Alice Winters. She studied what was left in her hand mirror — her true self, unmasked. Tired, wan eyes, naked without their embellishments, the small cluster of spots forming on her chin, the pale slice of her mouth pulled into a grimace. Bed and oblivion for a few hours would set things right.

But the winter house teamed with the comings and goings of its occupants. How noisy it was, when ordinarily it was sombre as a mausoleum. The crash of a pan from the kitchen, a caller at the front door, a delivery at the back. Half an hour later, Alice gave up all hope of rest, pulled the sleeping mask from her eyes and stared at the ceiling, studying the rose at the centre of her chandelier.

A smile crept across her lips as she recalled her dawn escapade on the trolley. Those few minutes provided more fun than the whole of her birthday party. Della. Not an easy person to forget. She liked the way Della talked to that obsequious waiter, the way her eyes sparkled and the unruly nature of her black curls. If only they hadn't ruined the cake. The memory caused the queasiness in her stomach to rise. Overindulgence and shame for the idiocy of the people she called friends. Alice couldn't recall who'd started the food fight, only at the time she'd found it hilarious. Part of her hadn't wanted the party at all, but she'd succumbed to the pressure to mark her twenty-first birthday in a suitably raucous manner.

Throwing back her covers, Alice pulled her robe over her pyjamas and made for the door. A deathly quiet now descended on the house as if it knew she was on the move, tiptoeing along the landing to the stairs at the back, the naked wood chill against her bare feet. She climbed to the top and hurried past the servants' rooms, where the musty smell of neglect contrasted with the scent of wax and Brasso that lingered in the polished realms of the main house. One thing she could rely on was that the servants rarely frequented their quarters during daylight hours unless one of them was ill.

The key was where she'd left it, beneath a dusty spider plant on the window ledge. Alice unlocked the door at the end of the corridor and slipped inside.

Rays of sunlight fell across the floor from the attic windows, catching dust motes dancing as if in the grip of a complex ragtime tune. Alice moved behind the folding screen which guarded her secret and revealed the easel in the centre.

She studied the painting before her — a portrait of Toby. It was all wrong, as she concluded the last time she analysed it and the time before that. There was something missing. His gaze appeared lifeless, even a little cold. Perhaps a manifestation of her ambivalence? It never did to work from memory, and she could hardly ask Toby to sit for her when he knew nothing of her clandestine hobby. Except it wasn't *just* a hobby, not really. It was the thing that gave her life meaning. Dramatic perhaps, but true. Alice hated to abandon work but now a new form assembled in her mind, one she couldn't ignore.

Retrieving a piece of sandpaper from a box of supplies she kept under an old daybed at the room's centre, Alice removed the rough edges of paint from the canvas. Next, she wiped the surface with a soft cloth then selected her thickest brush and set about erasing Toby with gesso. There was something satisfying about the act, a feeling she was disinclined to examine. It would take several coats but already she could see the outline of a new image taking form in her eye. The black curly hair as unruly as her name, the pale skin, the sharp cheekbones. Della Wilde would leap from the canvas as she leaped from life. Alice had to find a way to paint her.

CHAPTER 3

Della walked home that evening feeling ruffled, like the feathers on Alice's feather boa trailing in the yard, as if she too had been dragged through something murky. How had an MP's daughter ended up abandoned under the banquet table? That question troubled her all day.

Such was her reverie, she didn't notice the puddle. Her pumps oozed with ice-cold brown water, sending a shiver travelling down her spine. After the unexpected events of the morning, the day passed in a haze of breakfast rolls, warm on their platters sent down to the basement servery, afternoon tea, delicate sandwiches — no crusts, of course — and cakes brimming with buttercream. Della's stomach rumbled again, a side effect of her job. It wasn't easy working with so much food when the offerings at home weren't exactly plentiful. Everything about the café and its clientele screamed excess, but why was it the privilege of a few? People like Alice and her friends who saw a cake not as a work of artistry and a lavish indulgence, but as a mere frippery in a long line of disposable things. A bubble of anger surfaced, not at Alice — her mournful eyes told of their own troubles — but at the injustice of it all.

13

A gust of wind sent her skirt flailing over her stockings. She pulled her cloche hat down a little further and stuffed in an errant curl. It escaped and thwacked her again. If she were brave enough to get her hair cut like Alice, she wouldn't have this problem.

The strengthening breeze was doing its work on the laundered sheets slung in rows across the bricked-in yard when Della walked through the gate. She used the privy then entered the back of their terrace.

Her mother's cheek was warm as it brushed against hers in the kitchen. 'Anything left over today?' She eyed Della's satchel.

'Sorry, Ma.' After her disaster with the cake, she hadn't felt able to help herself to the stale bread that was sometimes on offer at the end of the day.

Her mother turned her back, a rebuke, and attacked the pan of potatoes with a masher.

Della hung her coat on the row of pegs by the back door. Six pegs for the six Wilde children, only four needed now. She slipped out of her wet shoes and put them by the stove to dry, then slid down her stockings and slung them over the rail.

Condensation misted the window. Puddles collected on the cracked ledge as she scrubbed her hands at the sink, pulled on an apron and rescued the pot of stew bubbling on the stove.

Five minutes later, the family assembled around the table. She took her place, squashed between Jack and Henry, older and younger respectively, while Samuel and Ma settled on the other side. Della couldn't fathom why her mother insisted they keep the head of the table and two seats empty when space was scarce. Almost seven years since the end of the war, it wasn't as if her dad and two eldest brothers were about to walk through the door.

She caught young Samuel's eye and threw him a wink as Ma put her hands together in prayer and they dutifully bowed their heads.

While Ma gave thanks, Della's mind strayed to Alice. Their meeting had brought a touch of glamour to an otherwise ordinary day. She couldn't picture Alice in a setting like this. Squeezed, shoulder to shoulder, jostling for space, the banter, the solemn reproach of the empty seats to keep their levity in check. Della struggled to picture Alice anywhere other than prancing up and down, lit by chandeliers, drawing every eye in the room.

'Della.' The table came slowly back into focus. Jack was eyeballing her, the pot of mash potato offered in his outstretched hand. 'What's got into you this evening?'

'I reckon she's sweet on that waiter she brought home,' Henry joined in.

'Shut up, Henry.' Della scraped the pan, pushing away the memory of William seated at this very table after he'd invited himself to tea. She sighed, ignoring their jibes, and forked lukewarm mash into her mouth.

Henry elbowed her to show he'd only been teasing. It was harmless banter to him. Della being the only girl, she was the butt of everyone's jokes. Tonight, she couldn't play the role with good humour. Her adventure with Alice hovered on the tip of her tongue, but Ma would find it unseemly, and her brothers tarnish it somehow. Instead, she filed Alice away. A secret for later.

'Any luck finding work today?' Ma asked Jack.

Della's back stiffened. Jack shook his head, his gaze focused on the thin stew. 'We can't all be like Della.' He muttered the words, but their bitter hue reached her ears. Ma met her gaze, the rebuke again. Why twist the knife when unemployment was through the roof and Della was the only one bringing in a regular wage? Would Ma rather she gave up her job to save Jack's pride? Sometimes she believed she would.

As soon as the meal was over, Della volunteered to do the dishes while her family dispersed to various parts of the house. Ma to the front parlour to take up her mending from the staggering pile that supplemented their income. Jack repaired to the yard to smoke. The clatter of feet on the stairs carried Samuel to a game in the attic. Henry's considered tread followed to his books and dreams.

Della took pleasure in the emerging quiet of the kitchen, save for the hiss of the copper boiler and the judder of a train pulling through St Thomas station, but Jack's resentment lingered in her mind. She recalled his face the day she came home with the news she'd got a permanent job at the Ambrose, eager to alleviate their precarious circumstances. To make Ma and Jack proud. His mask slipped long enough for Della to understand something had shifted between them. Jack had not long stepped into his role as man of the house, born too late to join Pa and their brothers at war, too early to live free of the burden of responsibility enjoyed by Henry and Samuel. She'd thought her job would ease his load. The opposite was true. All Jack could see was that Della — a mere girl — got to work, while he didn't. Never mind she'd trained long and hard for her place at the Ambrose, never mind that maybe she deserved it. Deserved more.

Outside in the yard, she could see Jack's cigarette, a spark against the darkening sky. In the old days she would have joined him, a ready ear for his woes, but her sympathy wasn't welcome anymore. Instead, while her hands plunged in the warm, soapy water, Alice reappeared in her thoughts. The image of her walking through the yard, dodging puddles of rainwater under the sodium rays of early morning. Della supposed they all had their secrets, and none was so disinclined to share as her.

16

CHAPTER 4

Alice followed Toby up the grand staircase, her fingers gliding the curvature of the banister to the gallery tables on the upper floor, offering a view of the bustling café beneath. The perfect vantage point to see the comings and goings of the Ambrose clientele, not to mention the staff, although now she recalled, Della hadn't been wearing a waitress uniform. Of course, she worked behind the scenes. Disappointment settled on her as Toby pulled out a chair, solicitous since he'd picked her up from the winter house, proud as a peacock in his new car.

They'd made up, or rather Alice decided to overlook his shortcomings for the opportunity to return to the Ambrose on his arm. The café band at the far end of the room raised her spirits and she tried to relax into the convivial atmosphere. When her gaze returned to Toby, he was studying her with a quizzical expression as if he were trying to work her out and wasn't entirely satisfied with what was being revealed. It was like looking into the face of a disgruntled parent rather than her intended. What effect might it have in the bedroom? All pre-emptive explorations suggested Toby was up to the job and he had experience. How ghastly to be a pair of innocents fumbling in the dark. When Toby finally took her to bed,

17

he'd know what was required and how to get the best result. If only she were a bit more certain about what that was. It struck her men had the better deal. A woman's body was a thing of beauty — soft, curvaceous, abundant. What did a woman get in return? A foreign landscape of muscle and hair, neither of which appealed. That rather bothered her too.

'I have some business.' Toby broke into her thoughts, gesturing to the basement room. 'Are you alright here for a while?' Without waiting for a reply, he stood and as an after-thought pointed at the menu. 'Order whatever you want.'

Alice watched him leave — the confident way his long legs took the stairs, the hint of pink at the centre of his crown where his hair thinned. He rounded the corner and disap-peared into the bowels of the café.

Her gaze roamed over the clientele. Ladies her mother's age, clinging to the fashions of the previous decade. Ankle-length dresses, large hats, ruffled necklines. Secretaries, smart in their work suits. Neat, bobbed hair under cloche hats, heads bowed in gossip. Alice was aware she didn't have close friends. There were always people to be found, parties to join, but no one who held her confidences and shared their own. After finishing-school in Lausanne, she'd returned to Exeter to languish at the winter house while her counterparts became engaged. Alice wanted more, had known it for years. The dusty attic room contained her dreams of art school, but were those dreams dusty too? Painting was all very well as a feminine accomplishment, but as a career? Mummy would find it absurd, not that she'd had the temerity to ask her. *Why foster rejection?*

A waiter whipped by in a gust of air and stopped at the next table. Alice recognised his voice as belonging to the man who'd accosted Della when she'd been hiding on the trolley. The memory teased a smile from her lips.

'Excuse me,' she called on impulse.

He came to her side, his dark hair slick with brilliantine. 'Are you ready to order, Miss?'

'There was a girl at my party the other evening, a girl who makes cakes.'

A brief frown then his expression cleared. 'That would be Della. She works in the kitchens. I hope the cake was to your satisfaction?'

Alice shifted in her seat, a flame of heat at her cheeks. 'It was wonderful. I wanted to thank her for the beautiful cake. I'm afraid we didn't treat it with the respect it deserved, and it's been playing on my mind rather.'

His puzzled expression suggested he found her reasoning strange.

'I hoped to speak with her so I might make amends,' she coaxed.

He dismissed the notion with a wave of his hand. 'Please don't trouble yourself.' His demeanour matched his obsequious tone.

'Oh, but I am troubled,' Alice pressed.

He brushed a piece of fluff from his sleeve, clearly bewildered or bored by her insistence. 'Della isn't suitably dressed for front of house. The Ambrose has certain rules. If you wouldn't mind coming to the corridor in five minutes—' he gestured to the doorway at the back of the balcony — 'I can have Della meet you there.'

'Excellent, you've been most helpful . . .'

'William,' he volunteered, then, bowing his head, hurried away towards what she presumed was the back corridor where the kitchen doors were concealed from general view.

Alice checked the clock above the band, who were playing a foxtrot. She tapped her foot in rhythm to the tune but despite its speed, time seemed to slow and still no sign of Toby.

He appeared as she stood. 'Where are you going?' That proprietorial hand on her arm again.

'Powder room.'

She sensed his eyes on her as she walked away. Would this be her life if they became engaged, a thing to be watched, questioned, owned? She squashed the thought and slipped into the corridor — the steamed-up windows of the kitchen, the clash of pans, the hum of raised voices. A secret world. Venturing towards the voices, nerves overcame her. *How to begin?* To invite Della to tea by way of apology for the cake would be crossing a line, but she wanted to get her to the winter house somehow, to have Della sit before her in all her splendour. She couldn't let this opportunity slip through her fingers.

CHAPTER 5

Della wiped her hands down her apron and pulled off her cap. An unruly curl bobbed up her forehead. She licked her fingers and attempted to flatten it. Ma said it was a cowlick, that her father had been exactly the same. She considered putting the cap back on, but the apron was mortifying enough.

Alice had her back to her when Della pushed open the doors. She paused to drink her in, the long line of her neck, the sculpted hair forming a V at her nape. Anthony came up behind with a loaded tray, forcing her through the doors. Alice turned, an uncertain expression quickly put away, her lips parting into a grin but her eyes betraying anxiety. Della grinned too, a shared secret. The trolley. The ludicrous escape.

She opened her mouth to speak. Alice got there first.

'I wanted to thank you again for yesterday morning and to apologise for the cake.'

'Think nothing of it, Miss.'

'Alice, please. I hope you didn't get in any trouble?'

Della shook her head. 'No trouble.'

Relief filled Alice's eyes. 'Good.'

Anthony returned, throwing her a bemused smile as he pushed past. A silence stretched out while Alice's gaze held hers. Neither seemed inclined to tear themselves away.

Della became aware of William on the other side of the window smirking behind Alice's head. Her cheeks flamed. Why did he have to goad her so?

'You have work to do,' Alice said, her anxious expression not so easily disguised this time. Della longed to put Alice at ease, but a wall of decorum stood between them. Instead, she gave a brief nod.

Alice rummaged in the embroidered bag hooked over her arm. For a mortifying second, Della thought she was going to give her money, and she drew breath. As much as it was needed, the embarrassment would be acute, the cheapening of the moment they'd shared. Her chest relaxed when Alice handed her a small, white card. Della turned it over between her fingers. Embossed in black ink was an address in St Leonards.

'Come soon,' Alice whispered, an urgent plea, a waft of expensive perfume, then she was gone.

Della didn't follow her progress but remained rooted to the spot, staring at the space Alice occupied only seconds before as if a trace was left behind. William shoved the door and a gust of hot air blew in her face.

'What did her ladyship want? You look like you've seen a ghost.'

Della rallied. 'Nothing to concern you.' She slid the card into her apron pocket and pushed past him, glad for the hub-bub of the kitchen.

* * *

That evening, she left for home having transferred the card from her apron pocket to her coat, the address now lodged firmly in her memory. Petrichor lifted off the rain-drenched cobbles — a packed tram rattled past. Working the card between her fingers, she worried over what Alice meant. There was something about the urgency in her whisper Della couldn't fathom. Was Alice scared or lonely? Did she feel the way Della . . . The idea was too dangerous to entertain. She tucked it away and considered other options. If Alice was in trouble, why choose a bakery assistant as her rescuer? It couldn't be that. And what an odd invitation — what time should she call and on which day? Was she being invited as a guest or something else? Should she use the back entrance? The house was bound to have one. What would she wear? Was Alice offering her a job? None of these options made sense when Della considered the mode of the invitation, if it could be described as an invitation at all.

These questions still troubled Della as she entered her home through the back door, pulled off her coat and read the room, as was so often required for the evening to get off on the right footing. The first clue was the absence of dinner on the stove, the second that Ma still wore her nightdress, her hair greasy and falling in clumps around her scalp. Samuel sat at the kitchen table, worry lines furrowing his usually smooth brow. He held her gaze with his large, brown eyes as if he were communicating something important only Della would understand. She searched her mind for the source of her mother's malady. Ma was prone on occasion to these dark episodes. A cloud would descend, and she'd take to her bed, sometimes for days. Della searched out the date and realised the cause. It was Pa's birthday.

She took Ma's rough hands, felt the bump on her finger from hours with a needle and thread. 'You get off to bed, Ma. Put your feet up. I'll take care of everything here.'

Ma's gaze met hers and it was as if she was noticing her for the first time. She nodded and, without another word, disappeared through the door.

'What's wrong with her?' Samuel's voice was small.

Della turned to face him. 'Ma's a bit sad. She misses Pa sometimes and it gets her down. She'll be right as rain in the morning.' How she hoped those words were true. Last time it was a fortnight before Ma found the wherewithal to engage with life again.

Samuel's young shoulders slumped with the weight of things he didn't understand. Della wrapped her arms around him and gave his slight frame a squeeze. 'Where is everyone?'

'Henry's upstairs reading. Jack said he had to go out and not to bother with dinner 'cos it didn't look like there'd be any bloody dinner.'

Della clipped Samuel's ear. 'You don't need to quote word for word.' She frowned. 'Out where?'

Samuel shrugged.

She didn't press him further. It wasn't Samuel's job to keep tabs on the eldest Wilde.

'Right.' Della forced a bright smile. 'Mash and stew for dinner again. You peel and I'll chop. Let me see those hands.'

He held up his small, neat hands for inspection.

'They'll do.' She searched the sack by the stove and passed her brother a peeler and a couple of sprouting potatoes, pushing Alice and her invitation from her mind. She had enough on her plate without adding the problems of rich girls who'd forgotten their place. There was an order to things, Ma told her often enough. It's them and us, the haves and the havenots. The Wildes were firmly in the latter camp and no good ever came from mixing the two. She glanced at Samuel, brow furrowed in concentration, wishing she could be so easily absorbed. The problem was, despite her resolve, Della wanted to visit Alice Winters. She wanted to know everything about her, even the dark bits, the dangerous bits. Especially those.

CHAPTER 6

Alice cursed herself through the rest of the meal, the short drive home and now, as she stood before the blank canvas. She couldn't have messed up her invitation to Della more if she'd tried. 'Come soon.' What did that even mean? Della looked confused and mortified. Who could blame her? It felt impossible to ask her to sit and yet she couldn't conjure another excuse. She circled the easel and Della's face filled the canvas, the potential for what she could create. Memory wasn't enough, she needed Della before her to capture the essence of the portrait in her head.

Her father's deep intonation from the floor below pulled her from her downward trajectory. Alice froze and listened. He was in her mother's bedroom — an argument, judging by the elevated agitation of their voices. She sighed, never more convinced they'd be better off calling it a day. If Father would only pay Mummy a little attention, perhaps she'd be less inclined to find fault. The voices faded, suggesting the disagreement had come to an end. Alice returned her focus to the canvas when the creak of a floorboard on the landing outside held her in place.

'Are you there?'

Her father, a softness to his tone. Did he know about her hiding place? She hovered with her hand inches from the handle, torn between revealing herself and the security of her secret. He muttered something indiscernible, and footsteps carried him away.

Overcome with curiosity, Alice waited a moment then emerged from the room. The narrow landing was empty, the servants' doors closed. She ventured to the floor below, again an eerie silence. In the entrance hall, she hovered outside his study, took a deep breath and knocked.

'Come.'

He sat in his wingback chair by the hearth, where a fire snapped in the grate, his attention focused on the papers in his lap. Alice cleared her throat and he raised his head, a hint of irritation dispelled by a bemused smile.

'Alice, what brings you to my door?' He gestured to the chair opposite. A rare invitation to linger.

'Were you looking for me?'

Father frowned. 'What makes you think that?'

If not her, then who did he seek in the attic rooms? She shrugged to hide her confusion and relief that her secret appeared to be safe. 'My mistake, I must be hearing things. How's Mummy?'

'Why don't you ask her yourself? I'm sure she'd appreciate your company.'

'I heard . . .'

'What did you hear?'

Alice shook her head, losing her nerve. 'Nothing.'

'Was there something you wanted, Alice? Because I have much to do.' He gestured to the papers in his lap.

Already on her feet, Alice made for the door. 'Sorry, I shan't bother you again.'

She hesitated on the other side. A curious racing in her chest always accompanied her dealings with her father, as if she feared and loved him intensely in the same moment. Alice wondered if it had always been like this or if the war and her years away at school muddied the picture of the man he'd been before. Hazy memories accompanied her up the stairs. Her arms hooked around his neck as he carried her across the beach at Exmouth, screams and laughter when he threatened to throw her in the sea. The tang of salt air and seaweed. The bristle of his moustache as he kissed her goodnight after a bedtime story. Alice knew his work put him under immense pressure, perhaps she was being oversensitive, but she wanted more than her mother now received. She wanted to make art, to exist in a world where she mattered for herself, not as a charming adornment to a cold man. Art could give her that, and not by privileged means but by hard work, talent and dedication. She opened the door to the room where she allowed herself to dream.

* * *

Della arrived at the winter house the following afternoon. Gillespie came to Alice after lunch while she was playing cards with her mother in the sitting room, determined to be a better daughter. Discreet to his core, he conveyed in a whisper that a person of a lower class had called at the front door. He'd sent her to wait in the kitchen. Alice shot up, almost upsetting the card table. Her stomach thrummed with anticipation as she followed the butler below stairs.

Della spun around when they entered, those sharp cheekbones flushed with embarrassment more than pleasure, judging by her pained expression. Alice wanted to put her at ease but settled for an awkward handshake conducted under Gillespie's curious gaze.

She turned to the butler, her voice overbright. 'Thank you, Gillespie, Della has business with me.'

He nodded and backed away at the tinkle of the bell coming from the sitting room.

Alice returned her attention to Della. 'I'm sorry, you shouldn't have been left to wait in the kitchen.'

27

Della shook her head. 'I had a half-day owed. You never said when to come and I wasn't sure the purpose of my visit, but I didn't like to keep you waiting in case it was important.' Her words tumbled out in a rush.

Alice saw her folly again, the worry she'd caused Della over something as trivial as social awkwardness. 'I'm glad you came. Would you like tea?'

Della cast around the kitchen before shaking her head. Alice gestured to the door. 'Shall we?'

Her guest looked relieved, her soft tread a deferential distance behind as they made their way up the back stairs. She was no better than Gillespie, taking Della to what was obviously the servants' quarters, but it was the only way to avoid running into either one of her parents. Her thoughts flitted to her father's visit to the attic. 'Not too much further.' She offered an encouraging smile as they passed the door to the first floor, but Della's eyes were engaged in her surroundings.

Hurrying to her secret studio, she extracted the key which she'd taken to carrying in her pocket and let them in. Della continued to gaze wide-eyed.

Alice felt the pressure to explain as Della took in the easel, the daybed and the box of artist materials ready to be hidden away afterwards behind the clutter of the remaining space. Understanding seemed to dawn before she uttered a word.

'Oh,' Della exclaimed. 'You want to paint me?'

'I'll pay,' Alice blurted.

Della frowned.

'I mean, I don't expect you to sit for free. Your time is valuable.'

'I work six days a week.' Della stared at the canvas while she said this as if she too could already imagine herself there.

Alice bit her lip. Of course Della would be working. 'When is your day off?'

'Sunday. The café isn't open then.'

Her parents expected her to accompany them to church, followed by an interminable lunch, usually with one of her father's constituents, the vicar or some other parish do-gooder. What could she say to get out of all that?

'I could do the afternoon once everyone's fed and occupied,' Della continued.

If Sunday was the only day Della could manage, she'd have to make it work — a headache here, a touch of fatigue there. 'Alright, Sunday it is.'

They grinned at the prospect, then as quickly as it had arrived, Della's smile fell away. 'You don't want me . . .' She gestured to the daybed.

Alice caught up with her thinking. 'Oh no, you can keep your clothes on.' She wanted to capture Della just as she was — striking, those cheekbones, the light from the window behind bringing a hint of copper to her dark curls. Aware she was staring, Alice averted her gaze. 'Do you have time now if I were to make some preliminary sketches?'

Della nodded and allowed Alice to usher her to the daybed, where she sat carefully as if she feared it might break. Alice took up her sketchbook and pencil. At first it was hard to concentrate. She was too aware of Della's self-consciousness, conveyed by her stiff back and the fact she kept gazing around the room and then apologising because she'd moved her head.

'It's alright, you're not made of stone, I don't expect you to sit like a statue.'

Della smiled at that, her lips dark red. She was all contrasts — dark lips, pale skin, dark hair. Alice wondered if it was rouge or if Della had a natural hue. Her own lips disappeared without adding colour.

'I don't mean to pry—' Della studied her hands — 'but how come someone like you got left to sleep under a table?'

It was a fair question, if a little direct. The answer settled like a tightness in her chest. She felt compelled to tell the truth, but propriety made her hesitate. How could she explain to this girl who saw her as someone with everything that she had nothing? A child of parents unable to show their affection, friendless in the intimate sense and knocking around with a man who saw

29

her as a fool. Saying those things out loud would bring relief, but she wasn't ready to expose herself. There was a balance to painting someone's portrait. It was she who should be exposing Della.

Instead, she forced away her melancholy, always ready to act the clown. 'Too much champagne and a naughty streak.'

Della's expression changed to something akin to pity. It wasn't the result Alice hoped for.

'Anyway,' she said, noting a haughty tone in her voice, 'I'm sure the café has many more outrageous guests than me.'

'I'm in the kitchens most of the time. You're my first outrageous guest.' Della glanced away, a shy smile on her lips which put Alice at ease.

Seeing an opportunity, Alice took the reins. Della's eyes lit up when she talked about her job, it was clearly a source of pleasure, which she rather envied. 'How long have you worked at the Ambrose?'

'Just over three years. Joined the week after my sixteenth birthday.'

'You like the work?'

Della shrugged but her eyes came alive. 'Mostly. I like the baking and the cake making, especially doing the decoration. It took a lot of persuasion, but Mrs H trusts me to do some of the fanciest cakes now, like your birthday cake.'

Again, disgust for the frivolity of her class bubbled to the surface. 'I'm so sorry, we treated your hard work appallingly.'

'Don't matter. It's the decorating that gives me pleasure, I don't really think about what happens after that. It's not as if the cake is destined for my stomach.'

Alice felt a hint of reproach but when she glanced at Della, her face was clear and serene. She'd started to relax. Alice realised she had too.

'Would you like that to be your job, cake decoration?'

'I'd love it. I was reading in one of the chef's magazines about this cookery school in Paris, Le Cordon Bleu. What I wouldn't give to train there.' Della's eyes shone.

'Why don't you?'

Her shoulders slumped. 'People like me don't get to go to Paris.'

'I've been.'

Della sat forward — eyes like saucers. 'What was it like?'

Alice set down her pencil while she considered her answer. 'Think of the most beautiful cake you've ever seen.'

Della blushed. 'Don't laugh if I'm saying it wrong, but a croquembouche. I saw it in the same magazine.'

'Describe it for me.'

Della's brow furrowed. 'Well, it's in the shape of a cone, like a big tower, and it's made of choux pastry profiteroles filled with cream and dipped in chocolate, each one as perfect as the last. But what brings it alive is the light. If you get the chocolate ganache right, it gleams.'

Alice grinned. 'Paris is like that. Exactly. Layers and layers of elegance in every direction, too good to exist in. Just when you think you've seen all the beauty your eyes can take, you turn another corner and it's outdone the one before, and all bathed in the most extraordinary light.'

'Blimey,' Della whispered, causing Alice to laugh.

The distant chime of the grandfather clock on the landing below broke into their reverie. Della shot up. 'Is that the time? I'd better go. Ma ain't well and I've got to get dinner for my brothers.'

Alice set aside her sketch. 'I'll see you out.'

They hurried down the stairs. At the first floor, she realised she hadn't paid Della for her time. 'Can you wait here for a minute?'

In her bedroom, Alice snatched up her purse and pulled out a note. She had no idea what to pay and hoped what she offered was right. When she returned to the stairs, Della's back was pressed against the wall.

'What is it?'

'The man who let me in passed through the corridor below. I don't think he saw me. I didn't think — well, I didn't know if you'd want . . .'

31

Alice offered the note. 'It's fine. Thank you for your help today.' When Della didn't take it, she pressed it to Della's palm and closed her fingers around the money. Della's hands were cold; she should have lit a fire. Neither of them moved. Their eyes met, a fleeting connection, until Della broke it by whispering her thanks.

At the back door, their awkwardness returned. 'You'll come on Sunday?'

Della nodded, pulled down her cloche hat and was gone. Alice watched her progress along the path to the gate, the dark green of her hat disappearing and reappearing along the garden wall until she was out of sight.

'I trust your guest found everything to her satisfaction, Miss Alice?' Gillespie made her jump.

She turned to look at him, his face as closed as a clairvoyant. 'Did Mummy enquire . . . ?'

'Your mother was satisfied you were having a rest after a phone call from Mr Tobias Roland.'

He'd covered for her?

'If that's all, I'll leave you in peace.'

Alice stared after him until the echo of his footsteps died away, wondering what other secrets he kept.

CHAPTER 7

Della arrived home with the note Alice gave her crinkling in her pocket, her fingers alive with the ghost of Alice's touch. Inside, she found Samuel perched on a kitchen chair, reaching for the matches above the stove. 'What are you up to?'

He turned at her harsh tone, almost losing his balance. 'I'm hungry.'

She took the matches and helped him down, cursing her brothers for neglecting the youngest Wilde, guilty for enjoying her afternoon off. The brief time in Alice's attic had left its mark. She wanted to be back there. Talking to Alice about her dreams made them more vivid, as if they were attainable and not hopelessly out of reach.

'What's for tea?' Samuel asked.

Della cast around the kitchen, the breakfast dishes still piled in the sink. A loaf of bread left out to go stale, its misshapen form suggesting it'd been hacked at with a blunt knife. The lid had been left off the butter dish too, leaving the scrap of butter to spoil. She sighed, her dreams dissolving in the chaos. 'Where's Ma?'

'In bed,' Samuel muttered. 'Can we have baked beans for tea?'

She squeezed his shoulder. 'In a minute, let me check on Ma.'

At the top of the stairs, the door to the boys' bedroom stood ajar. Della poked her head around. Henry lounged on the bed he shared with Samuel, nose in a book. He'd probably been there since they came home from school. She didn't begrudge her brother his solitude, but sometimes his ability to switch off from the world and become absorbed in a better life boiled her blood. Jack's bed at the far end was made and untouched.

'Where's Jack?' Della snapped.

Henry looked at her through his ill-fitting round spectacles. 'No idea.'

'Samuel was downstairs alone about to set the house on fire.'

He sat up. 'Sorry, Del, I should have checked on him.'

She could never stay mad at Henry — he was so damn reasonable. He slipped past as she returned to the landing and listened at her mother's door. Silence. The black mood would pass eventually but what she'd give for Ma to get up, even if that meant putting up with her criticism.

The kitchen was empty, no sign of Henry or Sam, when she returned downstairs. Loading dishes in the sink, the glow of the afternoon with Alice dimmed further as she confronted the mess before her.

Jack walked in, a newspaper tucked under his arm.

'Where've you been?' Della struggled to keep the irritation from her voice.

Her brother shrugged. 'Could ask you the same question.'

'I came home to find Samuel about to burn the house to the ground. The poor lad only wanted his tea. Ma's sick and I'm working, someone needs to take responsibility.'

He slammed the paper on the table and rounded on her. 'I've been out looking for a job, but remind us all why don't you, Saint Della, single-handedly keeping the wolf from the door.'

She turned back to the sink to hide the tears smarting her eyes. It never used to be like this. When had Jack's bitterness tipped over into hatred? 'Sorry, I didn't mean—'

Henry burst in from the yard before she could make amends, bringing with him a gust of cold air and the squeal of a train whistle, a bundle of newspaper in his arms. His glasses steamed up as he set the package down. The room filled with the aroma of salt and vinegar. 'I took Ma's purse and went out for fish and chips. There was only enough for two portions, but that should split between us all.' He looked at Della for approval. Her anger deflated under the intoxicating smell.

'Count me out.' Jack grabbed his cap from the hook and was gone.

Della summoned her brightest smile. 'Well done, Henry. Find Samuel and let's tuck in.'

'I'm here.' Samuel slid out from under the table. He'd witnessed the whole thing. 'Why doesn't Jack like us?'

Della ruffled his hair and grabbed three plates from the dresser. 'Jack has his own troubles, he'll be alright.'

Henry pulled off his glasses and gave them a clean with his shirt tail. 'What about Ma?'

'Better keep some back for her just in case.' If Ma refused to eat, Jack would soon polish it off when no one was looking. She took up the newspaper he'd left on the table, the *Workers' Weekly*, a communist paper. Disenchanted men sold them at the railway station. The unwanted. Men whose bodies told of the ravages of war. She scanned the headline. Two million unemployed. Times were desperate, maybe Jack had a point. Sliding it under a pile of Henry's books on the dresser, she joined her brothers, resolving to try harder to build bridges with Jack. Henry unwrapped the fish and chips and he and Samuel tucked in. Della put the plates away and followed their example. Ma would be appalled, but she wasn't here.

CHAPTER 8

After a never-ending morning of church and polite conversation, the minute hand on the mantel clock now appeared to move at warp speed as Alice spooned delicate morsels of fruit salad into her mouth. Della had agreed to come at 2 p.m. It was now past five to, and her predicament was made all the worse by the guests who'd joined them for lunch — among them, a diminutive rather charming French woman from her mother's WI group, a local judge accompanied by his wife who hadn't said a word and a deacon at Exeter Cathedral. They made an odd gathering, but her mother excelled at bringing disparate people together. An MP's wife to the core. Conversation meandered from the mundane to the political. The French lady — Alice hadn't caught her name — appeared keen to persuade her mother to learn her native tongue, while the judge harangued her father about the rise of communism among working men. Like Alice, the deacon kept glancing at the clock as if he too had somewhere else to be.

Martha came in to clear the plates. Alice set down her spoon with relief and smiled at the maid as if they'd conspired over the interruption, but Martha's focus remained lowered in deference.

'Shall we follow up with drinks in the drawing room?' Mummy, ever eager to make the most of company. Gillespie appeared with cigars for the men. Alice glanced to the window while she tried to conjure an excuse. Raindrops pelted the glass, stealing the opportunity to express a desire to take some air.

With their cigars lit, the men followed her mother and the other ladies to the drawing room. 'I don't feel terribly well,' Alice said to their retreating backs. Her mother paused. Alice put her hand to her head. 'May I be excused?'

'Of course,' her mother said before being drawn back into conversation with the French lady.

Alone with Gillespie, Alice searched for a way to communicate her dilemma when he met her with his shrewd gaze. 'She's in the kitchen. Where would you like me to convey her?'

Alice gathered herself, a frisson of electricity raising the light hairs on her arm. 'The first-floor landing at the back, please.'

At that moment the front doorbell chimed. Gillespie went to answer while she made for the stairs. Toby's voice travelled into the hall and her heart sank. Despite Gillespie's polite protestations, he entered the house.

'Alice, there you are.' He pulled off his cap and a pair of driving goggles, handing them to Gillespie. 'Your chap says you're not well, but I thought we might take a spin in the Bentley. I haven't had a chance to put her through her paces yet.' He threw Gillespie a hard look which slid off the butler like water.

'Sorry, Toby. I've got a headache.' She glanced at Gillespie too, unsure what help she expected him to offer.

'I'll be in the kitchen if you need me, Miss Alice,' Gillespie said, leaving the hat and goggles on the sideboard in the hall.

'Come on, darling.' Toby approached, taking her hands in his.

'It's raining.'

'It will clear soon. We'll head out to the coast. A bit of fresh air might be just the thing.'

All Alice could think about was Della, waiting in the kitchen. What a poor start this was to their portrait sessions. She rallied, determined to extract herself. 'I'm sorry, I really do have the most dreadful headache. I don't think a spot of fresh air is going to clear it.'

He dropped her hand, his jaw tightening. 'That's disappointing. I drove over here with the expectation of spending an afternoon with my girl.' He kicked at the corner of the rug.

'I'm sorry you've had a wasted trip, but you could have telephoned first.'

Voices carried from the drawing room. 'At least someone's having a good time.' Toby's smile was thin.

'My parents and their lunch guests.'

'Why don't we join them?'

'Because I have a headache.' Her patience was wearing out.

'I'll say a quick hello.' Before she could stop him, Toby popped his head around the door.

'Toby, how lovely,' her mother exclaimed. 'Join us. Is Alice with you?'

'She's here.' He beckoned Alice into the room, giving her little choice but to follow. 'I want to take her out for a drive, but your daughter claims she's got a headache.'

Alice gritted her teeth. 'I do.'

'Oh, go on, Alice. The fresh air will do you the world of good,' her mother coaxed.

Alice looked to the window and the brightening skies; even the weather conspired against her. She tried to come up with another excuse, when Gillespie entered and cleared his throat.

'Forgive the interruption but children were playing around your car, Mr Roland. I saw them off, but I can't promise they won't return. I'd hate for such a fine vehicle to be damaged.'

Toby rushed to the window. 'Little tykes.'

Her mother frowned. 'We don't normally get children playing in this street.'

'I don't think they were from around here, ma'am.' Gillespie's solemn expression didn't waver.

'I'd better not risk it. Can't have the Bentley damaged before she's even a week old.' Toby addressed her mother. 'My apologies.'

Alice followed him into the hall, where Gillespie offered him his cap and goggles. 'I'll be back for that drive, you know.' He gave her a peck on the cheek and was gone.

Once they were alone, she turned to Gillespie. He answered her question before she'd voiced it. 'You'll find her on the landing, as requested.'

Alice raced up the stairs. At the top, she paused. Gillespie was still hovering at the bottom. 'Were there really children?'

He offered an almost imperceptible shrug. 'There might have been.'

She smiled. 'Thank you, Mr Gillespie.'

* * *

Della looked relieved when Alice found her on the stairs, dark hair tucked inside the same green cloche hat which had seen better days. Her tweed coat was a little ill-fitting around the shoulders, as if it was made for a larger person. Alice put her fingers to her lips, and they glided like ghosts up the narrow stairs.

The attic room was as she'd left it first thing that morning, a chair placed near the window where the light would illuminate her subject. Della shrugged off her tweed jacket and pulled the hat from her head, allowing the abundant black curls to spring free like a jack-in-the-box. Her hair was unfashionably long, and the frizz could do with taming. Alice saw it so clearly — the way Della's hair could be cut to make the most of those razor-sharp cheekbones. In the right hands, she'd be transformed. Not that she wasn't striking. As if she sensed Alice studying her, Della glanced up. Alice took her jacket and hung it on the door handle to hide her blush.

'I'm sorry I was delayed.' Alice grabbed her sketchbook and perched on the daybed, gesturing for Della to take the chair.

'Your butler gave me a cup of tea but I ain't got long now, I'm afraid.' There was an agitation to Della today. She scratched her nose then fiddled with her hair before resting her hands in her lap as if she'd got something out of her system. Hardly surprising after she'd been left to wait. Alice needed to come up with a way to ensure this didn't happen again.

Aware of Della's eyes on her as her pencil made marks across the page, she tried to focus. There was nothing critical in Della's gaze, more a curiosity puncturing the wariness that cast her brilliance in shadow. If only she could open her up. Alice's thoughts turned to their discussion the previous sitting, the dream to train at Le Cordon Bleu. She was about to reintroduce the topic when Della suddenly stood and walked to the dormer window overlooking the street.

'Sorry, I can't seem to settle,' Della explained without turning.

'Is everything all right? I know coming here must be difficult when . . .'

Della faced her, a look of alarm in her eyes. 'It's fine to come here, better than fine.'

Something about the way the light caught Della's profile, giving her an almost transcendent glow, caused a fluttering sensation in her stomach. She forced a smile to mask her fascination. 'Good.'

'Your folks don't know, do they?'

Alice resumed her sketch but found she could no longer concentrate. 'Know what?'

Della gestured to the room. 'About all this, the fact that you're an artist, that you invite strange women here to paint.'

'They don't know about any of it and you're the first . . . strange woman.'

Della smiled at that. 'Ain't you worried they'll find out? What about that man, the butler . . . ?'

She decided to be direct. 'I suppose I am worried.'

'What will they do if they catch you painting and talking to the likes of me? I mean, it don't seem so terrible, not the painting part anyway. Shouldn't they be proud you've got talent?'

'Art isn't the sort of thing that impresses my parents.'

'What does impress them?'

Alice set down her sketchbook and felt again the over-whelming urge to spill the beans, to tell Della how she felt like a ghost in her own home, how her parents' idea of her was so wildly inaccurate she'd lost the desire to correct it. When she looked up, Della was studying her intently.

'They want me to get married, so I'll become someone else's problem.' She glanced at her engagement finger, surprised by her honesty and relieved that no rock yet existed there.

Della's gaze followed hers. 'You've got a beau?'

Alice slid her hand from view, unsettled. 'Toby. I chose him, not my parents.' *Why the defensive tone?*

'But they approve?'

Alice thought about his intrusion earlier, how he'd been greeted like one of the family, how eager Mummy had been that he take Alice for a drive. 'Yes, they approve,' she whispered, *but did she?*

'And all this?' Della gestured to the room. 'Will you be Alice the artist, or Alice the wife?' There was a challenge in her eyes.

Alice felt her back stiffen. 'Both.'

They fell quiet, and an uncomfortable silence stretched on. Alice couldn't work out what had gone wrong between her and Della, but something had. She felt judged in a way she didn't appreciate, but was Della doing the judging or was she? Alice couldn't tell.

Della fiddled with her hair again. 'I really should be going.'

Alice was dismayed. None of this had turned out the way she wanted it to.

'Can I see?' Della asked with her eye on the half-finished sketch.

'I've hardly started.' But still, she offered up the sketch and sat back, bashful at having her work scrutinised. Della studied the page for what felt like an eternity. When she handed it back, she stood and without comment retrieved her jacket from the door hook.

Perturbed, Alice opened the door to check all was clear and accompanied Della down the stairs, a little irritated her work had been dismissed.

At the back door, Della paused, her face inches from Alice's. 'Don't give it up for anyone. You're far too talented and it makes your eyes dance.' She stuffed her mane under her cloche hat and was gone. Alice closed the door, delighted by the compliment and sorry she'd have to wait a whole week before she could see Della again.

CHAPTER 9

'That posh girl's here.' William raised his eyebrows on his way through to the servery.

'Who, Alice?'

He paused his progress. 'On first-name terms now, are we? The party lady, the one who wrecked your cake.'

Della returned her attention to the mixing bowl, hoping to hide the flush of warmth on her cheeks from William's sharp gaze. When she glanced up, he was studying her in a way she wasn't sure she appreciated. 'What?'

'You're blushing.' He smirked.

'Shut up, William.'

'I didn't say it was a bad thing.' He reached over her shoulder and scooped chocolate buttercream from her bowl with his finger, his nose inches from her hair — she could have sworn he gave it a sniff — then went on his way.

Della shuddered and resumed her mixing, desperate to abandon her post and peek into the café, but she didn't dare when her face was flushed and her apron covered in cocoa powder.

William walked back through a few minutes later, a smug look on his face. 'She asked me to give you this.' He offered a sealed envelope but when Della went to take it, he lifted it out of her reach.

'Give over, William.'

'What's it worth?' With a grin, he tapped his cheek holding the envelope aloft.

Della had no plans to kiss him, especially in front of the entire kitchen.

'Fine.' The good humour vanished from his voice when she didn't meet his request. He dropped the envelope on the flour-dusted table.

Della snatched it up and threw William a glare until he took the hint and left her in peace. She ripped open the seal, relieved it hadn't been exposed to his prying eyes, and scanned the note.

Meet me at Northernhay Gardens, Sunday, 2.30 p.m.
Yours, A x

Just like the address card, it was written on embossed, thick paper. Della lifted it to her nose, a woody mix from the paper and Alice's floral scent. She stuffed it in her apron pocket and returned to the buttercream with renewed vigour.

* * *

Sunday dawned fine but with enough gathering clouds in shades of grey to make Della worry the outing would have to be cancelled. She made her way into town under the railway arches and over the river from St Thomas, then up the steep rise of Fore Street with its shuttered shops. The baroque archway of the Ambrose's entrance called to her in the distance as she turned into Queen Street and headed for the park.

Della walked through the heavy iron gates and along the path to the new war memorial. No sign of Alice, but she was a little early. A statue of Victory rose up on a tall plinth at its centre, surrounded by four figures in bronze — a soldier, a sailor, a prisoner of war and a VAD nurse. The sight brought up the loss of Pa and her brothers. Thomas would have been twenty-nine and George twenty-seven now. What a waste. She thought of her mother that morning, a lump under the coverlet of her bed, and let her resentments about being left to run the house fall away. Henry promised to take care of Samuel, but as for Jack, who knew what he did or where he went? It was his business, but still, it unsettled her.

Lost in her reverie, Della didn't notice Alice making her way up the path until she was almost upon her, dressed unlike anything Della had ever seen. Her hair was tucked under a flat cap, while a gentlemen's raincoat flapped open over trousers, a dress shirt buttoned up to her long, elegant neck and a waistcoat. The look was completed with a tie which she'd left loose, and a large satchel slung across her body. Her smile and iridescent eyes gave her away.

'Are you in disguise?' Della asked when they'd exchanged pleasantries.

Alice glanced down at her outfit and laughed. 'You don't approve? I was trying something new. Men's clothes are so much more comfortable, don't you agree?' She took Della's arm, leaving the question hanging. She liked Alice's outfit — she liked it very much. If Della tried such an attire, she'd be laughed into the middle of next week, but there was something about Alice's confidence that allowed her indulgences — perhaps that's what having money meant, the luxury of flamboyance. 'Thank you for meeting me here,' Alice continued. 'I thought we were less likely to be interrupted if we avoided the house. Why not sketch in the park? I'm relieved it's a lovely day.' She glanced skywards, where blue parried with grey as if to confirm her statement. 'At least, it is for now,' she added.

They meandered past the ruins of a Roman wall and the lofty elms, straining in the wind, that bordered the central walk. Alice paused at a bench in a relatively sheltered spot and gestured for Della to sit.

'When will you start the painting?' Della hunched her shoulders against the strengthening breeze as Alice pulled out her sketchpad and a set of pencils.

'I already have.'

'So why do you need to keep sketching me?' *Was it an excuse to see her?* She shouldn't entertain such foolish notions, but still, she felt a pang of fear their time was already at an end.

'I want to capture all of Della Wilde. That means from every angle, both in and out.'

Della nodded like she understood to mask the fact she didn't, not really. Alice's words made her feel exposed. 'I don't know why you want to spend time staring at my ugly mug.'

Alice remained focused on the sketch. 'Your mug is far from ugly.'

Della took pleasure in the complement, even though she'd fished for it, and attempted to maintain her pose, but the bench was hard and her thin jacket provided little warmth, causing her to rub her arms. 'Sorry, I ain't very good at keeping still.'

Alice offered up a distracted smile. 'It's fine. I'll finish this and we'll walk some more.'

Twenty minutes later, she declared herself done. Della was about to ask to see when a gust of wind made a snatch for the paper in Alice's lap. She watched, horrified, as the sketch flipped into the air. Alice stood, sending her materials to the ground. They ran, following the paper's haphazard progress across the damp grass until it plastered itself against a man's leg.

He crouched and pulled the paper from his trousers. Alice's face was flushed with their exertions. She was staring at the man with a curious expression. Della followed her gaze and gasped. It was Jack. He thrust the sheet into Alice's hand before he noticed Della and his features changed from mild irritation to intense curiosity.

'What are you up to, Della?'

She cast around. Why not speak the truth? It was bring-ing extra money after all, but then this was Jack. She couldn't deal another blow to his pride.

'Who's this?' He thrust a finger in Alice's direction. Della's cheeks flamed at his rudeness. 'Ma in her sickbed and you're out cavorting with a boy.'

Alice's peel of laughter refocused their attention. She put her hands on her hips. 'A boy? You sound like my mother.'

Now Jack's cheeks flamed, but Della could tell it wasn't with good-humoured embarrassment. She'd seen the flash in his eyes, the first indication of a gathering storm.

'Jack.' She said it twice before he tore his gaze from Alice. 'This is Alice. She's an artist and she asked to paint my portrait.'

Jack studied Alice again and finally saw what Della saw, sparkling blue eyes with long lashes, flushed cheeks and a delicate jaw.

She turned to Alice. 'This is my brother Jack.'

Alice grinned, pulled off the cap and stuck out her hand. 'Another Wilde, how delightful.'

Was Alice flirting or being polite? It bothered Della in ways she didn't want to comprehend. Her brother appeared confused more than anything. Was it the unveiling of Alice or her voice that identified her as set apart from them?

Jack recovered and returned Alice's handshake, his gaze roaming over her several times as if he were recording a mental picture to be studied later.

The three of them stood, an awkward triangle, until Della recalled Alice's art materials strewn on the grass. 'Your things.'

Alice nodded. 'Of course.'

Jack's gaze remained trained on Alice as she crouched to pick up her materials and stuff them in her satchel. Della felt the stab of something hot in her chest. She wished he'd go, that he'd never come.

Alice stood in one fluid movement. 'Well, I suppose I'd better be getting back.'

All Della could do was offer up a weak smile in commiseration for the loss of their afternoon.

They watched Alice wind her way to the Roman wall and disappear through the arch that would take her down to the gates and out of the park.

'Her sort ain't for the likes of us.' Jack walked the way Alice had gone, but Della remained rooted to the spot. He stopped and turned to face her. 'What were you thinking, Del?'

She pulled her old tweed coat, one of her father's, tighter around her and crossed her arms. She was thinking that maybe she'd made a friend, maybe she could have a life that had nothing to do with being a Wilde.

Jack shook his head and walked on. Della followed a few steps behind. The skies darkened, the threat of rain and missed opportunities.

CHAPTER 10

Alice reached the iron gates before looking back, but there was no sign of Della or her brother. A tram rattled to a halt at her side. On impulse she hopped on, enjoying the disguise her clothes afforded. 'Watch it, lad,' an elderly gentlemen muttered when Alice accidently stepped on his foot. She paid her fare and climbed to the top deck with a sense of freedom.

Settling near the back, her thoughts returned to the afternoon's encounter. Jack Wilde. Handsome, there was no denying it. He had the same sharp, defined features as Della, a strong jaw and the shock of Wilde black curls, but his eyes left her unsettled. There was danger sparring with intrigue. A challenge that seemed at once appealing as it was repugnant. He'd looked at her as if he knew her, not as an acquaintance but fully knew her, what beat beneath her chest, what was hidden in the depths. All of it.

Unnerved, Alice took solace in her surroundings, a fine view of the upper floors of grand Exeter buildings. As the tram trundled past the Ambrose, she pulled the sketch from her satchel, rather damp now, and considered its subject. Della's beauty was raw and undefined. Alice longed to transform her, cut that hair, put an elegant dress over that pale, milky skin, but perhaps that would destroy what made her so compelling. Even so, with the right clothes and hairstyle . . . Alice crossed her legs, disquieted by the now familiar sensation that had taken up residence there. She tore her gaze from the sketch to the view again. Despite the fading light, there was enough afternoon remaining for time in the attic. Her mother had been persuaded to take French lessons — why, Alice had no idea. There were no plans to visit France but at least it gave Mummy a focus. Father would be in his study, where he spent every minute when he wasn't at Westminster.

As the tram rattled on towards Heavitree, Alice rang the bell, now eager to return home, her fingers twitching to render her vision to the canvas. She let herself in at the back of the winter house and raced up the servants' stairs. A feverish need took hold as she pushed open the door to their quarters. In the narrow corridor, she came to an abrupt halt.

Voices. *Damn*, maybe one of them was sick, otherwise they were always out on a Sunday afternoon, visiting their own families and friends. She tiptoed past, still hoping to get to her studio, when the intonation of a familiar voice stopped her. Father. Alice backed away with a desperate need to put distance between herself and whatever was happening behind one of the servants' doors.

In her bedroom, she paced, turning over and over the scene building in her head. Her father and who? She hadn't hung around long enough to find out or ascertain which door, but it could only be Martha. Mrs Drummond was too old. She conjured the maid, a slip of a girl with mouse-brown hair and a rather limp curl. Her eyes were overlarge in an otherwise delicate face, giving the impression she was constantly surprised. She'd only been with them for about six months. The previous maid had left to work in a shop. Alice and her mother had agreed, despite her shyness, Martha was a great improvement on Jemima, whose sullen face would surely turn customers away. *Had Father come to appreciate this change in their household too?*

Mummy, in contrast, was a striking woman, with hair the colour of wheat, her beauty still evident if a little diminished by anxiety, and maybe that was it. Martha's guileless nature offered Father something her mother couldn't provide — but was it an act, a pretence at innocence?

She'd seen glimpses of the servants' rooms in the past and found them stark and sparse. A cast-iron bed, a threadbare rug over floorboards that creaked with age. A chest of drawers, a small mirror and the lonely sight of a single chair. Were her father's clothes slung over that chair? Did the springs of the bed strain under their combined weight? She closed her eyes tight against the vision as the full horror of what she'd surmised boiled to the surface. All those weeks ago when she'd thought he'd sought her in the attic, it was Martha he'd been hoping to find. Martha, the intended recipient of his tender tone.

Alice stood before her dressing table mirror with repulsion for what it reflected back. She pulled off the cap and slung it to the floor, discarded the waistcoat and ripped at the buttons on the shirt — one of her father's. The trousers came next, the socks. She discarded it all. How clever she'd considered herself that morning, leaving the house dressed in her disguise, how much she'd enjoyed the look of confusion on her mother's face.

Oh God, *her mother*. Tears sprang from Alice's eyes. Did she know of her husband's clandestine activities? Was that the deal struck between them?

Standing in her underwear and stockings, she dried her eyes and reapplied the make-up, ruined in her fury. From her wardrobe she chose a dress in soft pink, a favourite of Toby's. Next, she slid into a pair of silver heels, and completed the look with a string of pearls and earrings to match. Smoothing down her hair, Alice stood back and admired the transformation. Another disguise, but one that wouldn't invite curiosity.

She descended the wide staircase, a genteel hand resting on the banister to counter the shaking in her limbs. The telephone awaited her in the hall. Toby answered on the second ring.

'Take me out.' A tremor in her voice, breathy against the receiver.

'Alice, is that you?'

She hesitated, less confident in her quest. 'Who else were you expecting?'

'No one, darling. Take you out where?'

'Isn't there a party somewhere? There's always a party.'

A pause at the other end of the line, an almost imperceptible sigh. 'Alright, there is a party.'

Alice forced a grin even though no one could see her. 'Come now, please, Toby.'

He agreed and she hung up the phone, a reckless mania pitching in her stomach. She wanted to drink an enormous amount of alcohol and then she wanted the world to disappear.

* * *

Somewhere between nightfall and dawn, Alice moved her hips in time to the music, legs and arms a flurry of activity as if they'd gained independence from the rest of her body. The people around her shifted in and out of focus, vibrating limbs and staccato laughter. Who'd have thought a trip to the ladies' room could provide the perfect remedy to her troubling discovery? A sniff of white powder and the world was painted anew. It was all so delicious. Her flailing arms kept time to the beat with fascinating speed. She studied their tremors until Toby came to her side, risking injury as he leaned in to speak in her ear. Alice roared with laughter even though his words failed to penetrate the fug in her head over the jazz that held her body in its grip. Toby took her arm, his fingers like a vice. It hurt. She twisted free and snorted, all part of the game, but his expression suggested he wasn't playing.

'For God's sake, Alice.'

The people around her shrank back — friends until seconds ago, although she couldn't identify a single person. Toby lunged at her again, this time securing the soft flesh of her upper arm in a searing pinch. As he dragged her out, the room tilted. She cast behind, leering faces loomed, then the bright lights of the foyer hit her before cold air needled her senses under the shroud of night.

He let go with a shove. She didn't want to feel, she only wanted the numbness of the dancefloor, the heat of too many bodies, the gauzy fog of alcohol and smoke to dull her memories. But the chill air was bringing it all to the surface. The attic rooms, her father and Martha.

Toby spewed an incomprehensible stream of vitriol that made him look like a furious child. Despite her misery, she was laughing again.

Then his fist met her cheek, and she wasn't laughing anymore.

CHAPTER 11

Della followed her brother as he strode ahead through the empty streets of the city centre under a granite sky. At the junction with the High Street, she paused to glimpse the Ambrose. How she wished she could dive in there now, don her apron and sink her hands into flour. You could trust baking — as long as you followed the process, it wouldn't let you down. Mix eggs with flour, butter and sugar and you'd get a cake batter. Melt chocolate and whisk it with warm cream and you'd have ganache. Baking was dependable, reliable. If only life could be like that.

Jack paused his stride to study her from behind a haze of cigarette smoke. She fell into step beside him, no longer certain how to communicate with this man with whom she'd shared so much in childhood. With a year between them, they'd formed a natural bond. The middle children stuck between their heroic older brothers off to war and the little ones, although Henry had always been a loner and Sam too young to be anything but the baby. Where was that bond now?

'What were you doing at the park?' Even she detected the accusation in her tone. In truth, Della wasn't sure she wanted to know what Jack was up to these days.

His eyes said *mind your own business* and maybe that was fair enough.

He drew on his cigarette. 'I go there sometimes, to see the memorial and think about Pa, Thomas and George. I should have been with them.'

Surprised by this confession, Della waited in case there was more.

If there was, her brother didn't care to share it. She wanted to tell him she was glad he hadn't gone, that he'd stayed home and safe.

'I miss them too,' she whispered.

Jack studied her so intently she glanced away. Eventually, he dropped his cigarette and ground it out with his heel. 'Aye, I know.'

'Do you?'

'What's that supposed to mean?'

'You act like you're the only one whose hurting.'

He walked on, quickening his pace until Della couldn't keep up or didn't want to. They made their way home in silence, a fissure opening into a chasm. If Jack's confession offered an olive branch, she'd somehow caused it to snap. She was still mad about Alice, about his intrusion on their afternoon and the way he'd looked at her friend. She wanted to interrogate him, to make sure he wasn't going to interfere, but the words remained stuck.

They continued in silence past St Thomas station, where their father had worked as a signalman before the war. Jack used to hang around watching the trains, dreaming of the day he'd join his Pa. Now there was no work on the railways and those who did have jobs talked of strike over pay. What would Pa think of the country he'd given his life for?

Lost in thought, Della nearly crashed into her brother, who'd stopped to wait for her at the end of their road. 'Don't mention you saw me to Ma, and I won't mention your posh artist friend. Deal?'

She nodded.

They exchanged a brief look of surprise at the gate. Through the kitchen window she could see Henry at the table, nose in a book, and Samuel engaged in a game of whip and top. At the centre of it all was Ma, hair combed and clean, face flushed as she stirred a pot on the stove. The relief was palpable. Jack threw Della a brief smile and opened the door for her. She stepped over the threshold, hopeful that she and Jack might finally have found common ground.

* * *

The evening continued to play on her mind as she walked to the Ambrose the following morning, the streets still wearing their dawn cloak of navy. The Wildes at their best — a rare thing since the war. Samuel, his eyes wide with wonder as Henry regaled them with stories of knights, princesses and monsters — that boy was destined to be a writer one day — Ma cooking and humming, and Jack, watching, his eyes warmer than she'd witnessed for months. When Ma came out of one of her episodes and the ingredients of their personalities melded just right, it was a beautiful thing. This time, would it last?

As she turned down the side of the Ambrose, Della almost screamed when a ghostly figure stepped into her path. She staggered back, trying to make sense of the woman before her. Alice's face remained in the shadow of the building, but Della could tell something wasn't right.

'What's happened?'

Alice gripped her hand — it was freezing cold, her pale arms shivering in the chill morning air.

'Let's get you in the warm.' She led Alice into the building, uncoiling her scarf and wrapping it around Alice's exposed neck. Only the other bakers and cleaners would be in at this time of day. Even so, Alice seemed reluctant to move too far inside. Della led her to a basement cloakroom and flicked on the lights. She gasped at the sight of her friend. A livid bruise formed on her cheek, her eye make-up ran in streaks down her face and her body shook in the thin dress. 'What happened to you?'

Alice's gaze flickered to the glass above the basin. She gasped too and lifted her hand to her cheek. 'Oh God.'

'What happened, Alice?' Della couldn't keep the panic from her voice. Dark imaginings filled her head.

'You have to help me,' Alice croaked. 'I can't go home like this. Do you have any make-up?' She gripped Della's hand.

'You're freezing. Let me get you a cuppa, then we'll sort you out.'

'Never mind about that. Please, I need to cover this bruise.'

She searched inside her bag, pulling out a small compact, embarrassed by how cheap it was. Alice didn't seem to notice. She snatched up the powder and moved to the sink.

'You should be alright in here. I'll fetch you a cup of tea.'

Alice looked at her in the glass and nodded.

In the kitchen, only Leonnard was in, unloading sacks of flour. He glanced at her with his good eye, the other having been sacrificed to a bit of shrapnel during the war. Della threw him a wave, wishing she could bring Alice to the warmth of the ovens, but while Leonnard kept to himself, other more inquisitive colleagues would arrive soon. She was thinking of William.

A large copper teapot warmed on a hotplate. Della poured the tea and added a sugar cube for the shock. Giving it a quick stir, she hastened back downstairs, colliding with Mrs Hastings.

'Watch it, girl, you'll have an accident. Where are you off to in such a hurry?'

Della was early. She knew her boss wouldn't begrudge her a hot drink before the day began. 'Thought I'd have this outside, see the sunrise.'

Hastings shook her head as if confirming Della's madness and went on her way.

In the bathroom, Alice had worked her magic on the bruise. She was almost herself but for the way she held her body, the shake of her hands as she accepted the mug.

'I don't want to get you in trouble,' she whispered, taking a sip and wincing.

'Don't worry about me. What happened?'

Alice cradled her mug. 'It was silly. I went to a party yesterday evening with Toby. I was upset when he picked me up . . .' She trailed off and took another sip. 'I found out something about my father after we'd been to the park, something . . . Oh, it doesn't matter. Anyway, Toby and I had a row. It was my fault. I wasn't looking where I was going and bumped straight into—'

Della cut her off. 'If you tell me you got that bruise from a door or a wall or any other inanimate object, I'll march you down the police station and let them reach their conclusions.'

Alice's eyes filled with tears and she set her mug on the edge of the sink. 'Toby hit me. I made him angry, and he struck me. There, happy now?'

Della only felt more miserable. She smoothed a tear from Alice's cheek with her thumb, careful not to smudge the make-up Alice had so skilfully applied. Their eyes met. 'He had no right,' she whispered, scared of breaking the moment but too angry to let it go.

Alice turned away. 'You don't know what it's like.'

'Try me,' Della said, desperate to understand.

'I've got no one. My mother can't see what's in front of her nose and my father . . . well, he's full of lies. At least Toby cares, although last night isn't a good example.' Alice frowned as if realising the contradiction in her statement.

Della's anger resurfaced. How could Alice place so little value on herself? 'This is the second time he's abandoned you — first your party, now this. If he cared, he wouldn't rest until he made sure you were home and safe.'

'Keep your voice down,' Alice hissed. 'I can't be found here.'

Her eyes stung with the tears she'd been trying to control. 'Sorry, I hate seeing you hurt.'

Alice cupped her face. Della held her gaze, aware of the rise and fall of their chests in tandem, the pink of Alice's lips, chapped from the cold. The sense something was about to happen. All her hopes distilled in a single moment, so fragile Della feared her breath could shatter it.

And then something did. A crash from outside broke their trance and they sprang apart. Della watched Alice move to the mirror to check her make-up.

'Get me out of here, Della, please?'

She nodded, barely regaining her equilibrium. 'I'll check the coast is clear.'

In the corridor it was as if the previous moments had never happened. The sights and sounds of the Ambrose took control of her senses. One of the cleaners had abandoned her trolley. Della could hear her in the gents' next door. She stuck her head back into the bathroom and beckoned to Alice. They ran hand in hand to the back entrance.

At the door, she pulled off her jacket and slung it around Alice's bare shoulders.

'Thank you,' Alice whispered.

This time, Della didn't watch her go. Alice wasn't the same marvellous, powerful spectacle she'd been after her party. She was small and vulnerable, a thing to be pitied. Della couldn't stand to see her so diminished.

CHAPTER 12

The city was coming alive as Alice walked home through its rain-smattered streets. Grateful for Della's jacket, she slid her arms inside and hugged her body. Despite the tea, her throat felt arid and her limbs could find no warmth. The events of the previous evening rattled around her head. The bruise on her cheek smarted each time a wave of emotion bothered the muscles there. It was her fault — too much alcohol, a sniff of cocaine from a dubious friend, a compulsion to drown her life and all it represented. She'd embarrassed Toby, confused him with her ricocheting emotions, laughed when he'd attempted to rein her in. She'd wanted it in a way, to test what level of numb she could achieve. As it turned out, the sharp sting proved she wasn't numb at all. Far from it.

When Toby drove away, leaving her standing on the street outside the Royal Clarence Hotel in the early morning, enveloped by darkness — friendless and alone — of course, she'd thought of Della. Sweet, kind Della Wilde, whose coat smelled of soap and something musty, familiar, comforting.

Her heels echoed along the mansions on her approach to the winter house. Her father reinserted himself as foremost in her mind, the previous evening having done little to extinguish what she'd overheard.

Gillespie answered the door with the efficiency his status required. Alice could only manage a nod in greeting, unable to meet his eye, before racing up the stairs. Delinquent Alice, home from another night on the town, her absence unnoticed by all but the staff.

In her bedroom, she uncoiled the scarf then slid out of the jacket and hung it over the back of the chair, feeling its loss about her body. Not only the warmth and comfort of it, but the connection to Della. The simple gesture of care. Pulling off her dress and flinging on her robe, she drew a bath and sank into the hot, soapy water. It was only then she allowed her mind to venture to the Ambrose bathroom. The all-consuming moment when Della's vulnerable gaze had met hers, how Della's lips had parted as if she knew Alice wanted to kiss her. What would have happened if the cleaners hadn't yanked them from the brink?

Back in her bedroom, cocooned in Della's jacket once more, her make-up carefully reapplied, Gillespie knocked and let her know Toby was on the telephone.

'Tell him I'm indisposed,' Alice replied without looking up from the novel she wasn't really reading. She wanted to be upstairs working on the portrait, but the attic was tainted by what she'd overheard.

By early evening, after hours wasted in her bedroom, Alice emerged downstairs. Gillespie informed her Toby had left several messages. 'I couldn't find you, Miss Alice.' He studied her with an untroubled expression, and she was grateful he hadn't bothered to try. 'Your mother was concerned.'

'Thank you, Gillespie. If you could assure Mummy I'm well.' She pulled on her coat over Della's under his inscrutable eye. 'I won't be here for dinner.'

The blue hour was dry and crisp, bringing with it a chill. Damp leaves littered the pavement as she retraced her steps back to the Ambrose. Alice waited in the exact spot she'd stood that morning, a desperate wretch, hoping Della would come to her rescue. Now she intended to say thank you.

She thrust her hands in her coat pockets against the cold, delighted to find a half-full pack of Players and fished one free, accosting a passing gentleman for a light. Such was her reverie she almost missed Della among the staff who filed out of the café.

Della was wearing a man's raincoat that skirted her ankles. She smiled when she saw Alice, but it didn't reach her eyes. Alice shrugged off her coat and relinquished the tweed jacket and scarf, sorry to say goodbye to their comfort. 'I couldn't leave you to walk home in the cold, although I see you've found an alternative.'

Della followed her gaze. 'I might start a new fashion. Oversized coats. Do you think it will catch on?'

Alice laughed. 'You certainly wear it with aplomb.' She felt suddenly shy. 'I wanted to say thank you, properly . . . for rescuing me this morning. Would you let me treat you to supper?'

Della's face fell. 'I'd love to, but . . .'

At that moment the waiter Alice recognised joined them. 'You ready, Del?' He rested a proprietorial hand on Della's arm.

Della's cheeks flamed. 'William's taking me to the pictures, he lent me his coat,' she said, as if it were an obvious exchange.

'Another time.' Alice backed away, straight into a lamppost. 'Have a splendid evening.'

Della left with William's arm plastered around her back.

Alice drew on her cigarette, watching them disappear into the rapidly falling night. 'You stupid fool,' she whispered.

CHAPTER 13

Della wriggled free of William and paused at the corner to glance back. Alice was still outside the Ambrose, smoking, her gaze focused on the distance.

'Come on, Del, we'll miss the start.'

She fell into step at William's side, cursing her decision to go to the cinema with him. She'd only agreed because he'd begged and lent her his coat, but the real reason was what passed between her and Alice that morning. Della rationalised it as some sort of mistake on Alice's part, like her injury had left her confused. What frightened her was none of that was true. Alice had wanted to kiss her. She'd seen it in her eyes, felt her soft breath on her lips. Now Alice had invited her to supper, and Della wanted to go. What must Alice have thought, seeing her stepping out with William? It irritated her, the way he'd put his hand on her arm, staking his claim.

Abruptly, she came to a halt.

William took a moment to stop too. He turned to face her.

'Sorry, William, I can't . . .' It was rude, but this wasn't about being polite, it was about what she wanted in her very core. Pulling off his coat, Della handed it to him and slid on her tweed jacket, the faintest hint of Alice's perfume lingering at the neck.

He tugged on his coat, shaking his head, his voice hard. 'It's not normal, you do realise that? People will think you're weird.'

Della stared at him. She could only guess at what he was implying.

He sneered. 'Every time you see her, it's written all over your bloody face.' With that he walked away.

Trying to shake off his words, she retraced her steps, breaking into a run. Of course, Alice was gone. She stood for a few moments, frantically scanning the street, then she glimpsed her, walking in the direction of St Leonards. She was about to call out when a man approached Alice. Della drew closer until she could make out the familiar profile. Jack. They exchanged a few words, then Alice threw her head back and laughed. He could be charming when he put his mind to it. Tears formed in Della's eyes as her brother offered Alice his arm. After a moment's hesitation, she took it and they walked away.

* * *

Della waited up for him in the kitchen with the lights out, while the last of the embers from the stove sputtered in the grate, the events of the morning keeping her company. The kiss might not have happened, but the anticipation in those moments before was everything she'd believed a kiss could be. Better than William's clumsy approach at the Christmas party. His words punctured her thoughts. *It's not normal, people will think you're weird* . . . Maybe he was right.

The creak of the back gate snatched her reverie. Della sat up, unsure of her next move. What in all honesty had Jack done wrong? Been there, that's what. It couldn't be a coincidence.

He closed the back door carefully, as if fearing waking the rest of the house, the spark of his fag end marking him out in the room.

'Hello, Jack.'

'Blimey, Del, you scared me half to death.'

'Nice evening?' She couldn't keep the derision from her voice.

Jack pulled up a chair in front of the stove and rubbed his hands, the sour smell of beer lifting off him. 'Yes, as it happens, not that's it's any of your business.'

'Alice is my friend.' Della winced at her childish tone.

Jack chuckled, which only made her fury burn.

'How did you know?'

'I saw you pick her up outside the Ambrose. What were you doing there?'

'Pick her up? You make her sound like a cheap tart.'

'Don't talk about her like that.'

'I didn't, you did.' He drew on his cigarette. 'Proper lady that one, until she's had a few drinks.'

Della focused on the embers, determined not to rise to his bait.

'Fancy house she lives in.'

'You went to her house?'

He threw his cigarette in the fire. 'I went to her bedroom.'

Nausea pitched in her stomach. Jack's sharp laugh pulled her from the nightmare.

'Of course I didn't go to her bloody bedroom. I saw her to her front door and bid her goodnight like the gentleman I am.' He leaned back, pleased to have got under her skin. 'What is it with you two? You're weird about her, and she was just as bad, spent half the time asking me things about you.'

Della shrugged, her anger receding at this news. 'What kind of things?'

Jack yawned, tired now he'd had his fun. 'I'm off to bed.'

She listened to his tread on the stairs, the creak of the floor in the room above while she mulled over his words. Jack's cigarette sparked against the dying embers like a beacon of hope.

CHAPTER 14

Alice shifted onto her side, content to linger in bed after the events of the previous evening. Jack Wilde, what a fascinating individual. Surprisingly intellectual in an earthy way. Inscrutable too. She couldn't work him out, but he'd provided a much-needed diversion from the sight of Della walking away on the waiter's arm. They'd gone for chips, hot and greasy from their newspaper packaging, unlike anything she'd known. He hadn't made a pass at her either and she'd appreciated that. How odd a man with so little breeding could treat her better than Toby, a man who'd enjoyed every privilege.

A car horn dragged her to the window. She peered out to see Toby emerge from his Bentley behind the most ridiculous bouquet of flowers. The thing was so big, all she could see were his legs. The chime of the doorbell preceded muffled voices in the hall and the measured tread of Gillespie on the stairs. A light knock came against the door. Alice ignored it and eventually his footsteps retreated to convey the bad news.

An hour later, she stood before the painting of Della, a brush poised in her hand, a palette at the ready. During her carefree evening with Jack, she'd decided not to allow her father's selfish desires to trample upon the very thing that brought her joy. Besides, it was proving impossible to keep away from the painting. She'd made an outline of Della's face — her eyes looking off at something in the distance, windows on her soul. It was more painful than she'd expected. The portrait made her think of Della in the Ambrose bathroom, the lure of her lips, how close she'd come to losing control. Alice set down the brush. The whole thing made her depressed and embarrassed, and something else she couldn't or didn't want to define. But she wouldn't let it distract her from making the portrait everything she believed it could be. Alice picked up the brush again, dipped it in the palette she'd mixed for Della's skin and started in broad strokes, building up the layers, trying to remain objective. Looking but also not looking.

At lunch, Alice did little to acknowledge her father, not that he noticed, his attention focused on a newspaper. The flowers dominated the conversation with her mother. How expensive they were, how beautiful, how close Toby must be to dropping on bended knee. Alice nodded her way through until her mother set down her soup spoon and peered at her as if seeing her properly for the first time.

'Alice, what's happened to your face?'

She winced. The bruising had bloomed, and she'd forgotten to check her make-up was intact before coming downstairs.

'I bumped into . . .' She cast around the room for inspiration. Gillespie met her gaze and held it for a moment too long, before he resumed his close inspection of the wall above her father's head. 'The wall,' Alice said weakly.

'How on earth did you manage that?'

'I tripped on my bedroom rug.'

'Goodness, dear, you must be more careful. Gillespie, have a look at the rug in Alice's bedroom please.'

'Very good, ma'am.'

'Robert, have you seen Alice's bruise?'

Father glanced up. 'What was that?'

'I'm fine, Mummy, there's no need to make a fuss.'

He returned to his newspaper with a furrowed brow, not even distracted when Martha entered to clear their plates. Alice couldn't look at her either, instead making a study of the embroidery on the tablecloth until she was gone.

'Damned journalists,' Father muttered from behind his paper, then shook his head as if he realised he was in front of the wrong audience.

'What's wrong with journalists, Daddy?' Alice leaped at the opportunity to divert attention from her bruise.

He threw her a sharp look and folded the paper away. 'Forgive me, my dear, I spoke out of turn.'

She glanced at Gillespie, who continued his study of the wall. Did Gillespie know of her father's indiscretion? Did he help them meet? Her thoughts meandered back to the conversation in hand. When she returned her attention to her father, she found herself the object of his steady gaze.

'Perhaps you do need to know. We can't cosset you forever.'

Alice sat a little straighter, bemused by this turn in conversation. She focused on her father with expectation, ready to be educated by this man who was casting himself anew in her eyes. An adulterer, and now, apparently, a hater of journalists.

He cleared his throat as if about to launch into a speech for his constituents. 'The press are exaggerating the threat of communism, which in turn is inflaming the working man into violence and strike action. I don't say their grievances are unwarranted, but aggression should never be used as a tool for negotiation.' He shifted in his seat, his handsome, angular face furrowed as if he were at odds with himself.

The distant chime of the doorbell brought his explanation to an end before it had got going. He looked relieved, evidently puzzled by this changing world and his inability to articulate it. There was no doubt society was undergoing something of a transformation. Even Alice noticed the differences between the women of her generation and those of her mother's, not that they'd seen fit to trust women her age with the vote. She'd seen it in the eyes of the disillusioned who begged in the street, limbs offered up to the war. She knew not all wounds were obvious. Her father never spoke of the war, nor did Gillespie for that matter, yet they'd gone through it together. While other men returned with scars, her father returned with a Gillespie. Given his class, could he be a communist? Was Jack Wilde? It wouldn't surprise her. A smile arrived unbidden. She took a sip of water and reset her features.

Gillespie left to answer the door and they waited to discover who had the poor manners to interrupt them during luncheon.

The butler returned moments later carrying a small bouquet of what appeared to be flowers, although judging by the state of them, they'd been through several trials before reaching their destination.

'For you, Miss Alice. They were left on the doorstep.' Gillespie offered the depleted blooms.

Alice thrust back her chair and dropped her napkin. 'Thank you.' She took the flowers, finding a small card enclosed within the folds of brown paper and plucked it free. 'Put these in water, please.'

Gillespie's expression suggested he didn't think the flowers were worth saving but he left without comment.

Alice tore open the seal. The handwriting on the card read: *Thank you for a lovely evening. Yours, Jack Wilde.*

She bit her lip, half amused, half appalled. Could Jack Wilde seriously be attempting to court her?

Gillespie returned with the flowers artfully arranged in a small vase. He set them on the sideboard next to the enormous blooms Toby had sent that morning, distributed over several vases. The dining room resembled the scene for a wake.

Her mother eyed the flowers. 'Goodness, dear, Toby is keen.'

Alice wanted to be free from the stifling room. 'I think I'll take a walk.'

In the hall, she donned her hat and coat, swapping the heavy interior atmosphere for an exterior one where clouds threatened rain.

She'd barely reached the end of the road before she heard her name. Toby leaned out of the window of his Bentley, which he'd parked discreetly on the opposite side. He opened the door, inviting her in as raindrops danced on the roof. Alice hesitated before a droplet slid down her neck, causing her to relent. The car was at least dry, the windows misted with his breath.

'What do you want, Toby?'

He sat forwards, expression earnest. She turned her bruised cheek in his direction, giving him a full view of his work. 'Darling, I'm sorry.' His hand enveloped hers, warm, dry. Alice snatched it back and shifted a little away in her seat. She wasn't remotely scared — if anything, she pitied him — but that didn't mean he was forgiven. 'You don't know how you frustrate me. A chap can't be taken seriously if his girl shows him up in front of everyone.'

Alice grimaced, recalling how she'd laughed when he'd asked her to rein in her dancing, how he'd grasped her arm and led her away. How he'd reduced her in the eyes of his friends. Shame gave way to anger. She looked through the glass; the deluge had slowed. Alice was gripped with a need to leave, to leave all of it. *Where would she go?* The Ambrose. She'd find Della — but of course, there was the waiter. A drink then, perhaps she'd run into Jack, but where?

The look of defeat in Toby's expression suggested he'd already seen what was coming. Alice set her hand on the door handle to expedite a fast escape. 'I don't want to see you again, Toby.' Then she was out of the car and walking up the road, relieved at the silence accompanied by the gentle patter of rain. She headed in the direction of the city, in pursuit of one Wilde, while longing to see the other.

CHAPTER 15

Della funnelled cream into the centre of the éclair, her hand steady, her mind anything but. She replayed her conversation with Jack the previous evening, dissecting each part, studying it from every angle, returning to the same point. *You're weird.*

William slouched by, wearing a scowl. His anger was palpable from the moment she'd arrived at work that morning and he'd failed to acknowledge her existence or accept her second apology. Part of her wished she'd gone with him, that she'd let him try and kiss her in the back row, that she could conjure those feelings like other girls. *You're weird.* Hadn't he said it too?

The final éclair on the tray done, she stepped back and mopped her brow, surveying her handiwork, the neat rows of pastries gleaming with chocolate ganache. William walked past again, finding something about the floor fascinating. 'These éclairs are ready to go to the servery,' she said to his passing figure, hoping his mood had lifted.

'Ask someone else,' he shot back.

Hastings approached. 'What's got into that lad? He's had a face like a gathering storm all morning.'

Della shrugged. 'Search me.'

Hastings threw her a knowing look. 'Be gentle with him. He's carried a torch for you since your first day. The lad isn't made of stone.'

Della suppressed a sigh. 'I'll speak to him.'

'You're a good girl.'

Was she good? Della wasn't so sure. She didn't feel a shred of goodness when she thought about Alice and her brother. No, that didn't make her feel good at all.

* * *

Despite her resolve, by late afternoon, her promise had faded into a busy day. Grateful for the distraction of work to keep her mind from straying to Alice and Jack, she was easing a sponge cake from its pan onto a cooling rack when she sensed a presence at her side. Della glanced up, expecting William. Instead she looked into the face of Mr Voisin, the head chef, his stiff white hat adding height to his otherwise stocky frame.

'Della, isn't it?'

She wiped her hands on her apron. 'Yes, sir.'

'You were responsible for the éclair's this morning?'

She gave a brief nod. A nugget of fear worked its way into her stomach. What had she got wrong?

'Don't look so worried. I merely wanted to congratulate you. The piping was exceptional, the ganache perfection. We had several compliments passed onto our waiting staff.'

Relief replaced anxiety in her knotted stomach. 'Thank you, sir.'

He nodded, turned on his heel and walked away. Della stared after him, elated to have her work noticed by a man who was said to have trained at Le Cordon Bleu. Perhaps it didn't do to entertain ambitions beyond her reach, but Voisin's compliment had brought her a step closer to making her dream feel a little less ridiculous.

William appeared in her periphery, dispelling her reverie. Della took a deep breath before calling his name.

He marched on as if he hadn't heard — but half the kitchen had, judging by the number of her colleagues who looked up, Anthony among them. Della returned her focus to the cooling sponge, hoping to hide her humiliation.

She was mixing the filling when Anthony approached. 'I hear you've been breaking hearts?'

Della sighed. 'I don't know about that, maybe his pride.'

'I wouldn't be so sure. He's been in a temper today.'

First Mrs Hastings, now Anthony. Della didn't know what to say.

'Hey, I was only joking.' Anthony evidently noticed her pained expression. 'I have a talent for saying the wrong thing, just ask my missus.'

Della hoisted a smile. 'I'm sorry William's giving you a hard time on account of me.'

'It's nothing, imagine living with him in the trenches.'

'I didn't realise you went through the war together?'

'Yeah, quite the hero you've passed up there. I could tell you a few stories.'

Hero? Della couldn't picture it, but she nodded. The war was never a topic she wanted to dwell on.

'Anyway, like I said, ignore me.' With that he sauntered away, whistling as he went.

By the time the café closed its doors, Della was thoroughly fed up with the muddle in her head. She pulled on her coat and trailed behind her colleagues. William was leaning against the lift when she emerged from the kitchen. After a day of suffering his withering looks, Della didn't have the energy to muster another apology, but he stepped in her path as she made for the stairs.

Heeding Hastings' words, she tried to be gentle. 'I'm sorry, William. I shouldn't have agreed to go to the cinema when—'

'You're not like her.' He cast around as if to ensure they were alone. 'That Alice.' His lip curled. 'One of them *sapphic* types.'

Heat found her cheeks.

He took a step closer, making her acutely aware of his height and breadth. A heavy scent of brilliantine lifted off his hair.

'William, I'd just like to be friends.' Her voice sounded feeble.

He frowned and rested his hand against the wall above her shoulder, blocking her escape with his arm. 'Is there someone else?'

Her thoughts went to Alice, but that was wishful thinking. She shook her head.

The lift creaked to a halt and Leonnard emerged with a trolley stacked with sacks of flour. As if he sensed the atmosphere, he paused.

William took a step back. 'What are you bloody staring at?'

'Don't speak to him like that.' Della found her courage. Leonnard hurried away.

'One-eyed freak,' William muttered. 'Is it him?' He glared at the back of Leonnard's head as the kitchen doors swung shut behind.

'I don't want to go out with you, William. I'm sorry if that's upsetting to hear, but surely it's better if I'm honest.'

His neck glowed, his anger so evident she could almost see the vein pop in his forehead. He entered the lift and slammed the gate across. With his eyes drilling into her, it felt like an eternity until the lift carried him away.

Della returned to the kitchen to check Leonnard was alright after William's offensive remark. He was unloading the flour and placing a sack by each bench, ready for the morning.

'I'm sorry William was rude.'

Leonnard studied her for a beat then shrugged his broad shoulders. 'You're not his keeper. Anyway, I've heard worse.'

She didn't know what to say. That anyone would treat Leonnard so appallingly because of an injury he'd sustained in the war made her burn with fury. 'Even so, he shouldn't have spoken to you like that.'

He lifted another bag of flour into place. Leonnard had been with them for about a year, but they were all guilty of taking his work for granted. Sacks of flour, bags of sugar, an endless supply of clean mixing bowls and cake pans — they all made their way into the kitchen by Leonnard's hand.

Lost for what else to add, she watched him move further away. 'Bye then,' she called and left.

* * *

On the walk home, the accumulation of all her anxieties weighed heavy, as if she too were carrying a bag of flour. The ghost of her confrontation with William lingered, but as she neared the house, Jack and Alice reinserted themselves in her mind too. Only Mr Voisin's compliment lightened her load, but the thought of Le Cordon Bleu brought her back to Alice, the only person with whom she'd shared that ambition.

She let herself in and froze at the sight she dreaded. The kitchen in disarray, the *tap-tap* of Samuel under the table, knocking his whip and top against the legs. It could mean only one thing.

'What's happened?' She crouched to see Samuel's face.

He gave the table another good thrash. 'Came home from school and Ma were crying at the stove. Henry took her to bed.'

Della crawled underneath to join him, gently extracting the toy from his hands. 'She'll be alright after a rest.'

Sam's focus remained on the floor; hers did too. What if Ma didn't get up? What if this downturn carried on for weeks, months, years? Suddenly she wished she could talk to Jack, not to argue but to figure out a plan, like they used to before life set them on opposing paths.

An hour later, with order restored to the kitchen, three of them sat down to a tea of bread and jam, Jack conspicuous in his absence.

'Maybe he's got some work,' Henry offered from the depths of a book. Reading at the table was not a habit Ma would encourage.

So long as he isn't with Alice. The thought sent Della plummeting new depths. Five interminable days until Sunday. After the events of the previous evening, she had no idea if Alice was expecting her or even wanted to see her, but right then, she decided to go. Whatever this thing was between them, she needed to know if Alice would join her on the precipice. If she'd take her hand and fall.

CHAPTER 16

Alice took a seat at the dining table, the detritus of her parents' breakfast yet to be cleared away. A headache pressed at her temples. She wasn't in the mood for food, but experience taught her a plate of Mrs Drummond's eggs might counter the effects of the previous evening's overindulgence. Pity it couldn't steer her through the labyrinth in her mind.

Martha darted into the room and startled. 'Beg pardon, ma'am.' She scooped up the plates with her deft hands, clearly desperate to be away. *Guilt?* Alice watched her leave. If she couldn't countenance Alice, how on earth did she manage to attend to Mummy, the true victim of her affair?

Gillespie entered the room with a fresh pot of coffee, putting an end to her speculation. The aroma was enough to make her weep with gratitude.

'I trust you had an enjoyable evening, Miss Alice?' He eyed her, the only member of the household with any idea of her nocturnal activities. Since breaking up with Toby, days had dragged, each one punctuated by regret and ending with new friends at the Zodiac bar. Having attempted to cauterise her wounds with champagne cocktails, she was now paying the requisite price. Each time she'd rolled in at an unearthly hour,

Gilliespie had been reading in the kitchen. He never made any comment, but there was something comforting about the way he bolted the back door as she climbed the stairs, as if he'd been waiting for her safe return before considering his day at an end. The man must hardly sleep. She really should be less selfish.

'I did, thank you,' Alice rallied. 'Are my parents out?'

'Your father caught the early train to London and your mother has a French lesson.'

A French lesson? Her second that week. Alice was pleased by this news. A full day in the attic.

'Eggs?'

She nodded. 'Thank you, Mr Gillespie.'

* * *

But time in the attic didn't offer the inspiration Alice hoped to find. It wasn't only the headache and the queasiness in her stomach. As she stood before the portrait, she finally admitted to herself it wasn't working. Her vision of the painting, so clear upon first meeting Della, had muddied and Alice couldn't fathom why, or perhaps she could. The complex turn in their relationship had ruined her ability to capture the essence of her subject. How could she fix it when her feelings remained ambiguous too? This was all her father's fault. If she hadn't discovered his secret, she wouldn't have gone off the rails with Toby, wouldn't have almost kissed Della . . . Toby never made her feel like that — naked with desire.

Alice cleaned her brush and packed her materials away with the Della in the portrait watching as she moved around the room. She took one last glance at the woman who filled her waking thoughts before covering the canvas with a sheet and making her way downstairs. Two days until Sunday, then perhaps she'd have a chance to put things right, but where would she be if Della didn't turn up?

* * *

Sunday dawned with another headache after a further night of trying and failing to forget. Alice stood at the attic window looking out for Della. Part of her hoped she wouldn't come after her humiliation at their last meeting. She'd ruined things with her clumsy reading of the situation.

A large black bird — a raven, a crow? — chuckled from the opposite tree as if calling out her lie. Of course she wanted to see Della. She always wanted to see her. That was part of the conundrum.

The bird called again — a raven, she decided, for its ominous sensibilities. A shock of dark hair caught her eye. Della walking down the street, black curls bouncing in a long plait, her hat removed and clutched in her hand. The bird flew off as if its job was done.

Alice raced from the attic and down the servants' stairs, darting past a baffled Gillespie as he smoked a cigarette in the kitchen. She flung open the back door for Della, who'd lifted her hand to knock. Her face was flushed, making her cheeks stand out, two circles of pink against her pale skin.

'I wasn't sure . . .' Alice halted as Della uttered the same greeting. They laughed, an incandescence to Della's eyes.

Alice stood to one side. 'Come in.'

As they climbed the stairs, she was aware of every step Della took behind. She'd brought in with her the fresh smells of a chilly spring day and the scent of something earthier. Whatever it was, Alice liked it.

When they made it into the attic room, its contours felt too confined for what she was feeling. Della unwound her scarf, letting her long plait fall down her back.

'I should have lit the fire,' Alice ventured, pointing at the grate, where the ash from a week ago lay like tarnished snow.

'I'm warm from my walk.' Della held Alice's gaze until she was compelled to look away.

This coyness that appeared to have taken her hostage was not only ridiculous but quite unattractive. She cleared her throat in a bid to assert control over her senses. 'Did you enjoy your evening at the cinema?'

'Oh, that.' Della studied her hands. 'I didn't go. I mean, I changed my mind after I saw you. I'd only agreed because William lent me his coat and he does go on so.'

Alice couldn't explain the warm feeling in the pit of her stomach.

'I came back actually, to find you, to go to supper, but . . .'

She now recalled Jack, the chips, the salt on her tongue, the vinegar hitting the back of her throat. She hadn't bothered to seek him out again. 'I, um . . .'

'You went out with my brother.' Della was studying her, a slight frown. An accusation?

'He told you?'

'I saw you leave with him, but yes, he couldn't resist gloating.'

Alice felt suddenly tired by it all. She sat on the daybed, gesturing to Della to sit too. Della settled herself, sweeping her plait from her shoulder. Alice had the urge to untie it, run her fingers through those long curls and free them from each other, but it was her feelings that needed untangling. 'If I'd known you were available — well, I was rather wounded when you went off with William, so . . .'

A smile tugged at Della's lips as if she were pleased by this news. 'How's your face? The bruise, it don't look so bad today.'

Alice touched her cheek. 'It aches a little.'

'Does he often do that, your beau?'

'He's not my beau anymore.'

'Pleased to hear it, bleedin' cheek. I'd like to give him what for.' Della clenched her fists.

Alice stifled a laugh.

'What?' Della seemed genuinely angry.

'Nothing, you look delightful when you're furious.'

'Delightful?' Della blushed, her gaze directed to the window before it swept back to Alice. 'Are we . . . weird? That's what William said, Jack too.'

Alice glanced away, unable to answer, unsure if she wanted to name it, this thing with Della, or pretend it wasn't happening. There were times, like in the Ambrose bathroom, when it became too big to contain. She stood, irritated by her inability to face it head on. Sensing Della's eyes on her, she moved to the easel, the canvas providing cover. 'I need to get on with the painting.'

Della nodded slowly, as if taking it in, this rebuff of her perfectly fair question. 'Can I see it?' There was the hint of strain in her voice.

'Not yet, silly. Not until its finished.' Alice detected her own shrill note. She picked up a brush at random and spent an unnecessarily long time over the mix of paint. All the while Della's presence filled the room like something ethereal. When Alice finally looked at her, she could see her anew, with a short crop of black curls, how it would transform her. How it would distract them. 'Have you considered cutting your hair?'

Della, clearly surprised by the abrupt change of subject, shrugged. 'I dunno. I know my hair's not fashionable.' She fingered the end of her plait. 'I've always worn it like this, and I can't afford to go to one of them hairdressing places.'

Alice moved to the daybed, her inhibitions shed by something stronger. 'I could cut it for you.' She was gripped, convinced this was the thing to do.

Della's eyes widened. 'What, now?'

'Why not?'

'Don't you want to paint? I mean, isn't that the point of me being here?'

Alice nodded, but it wasn't the point. She could admit to herself, if not to Della, she wanted her there. 'There's time, and I'd love to paint you with short hair. Please?'

'Alright, if it means that much to you.'

Alice grinned, relieved to have a diversion and one she'd enjoy. 'Don't move, I'll fetch scissors and my comb.'

In her bedroom, she found the items, catching her reflection in her dressing table mirror. Her cheeks were flushed, her

81

eyes alive, the bruise no longer sore. A bloom of happiness. *Are we weird?* Why didn't she have the mettle to admit it. Yes! She wanted to scream it. Yes! And I don't care.

'Alice, is that you?' Her mother's voice from the landing.

Alice slid the comb and scissors into her pocket and opened her bedroom door. Her mother was wrapped in an elaborate brocade shawl her father had brought as a gift from his last trip to London. Did he buy gifts out of guilt? He'd got Alice a beautiful slide for her hair. She tried not to think of it as tainted. 'Are you cold, Mummy?'

'I am rather. Gillespie's lighting the fire in the drawing room so I can play cards. Why don't you join me?'

'Sorry, I'm going to take a nap.' She yawned for effect.

Her mother lifted her hand to her cheek. 'Your bruise is healing nicely.'

Alice tried not to flinch at this rare affection.

Her mother smiled. 'Well, if I can't tempt you.'

She watched her make her way down the stairs, a pale slender hand gliding the banister, resolving to spend more time with her, to make up for her father's neglect.

As Alice climbed the stairs to the attic, she tried to put the guilt away and capture some of her earlier happiness.

Della was seated as she'd left her. 'You didn't peek?' she gestured to the easel.

'I was tempted.'

Alice retrieved the comb and scissors. 'Ready?'

'Don't make me look like a scarecrow, Alice Winters.'

Alice sat beside her, enjoying the sound of her full name on Della's tongue. She gently took hold of the plait. 'I'm going to chop at the top of this plait and then I'll tidy what's left.

'Eeek,' Della squealed. 'What am I doing?'

Alice felt the weight of the hair in her hands, as heavy as the responsibility at the task she was undertaking, but there wasn't a whisper of doubt in her mind. Della would look stunning with short hair. She took her time, feeling the soft hairs on the back of Della's neck brush against her knuckle as she cut. The hair was thick, the scissors only just up to the job.

Della gasped again as the plait came away. Alice held it up, shocked herself by how much hair she'd cut. What was left came loose around the nape of Della's neck, her natural curl requiring little work to make the cut smooth. She lifted Della's chin and pulled the sides of her hair down, taking a little off the left to even things up. Della's eyes met hers. There was anxiety there but also a sparkle of excitement. A few more cuts and she was done. The transformation was remarkable. Della looked sophisticated and vibrant, as if the plait had been weighing her down. Alice couldn't stop staring.

'Can I see?' Della whispered, her voice a little uncertain.

She stood, letting the plait fall to the floor. 'Of course. There's a mirror in the bathroom.'

On the narrow landing, Alice listened for signs of life before directing Della to the bathroom the servants shared. A rather mottled square of glass was propped on top of the radiator. She felt ashamed her parents offered their staff so little. Della didn't seem to notice, but took up the glass and stared into it, her fingers grazing her neck as if to ensure there really was no hair.

'Blimey,' she whispered, her expression grave.

Alice felt aghast. 'You hate it.'

Della returned the glass to the radiator and turned to face her, her hair falling in perfect soft waves. 'Oh no, Alice, I love it.'

Alice swept a curl from Della's eyes. Her gaze roamed over her face, stalling at Della's lips, parted and dangerously close to hers. She was back in the Ambrose bathroom with every sinew in her body crying out with need. Della's lip quivered and she tilted her head. Alice met her gaze, seeking permission. Then they were kissing. It was everything she'd imagined and so much more. Her fingers entwined in Della's hair, exploring the thick, lustrous locks at the nape of her neck. Even the radiator pressing into her thigh couldn't detract from her heightened senses, mini explosions sending goosebumps scattering along her arms.

At the creak of a floorboard, Alice reeled backwards. They froze, eyes locked in panic. A man cleared his throat. *Gillespie?*

Alice put her finger to her lips. A door further down the corridor clicked shut. After a moment, she checked the landing and, finding it empty, ushered Della back into the attic room.

The heat from their bathroom exchange evaporated. Della continued to fiddle with her hair, running her fingers through it, pulling at the back as if she were trying to make it long again. Alice watched all this from the closed door she was leaning against, her mind half preoccupied by the kiss, half terrified at what Gillespie had heard. He'd kept her meetings with Della in confidence, but who else's secrets did he keep? Her father's? His affair that could bring the winter house to its knees.

Della picked up her discarded plait and weaved it through her fingers. 'I should go,' she whispered, with one eye on the fading afternoon light.

Alice nodded, both disappointed and relieved. 'Thank you for coming.' It sounded so cold.

Della lifted her fingers to her neck again. 'Thanks for the haircut. Might be able to sell the plait.'

'Gosh, really?'

'There's folks that need real hair for wigs and what not.'

Alice ran her fingers through her own short tresses, wondering if the hairstylist had sold her golden locks. 'Well . . .' This awkwardness was unbearable. 'I'll take you down.'

There was no sign of the butler as they traversed the stairs and the kitchen. At the back door, Della paused. 'Do you need me again?'

Alice frowned.

'For the painting?'

'Oh . . .' Yes, she needed her again, but was that wise? The moment's hesitation answered for her.

'It's fine.' Della's tremulous smile failed to reach her eyes. 'I'll see you around.'

Alice watched Della walk away, knowing she'd broken something, not just between them but within her too. She closed the door and turned back inside.

Gillespie stepped out of the shadows.

CHAPTER 17

Tears came hot and fast as Della walked away. Alice had done it again. No, worse. This time, she'd actually kissed her and then withdrawn, leaving her feeling used. *I kissed her back.* It was true, she had, but Alice's response was equally hungry. William and Jack's words resurfaced. Alice hadn't answered when she'd asked if they were weird, perhaps Alice knew it too. There was something wrong with them, and now it was over. More tears fell as she reached the Magdalen road and struck out for home.

The house was eerily quiet as she slipped in at the back, the stove cold and the table littered with the remnants of lunch. Della made for the stairs, wanting to stow her plait in her bedroom. If she was going to sell her hair, that was her business and no one else's.

On the landing, she paused outside Ma's room, hearing laboured breathing from within, then continued up the stairs, wiping away fresh tears with her sleeve. In her attic bedroom, she put the plait under her pillow and glanced in the mirror, surprised by her own reflection. Her eyes might be red and puffy, but the sight of her new hair helped her recover. She was a woman now.

In the kitchen, her newfound status ebbed as she lit the stove and cleared the table, puzzling over the absence of her siblings. How long would the dark cloud hover over Ma this time?

Pa was a willowy man with jet-black curls, a good-humoured soul, a foil to Ma's anxious nature. The day they brought the telegram, Ma dropped to her knees and howled. It scared her, it scared them all. Samuel was still a babe in arms, tottering about on chubby legs, hadn't even met his father. Ma stayed in bed for a month, not a word uttered from her lips. They'd subsisted on jam sandwiches and anything neighbours could share. Only Jack held it together. Been a rock for them all to cling to.

Henry crashed through the kitchen door, his glasses hanging off his nose, one of the arms bent in two.

'What's happened to you?'

'Just some lads.' He shrugged as if being set upon by a group of lads was as regular an occurrence as taking a bath.

'What lads?'

'Drop it, Del.'

She did as she was asked and turned back to the stove. 'Where's Sam?'

'Dunno.'

Della turned on him again. 'We need to make sure he's not left alone. He's not old enough to take care of himself.'

'He's ten. Anyway, you weren't here either.'

It was true, she'd gone to Alice's without so much as a by your leave.

'What did you do with your hair?'

Della touched her neck, distracted. 'What do you think?'

'Did some lads set upon you too with the garden shears?' Henry was smiling. Nothing could ruffle his feathers.

She threw the dishcloth at him and set about slicing the loaf, her attention returning to Sam. Things were getting bad with their mother. If she carried on like this, they'd have to work out a rota so Sam wasn't left to his own devices. She

86

glanced at her brother, now seated at the table, nose stuck in a book. Henry didn't make life easy on himself but at least he was smart. Perhaps one day all that learning would get him somewhere, and them by association.

The door swung open so fast, it smacked into the work-top. There was Sam, a grin on his face, Jack behind, carrying a brace of rabbits which he dumped on the kitchen table.

Sam rushed up to her then stopped short. 'What have you done to your hair?'

'Cut it off. What have you been doing?' She glanced behind to Jack, who was studying her from under his cap.

'Me and Jack went to—'

'Shush now, Sam. If you tell her, it won't be our secret.' Jack winked. Della didn't like the cut of the smirk slicing across his features.

Sam looked conflicted. 'We got rabbits for a stew,' he said, his face brightening.

'So I can see.' Della approached the poor creatures. 'Who's going to skin them?' She glanced to Jack.

'I only provide the food.' He pulled out a chair and sat down, feet on the table.

Skinning rabbits and defeathering chickens was usually Ma's job. Her gaze lifted to the ceiling as if she could wish her into the room. 'I suppose it's down to me.'

With Ma's largest knife in her hand, Della laid the first rabbit across a sheet of newspaper. Her insides curdled as she sliced through the gut, inserted her fingers and tugged the skin away. It didn't give easily, the creature sliding from her grip as she pulled with all her might. The metallic scent of blood mixed with earthy, gamey smells had her heaving. Sweat pooled at her spine — disgust for the work, irritation that her brothers were useless and curiosity over where Jack had been with Sam. It was one thing to keep his counsel about his own activities, he could please himself and always had, but Sam was a different matter. She resolved to keep a closer watch over the youngest Wilde.

87

Half an hour later, the stew was bubbling. Della scrubbed her fingers under the tap, appalled at the memory of the soft, warm flesh. Another experience she'd gladly forget along with Alice's kiss, not that there was any similarity between the two. The kiss made her feel alive, but in the same way she'd pulled the skin from the rabbit, it had left her exposed and now bereft.

Jack broke into her thoughts. 'What's with the hair?'

'I figured it was time I caught up with the rest of the world.' There was a defensiveness to her tone. She turned, surprised to find they were alone.

He lit a cigarette and expelled a plume of smoke. 'Suits you.'

Della shrugged, unsure what to do with this rare compliment.

'Was it Alice?'

The skin on the back of her neck prickled at the mention of her name. Unable to trust herself to speak, she gave a quick nod.

'Thought so.' He looked pleased, like he knew Alice better than her, like he'd put Alice up to it.

She turned back to the sink and took a moment to compose herself. Outside, dusk had blanketed the yard, making shadows of the familiar. 'Where did you get them rabbits?' Her voice came out, steady and sure. She was back in control.

'A bloke.'

'Where did you take Sam this afternoon?'

'Out.'

Jack knew exactly how to cause maximum frustration. She needed to remain detached, disinterested. To probe further would only give him more ammunition. 'Stew will be ready in an hour. Make sure it doesn't boil dry. I'm going upstairs to check on Ma, see if I can't coax her out.'

On the landing, Della paused, but she didn't go to her mother. Sam was already there, chatting in his sing-song voice. Her heart broke for his upbeat demeanour, ploughing on with so little response.

In her bedroom, she stood before the mirror once again. Her hair might be gone, but underneath everything was exactly the same.

CHAPTER 18

Gillespie set the teapot on the kitchen table between them. Not the fine china one her mother used, but a brown betty, chipped at the spout, the victim of dedicated service and Mrs Drummond's clumsy washing-up. He eyed the pot too, as if he could see into her mind. Would he read the leaves after their talk? It wouldn't surprise her, but what would he find?

It was odd to think of this man, so apparently unruffled, sharing tea, her secrets hidden behind the wall of propriety they lived by. Alice wondered again at what he knew about the inhabitants of the winter house.

He pulled out a chair opposite. 'Shall I be mother?' He gestured to the pot.

Her mouth twitched with amusement. This bear of a man, with the refined delicacy of an English Rose. It certainly took her mind off the turmoil in her heart.

Taking her silence for assent, he lifted the pot, took his time with the strainer, serving her first. She watched him add milk and one sugar. There was no need to enquire how she took her tea — it was his business to know. How she liked her tea, her coffee, her preferred evening drink. Gillespie knew this family better than they knew themselves.

He sat back, studying her with an open expression. Alice felt exposed. Was she supposed to speak first? It was his suggestion they sit down like this. He'd witnessed her distress on closing the door behind Della, observed the tear slide down her cheek and offered his crisply ironed hanky to catch it.

Gillespie cleared his throat. Here it was. 'You're an exceptional artist.'

Alice stared at him. Surprised. Flattered. Confused.

'Why haven't you told your parents you paint?'

She frowned. 'They wouldn't understand.'

'You underestimate them.'

Impertinence. She pushed the thought away. His comment was kindly meant.

He sat forward, brown eyes focused intently on hers. 'I'm not paying you lip service, Miss Alice. You have talent. That's a fact.'

Alice nodded, still on guard. Why couldn't she be gracious? 'Thank you.'

He lifted his cup, dwarfed in his large hands, nails neat and clean. 'The girl who comes here, she's your muse?'

She hadn't considered Della in those terms. Was it normal, to feel this way about a muse? Was that all that was the matter?

'Does she inspire you to paint? Do you think about her when she's not around?'

'I suppose so.'

'Whatever happened between you to cause an upset, put it right or your work will suffer. Don't overanalyse it,' he continued, warming to his subject. 'See her as much as you can.'

'I doubt that's possible.'

'A lovers' quarrel?'

He did suspect and yet he showed no hint of shock or revulsion. 'I don't know.' It was the most honest she'd been in weeks. How odd that this man should pull from her such truths about something she struggled to define herself. Perhaps he was a clairvoyant after all. 'Why are you saying all this?'

He drummed his fingers against the table. 'Because I don't like to see talent wasted. If you've been granted a gift, use it. Don't fritter it away.'

She wanted to ask if he was speaking from experience and to whom he was referring, but his face had closed, his eyes muddied by something personal. Alice sipped her tea, finding it provided the comfort she needed. The silence that followed felt heavy, perhaps from the weight of their conversation or the unravelling of her secrets. Either way, she didn't know how to circumnavigate this awkward moment. She was at once flattered and moved by his words, while fearing she'd made a grave error with Della. Wasn't it better to stop this now? *See her as much as you can.*

She set down her cup, finding herself the object of his inscrutable gaze. That sense he could read her. 'How did you discover my painting?'

'It's my job to know what goes on in this house if it relates to its security and the comfort of my employer. I have a key to every room.' Alice must have failed to hide her consternation because he added, 'I don't use my position to pry but I do check the unused rooms as a matter of maintaining the property.'

It was fair enough and she should have realised that herself. 'You won't tell my parents?'

A smile tugged at his lips, a rare moment of levity. 'Your secret is safe with me, but you should consider telling them.'

Alice wondered which secret he referred to, her art or Della? 'I can see how that would play out. Daddy would frown and go off to his study, Mummy would tell me not to be absurd. They want me married and out of here.'

He rubbed his chin as if weighing up her assessment. 'You have the measure of them in your mind. Is it fair?'

'All evidence so far has led to that conclusion.'

'If you don't challenge the status quo, how can you be certain they aren't capable of change and understanding beyond your imaginings? How can you know they wouldn't welcome your honesty? Have you led them to believe it's you who wants to be married off? You play your part well.' He let his statement hang while he finished his tea, then pushed back his chair.

Alice watched, confounded, as he cleared away their cups and took the teapot to the sink. It seemed their meeting was at an end.

CHAPTER 19

Work claimed Della's focus in the following days. February turned to March. Daffodils bloomed, bitter frosts gave way to damp. She tried not to think of Alice or worry about Samuel and who was taking care of him after school while Ma kept to her bed. Henry disappeared so far into his own world, he hardly noticed the other Wildes. And as for Jack, who knew what he did with his days? But it was all there, floating in the soup of her mind, seasoned with anxiety.

The ping of the kitchen timer pulled her from further contemplation. She went to the ovens, where four trays of sponges were baking. Della picked up the peel and slid them out, pleased with their rise.

'They look good,' Leonnard commented as she eased them onto a cooling rack. His arms were filled with a stack of clean cake pans.

'Thanks. They're for the mayor's banquet this evening.'

Leonnard nodded, a little downcast. She'd noticed the way he studied the other bakers. He clearly had ambition, but to those in charge, his missing eye held that ambition in check. He stowed the pans under the work bench and walked away.

She tucked a stray curl under her cap and assembled the other ingredients. Her haircut was old news now. 'Well, look at you,' Mrs Hastings had said on Monday, after Della pulled off her hat to reveal her cropped hair. 'Goodness, Della Wilde, it looks so modern, so sophisticated. You need to be out front, showing off, not stuck away in here.'

Despite the attention her new do invited, she was relieved when it reached its end. She wanted to remain hidden in the comfort of the kitchen and absorb herself in her creations, like the one she was working on today. The dinner was to be held in the banqueting room that evening, a stuffy affair, men in suits, accompanied by their wives in the finest couture Exeter could offer. Her petit fours would be the centrepiece. Hastings was giving her more responsibility and she was eager to learn. Leonnard reappeared in her periphery, dragging a bag of flour. She'd have a quiet word with Mrs Hastings, see if he couldn't be given an opportunity too.

While her sponges were cooling, Della picked up the *Le Cordon Bleu* magazine which had been left in the servery. She thumbed the worn pages and lost herself in recipes — one for pineapple upside-down cake, which was said to be taking America by storm — but her attention couldn't be diverted for long. The banquet would be a welcome distraction, a delay to the return home and the reality of no Sunday visit to Alice to brighten her week.

Two hours later, her back ached with the effort of decorating the exquisite petit fours. Each one had to be even and as perfect as its predecessor. There were mini Victoria sponges, delicate squares of gateaux, éclairs, and tarts glazed with forest fruits. She wiped her brow and lifted her gaze to the clock above the kitchen doors. One hour to go.

At 7 p.m. Della watched Anthony transfer her work onto the cake trolley, taking her back to her first meeting with Alice and the clandestine escape. She pushed the memory away as the last of her creations were arranged on decorative stands. Anthony took the helm. At least it wasn't William, and the petit fours made an impressive display. Despite having scrubbed her hands, her fingers were still sticky with sugar. She could only hope the fruits of her labour arrived without mishap and that the guests were more refined than Alice's friends.

At the door, Anthony paused. 'Aren't you coming to see your hard work make its maiden voyage?'

'What, dressed like this?' She gestured to her flour-smeared overall.

'You're decent underneath, aren't you? Why don't you grab a clean apron from the stores? To be honest, I could do with the help. There's a lot that could go wrong with a trolley full of cakes. Apart from the obvious, I need you to stop me eating them.'

Della smiled. She'd put on a plain navy dress that morning — like all her clothes, a little dated but presentable. 'Give me a second.' She ran to the staff changing room, removed her cap and unbuttoned her overalls. Fluffing her hair, she returned to the kitchens via the linen stores for a fresh apron and accompanied Anthony up in the lift.

'Your new hairdo makes you look like Mary Pickford, only prettier,' Anthony observed.

'Does your wife know you talk to women like that?'

He chuckled. 'She encourages it.'

Della lightly punched his arm. 'Liar.' Still, she enjoyed the compliment, and coming from Anthony, she knew it was kindly meant.

As they emerged from the lift, William stormed past.

'Still sulking?' Anthony enquired once he was out of earshot.

'It appears so.'

'He'll get over it. We're all a bit curious about you, Della Wilde.'

Della was going to ask him to elaborate, when Mr Voisin approached to inspect her work. A frown furrowed his brow as he studied the petit fours from every angle. Della's stomach tightened. His sharp gaze met hers. '*Très bien.*' Voisin glanced at her outfit and gestured to the door.

Della's smile fell into a gasp. 'Me, go in there?'

'*Oui*. Hurry, they are hungry for decadence only the Ambrose can provide. Don't keep them waiting.' He raised his eyebrows and was gone.

'You heard the man.' Anthony pushed the trolley to the door.

The tables were arranged in long rows a bit like a school dining hall but decorated with starched linen cloths and silverware. The guests, dressed in their finery, gossiped to the accompaniment of a jazz quartet. Della cast over the room — many of the clientele were middle-aged. Men with moustaches and balding heads, the women either adorned in the latest fashions or clinging to the previous decade. Perhaps that's why Alice stuck out among them with her abrupt crop and her emerald-beaded dress.

Della felt colour bleed into her cheeks as she took her place beside Anthony. Mr Richards, the Ambrose's master of ceremonies, cleared his throat, the band brought their tune to an end and a hush spread over the room. Alice, who'd been engaged in conversation with a gentleman to her left, looked up.

'That's the MP, Robert Winters,' Anthony whispered as if she'd expressed her curiosity about Alice's companion out loud.

Mr Richards introduced dessert and the room erupted into an enthusiastic round of applause.

'Can you help me serve, Del? I dunno what's happened to William.'

Della nodded, a trance-like state taking command of her limbs. Anthony's steadying hand found her arm and together they lifted the trays of petit fours onto the top table so guests might serve themselves. All the while, Della was too aware of Alice in the room.

At the first opportunity, she hurried back to the kitchen and took her time packing away her work bench, cleaning down the surfaces and ensuring everything was properly stored. The room was empty, the other bakers had gone home, but something or someone made her linger. It was absurd; after their awkward parting there was no reason for Alice to seek her out. She wouldn't find her way to the kitchen, let alone be able to conjure an excuse to visit. And yet, when Anthony appeared with the cake trolley ten minutes later and Alice emerged from underneath, Della wasn't at all surprised.

CHAPTER 20

'Your face.' Alice grinned at Della once the waiter had departed. Unlike the surly William, this one was charming. He'd taken it in his stride when she'd asked if he might sneak her out of the banquet so she could visit her friend.

Della was staring at her from behind a long table.

'Aren't you going to say hello?' Alice was rapidly losing her nerve. The silence continued. 'Your hair looks . . .' She gestured to Della's crop. It looked amazing and that had nothing to do with who'd wielded the scissors. It was all Della, her crisp cheekbones, her alabaster skin, those eyes, studying Alice with such uncertainty.

Della dropped her gaze to the tabletop. 'What are you doing here?'

'That's hardly a warm welcome.' A prickly response to a prickly question. She tried again. 'I'm here with my father. Mummy had one of her headaches and I thought if I could see you, it would be worth sitting through a dinner tainted by boring conversation.'

Della appeared to find the tabletop fascinating. 'I don't normally work in the evenings.'

'No, but you do work at special occasions. Who but Della Wilde could make such a fabulous dessert?'

'You weren't particularly bothered about the last one.'

It was Alice's turn to study the table surface, pockmarked with overuse. This was proving harder than she'd imagined. It was clear she'd injured Della, but Gillespie's words had settled in her head and her heart. She mustered her reserves of courage. 'I'm sorry for saying I didn't need you anymore. It wasn't true. I do need you.'

Della met her gaze. 'So you can finish the portrait?'

'That and . . . I want to see you. I can't pretend to understand. I think you're my sort of muse. It's rather irritating. Every time I try to deny it, the need to see you gets stronger.'

Della was wrestling with a smile, her lips curled into a grimace, but her eyes gave her away. Alice relaxed a little, feeling the warmth of the expansive room lingering from the ovens, the ordered chaos. Large mixing bowls on stands, big enough for a baby to bathe in, sacks of flour and sugar, pans in every shape and size imaginable.

'Do you want a tour?' Della had followed her gaze.

If this was a peace offering, she'd take it. 'Please.'

Della led her from section to section, a light in her eyes, her fingers gliding over the precious tools of her trade.

From the kitchen they made their way through the first-floor servery, where gleaming silver teapots and coffee pots waited for breakfast. On they went to the china store, stacked with every kind of crockery imaginable, the silver store, rows of candlesticks for elaborate dinners, and the linen store, where starched tablecloths and napkins lay in wait. Eventually, they passed through the ground-floor servery and into the main café, where Alice had sat with Toby, the balconies overlooking the basement, the tables dressed in their morning attire.

Back in the kitchen, Della seemed to deflate. 'Sorry, was that boring?'

Alice shook her head. 'You're proud to work here and you're very talented. The petit fours looked and tasted incredible. Everybody agreed.'

A blush crept across Della's cheeks. 'Incredible how?'

She was taken aback. 'Surely you tried them?'

Della shook her head. 'Only the offcuts. Cakes like that aren't for the likes of me.'

Reality dawned — her privilege stark, an embarrassment — but there was only curiosity in Della's gaze. Alice understood she really wanted to know. 'The sponge was as light as air, it melted on the tongue. The buttercream was rich and . . . creamy?' She was clutching at straws, frustrated by her inability to capture the experience for Della.

'Go on,' Della encouraged.

'The fruits were sweet, but with a tartness so as it wasn't overbearing.'

Della was grinning now.

'What have I said?'

'I like hearing something I've made has been appreciated, that's all.'

Alice nodded, delighted. 'Will you come on Sunday?'

Della's expression closed. 'I don't want to feel like I did last time.'

Heat filled her cheeks as she cast around to ensure they were still alone. 'I can assure you I won't try and kiss you again. I'll be on my best behaviour.'

'I don't want you not to kiss me, I just don't want the bit that comes afterwards where it goes all awkward and then we fall out.'

Alice let Della's statement sink in, a fluttering in her stomach, elation crashing with fear. She took a step towards Della, cancelling the space between them, and glanced at the door before cupping Della's chin.

'Not here,' Della whispered when their lips were so close she could taste what was coming.

Della took her hand and led her out of the kitchen.

* * *

Alice was still in a daze the following morning, standing before the canvas. Sunlight crept across the attic room, warming her

100

bare feet poking out from the bottom of her pyjamas. The servants had risen and made their way downstairs, Martha among them, humming to herself. *What did she have to be so happy about?*

Squashing the thought, Alice tried to focus. She'd sneaked up here after the banquet to wipe down the portrait and prepare the surface anew. It was a poor rendering — she could see what was wrong with it now. The previous evening had unlocked something, left her changed. Gillespie was right, she needed to accept this thing with Della, to give it air, and they had — in the Ambrose's linen store. No drama, just soft lips against soft lips and afterwards a sense they'd advanced into new territory.

Now, the fervour to get what was in her head out had her in its grip, but something was still wrong. Della's hair looked flat. She stepped back, hoping for clarity.

Outside, the call of a bird diverted her attention. Alice set down her brush and moved to the window. The raven was back, on the branch of the tree opposite, a beady eye in her direction. She met its stare, momentarily arrested by this creature. It emitted a gurgling sound, as if it were laughing at her, then took flight, leaving her to work out its message while scolding her superstition. Unsettled, she returned to the painting, where the solution to the problem of Della's hair materialised. The raven's jet coat, how the light gave it a silvery film. She snatched up her brush again. Another hour passed.

* * *

By the time Alice stepped away from the canvas, her arm ached, and her throat was parched. She could no longer look at the painting, but sensed it was her best work. Footsteps on the landing pulled her from further reflection. She set her brush in the murky jar and tiptoed to the door. A heavy tread — surely not Father? Martha would be attending to her mother now. A spike of anger passed through her, but she still couldn't be sure what she'd heard or from which room, and Father had been kind the previous evening, taking her to the banquet, showing her off to his stuffy friends. A doting parent.

Something was placed on the floor directly outside the room, then the footsteps died away.

Alice waited, all too aware of her heart thudding against her chest. After a few moments, she eased open the door. Before her was a tray containing a pot of tea, a rack of toast, a slab of butter and a boiled egg under a knitted cosy. She crouched to retrieve her breakfast, the smell waking up her hollow stomach. Of all the people in her life, Gillespie's simple act of care and faith in her work left her undone. She settled on the daybed and tucked in, exhausted but happy.

* * *

It was late afternoon before Alice emerged from the attic and took a long bath. Such was her fatigue she almost fell asleep in the suds. She was dressing for dinner when a light tap came against her bedroom door. Martha entered carrying the evening dress Alice had worn to the banquet, pressed and ready to be hung in her wardrobe.

'Thank you, Martha.' She couldn't help studying this woman, wondering at what her father saw, if indeed he saw anything.

'Can I help you, Miss?' Martha gestured to the dress Alice was about to pull over her head. Before she could answer, Martha was there, gently easing the soft fabric down her arms and straightening the skirts around her stockinged legs.

Alice nodded her thanks, unable to put the picture building in her mind of her father and Martha to one side. The evidence was scant, but the seed had been planted.

At dinner it continued to plague her. She made a study of Father and Martha while attempting to remain present in the room, but if there was something between them, neither betrayed it. In fact, Father behaved as if Martha didn't exist. Only Gillespie was the beneficiary of his occasional attention. By the end of the meal, she was thoroughly bored by her internal dialogue and desperate to be elsewhere. Alice pushed back her chair. 'I'll be out this evening,' she announced to her parents.

In the hall, Gillespie was ready with her coat.

'Thank you for breakfast this morning.'

He held the coat open for her and she slid her arms inside.

'I trust you had a productive day?' He passed her a matching cloche hat.

'Indeed.' She pulled it on, eager to be on her way with the slim hope she might catch Della at the Ambrose.

At the front door, he retrieved a newspaper cutting from inside his jacket and handed it to her. It was an advertisement for entry to the Royal Academy annual exhibition. She'd never dreamt of showing her work to anyone else, let alone making it public and in such a grand institution. Still . . . *could she?* Gillespie clearly believed she could. Alice met his gaze. He gave her a brief nod as if the thoughts in her head had spilled into his and he was merely confirming what she already knew. She pocketed the cutting and walked into the night.

CHAPTER 21

'You're here late again, Della.' Mr Voisin appeared at her side. 'Your petit fours were a triumph last evening.'

Della felt herself blush. 'Thank you, sir. I wanted to finish this pie crust for tomorrow.'

He broke off a piece of pastry from an edge she hadn't yet neatened and popped it in his mouth. 'This is excellent. Buttery, flaky. You take real pride in your work.'

Her blush deepened. 'I try my best.'

He studied her with a broad smile, a crumb of her excellent pastry caught between his teeth. 'I'm going to keep an eye on you. I think you're destined for great things.'

Della revelled in his words as his footsteps died away, and returned her attention to the pies. She hadn't got much sleep after the banquet, which had everything to do with Alice kissing her in the linen store. The appearance of Ma, dressed and washed in the kitchen when Della came down this morning, soon brought her back to reality. 'Blimey, what have you done to your hair?' Ma had said from the kitchen door, a chamber pot between her hands. It was good to see her having the wherewithal to empty it, a task Della had undertaken while Ma was unwell. Without waiting for a reply, Ma moved past her into the yard and the privy beyond. Della poured tea into a fresh cup and watched her retrace her steps. She looked tired for someone who'd been in bed for over a week, but otherwise her hair had been combed into a chignon and her blouse and skirt were clean. Ma still wore the fashions of the previous decade, dressed in the way Pa would like. They didn't discuss the fact she'd lost a week, and Della's hair wasn't mentioned again.

The swish of the door from the servery brought her back into the room. Della glanced up from her pies expecting to see Mr Voisin, but no one was there. It was time to call it a day. Now Ma was herself again, there was less pressure to rush home for Samuel — but as ever, she questioned how long it would last.

Ten minutes later, Della made her way to the back entrance unable to shake the sense she was being watched. Exeter was full of old buildings like the Ambrose. It would hardly be surprising if its ghosts were drawn out in the evening, when the living dominated the day. A shiver travelled down her spine as she stepped outside into a squally wind. Tugging on her hat, she dug her hands in her pockets and readied herself for a damp walk home.

At the corner, she was surprised to see Alice, who looked immaculate in a crimson coat and matching hat. 'Thank goodness, I feared I'd missed you.'

'You almost did.' Della tried to subdue her elation, but her smile only got wider.

'I've nearly finished the painting.' Alice's eyes gleamed.

She felt a stab of disappointment — no more Sunday afternoons. Alice took her arm as if reading her mind. 'Our Sundays are sacred.' She winked.

Swept up in Alice's presence, Della knew she should be making her way home, but Alice was leading her in the opposite direction. It was then she noticed William watching them from the other side of the street.

'When can I see the painting?' she asked to distract herself.

'Not yet. Not until I'm certain it's ready.'

'When will you be certain?'

A frown creased Alice's brow while she considered the question. 'When I stop wanting to add to it.'

'Right,' Della said as if that made sense. In a way she did understand. When she was decorating a cake, there was a perfect moment of balance where any further embellishments would distract from the main feature and overcrowd the spectacle.

She checked behind, relieved William was gone.

They approached the Cathedral Green, the wind gaining strength, the air scented with the coming deluge.

Alice ducked into the entrance of the Royal Clarence Hotel, taking Della with her. 'Let me treat you to celebrate.'

'I'm not dressed for this,' Della protested.

'Nonsense.' Alice marched her through the sumptuous foyer and into a bar named the Zodiac. She was clearly on home turf. They sank into deep leather armchairs. Alice reached for a cocktail menu and studied it while tugging off her gloves and hat. 'What will you have?' She offered the menu.

Della shrugged. It may as well be written in a foreign language. A nugget of anxiety about Samuel crashed against her desire to be with Alice, to appear relaxed and worldly.

'I'll choose for you.' Alice sprang from her seat and approached the curved bar, where a penguin-dressed waiter took her order. Behind were rows and rows of bottles capturing all the colours of the rainbow, the like of which Della had never seen.

'What's worrying you?' Alice asked, sliding back into her seat. 'I can tell there's something wrong. Don't you like it here?'

'It's not that. I should be home. Ma relies on me.'

'There's a phone at reception. Why don't you let them know you'll be late?' Alice rummaged in her bag. 'I'm sure I've got some coins here somewhere.'

'We don't have a phone.'

'Oh.' Alice failed to hide her surprise. Della could see so clearly what Alice seldom noticed — their gaping differences. Alice's shoulders deflated a little. She felt terrible for bringing her down. One drink wouldn't hurt, and Henry would be around if Ma had a relapse.

She rallied. 'It's fine. They can manage without me for once.'

The drinks arrived, and the waiter set a yellow concoction in a coupe glass before her. Alice raised her glass in a toast. 'Cheers.' Della watched her take a sip. 'It's a "Bee's Knees",' Alice added. 'Gin and lemon. You do like gin?'

'Of course.' She took a tremulous sip. The alcohol hit the back of her throat. She stifled a gag and let it settle in her empty stomach, where it fizzed and gradually warmed. She took another.

'Steady on. You're not supposed to drink it like water.'

Della's cheeks grew hot, her lack of sophistication plain. Grateful for the low lighting in the bar, she set down her drink and tried to relax.

A group of women entered, their exuberance claiming Della's attention. Her gaze swept over their beautiful dresses, immaculate beading catching the light. She envied their confidence and sense of belonging.

One broke away, approaching their table. 'Alice, I thought it was you.'

Alice stood to kiss the woman's rouged cheek. 'Hello, Fliss, how are you?'

Fliss's gaze flickered to Della and settled there like a bird of prey eyeing a mouse. 'Are you going to introduce me to your friend?'

Alice's smile seemed a little forced as she introduced them. Fliss offered a manicured hand. Della wasn't sure if she was supposed to shake it or kiss it. She went for a handshake under Fliss's gimlet stare. 'What an interesting coat. Does it belong to a man?'

Before Della could answer, Fliss returned her attention to Alice. 'Where have you been hiding lately?' She leaned in. 'We were sorry to hear about you and Toby.'

Alice smirked. 'Not half as sorry as Toby.'

Fliss threw back her head and laughed. 'Good for you.' She pulled a silver cigarette case from a sequinned bag and offered them one. Della hesitated. 'You don't smoke?' Fliss's sculpted eyebrows shot towards the ceiling.

Alice took a cigarette and accepted a light. She leaned back, clearly at ease.

'Have you even tried?' Fliss pressed, taking a seat next to Alice.

Della hadn't tried, never felt the temptation, but accepting seemed easier than setting herself even further apart from Alice's world. She took the proffered cigarette, brought it to her lips and leaned in for Fliss to light. She'd seen Jack smoke enough — it couldn't be that hard. Her eyes stung as she inhaled a lungful then her mouth burst open with a hacking cough. Fliss didn't bother to stifle a giggle. Her humiliation drew the eyes of the room.

She grabbed for her cocktail and took a large gulp, the acrid liquid adding to her problems. For a brief moment the room rocked. When she regained her composure, Alice was looking concerned and Fliss was doubled over with amusement.

'Are you alright?' Alice reached across and rested her hand over Della's. It made up for the last few minutes of shame, but her eyes were watering so much she couldn't focus.

'No,' Della squeaked.

'I'm sorry.' Alice gave her hand a squeeze, genuine concern furrowing her brow.

'Oh, how funny, what a sweetheart.' Fliss recovered. 'Where did you find this one, Alice? She's as green as a frog.'

A wave of nausea sprang from nowhere. Della dropped the cigarette in the ash tray and slapped her hand across her mouth before dashing to the foyer. A sign for the toilets indicated they were on the next floor. She took the stairs, two at a time, crashing into a bathroom to rival anything the Ambrose could offer, dizzying further at the sight of a chandelier hanging from the ceiling.

In the cubicle, she heaved but nothing came out. After a few moments, she closed the lid and sat, attempting to keep tears of humiliation at bay as the nausea retreated. What a disaster. How could someone like Alice, beautiful, sophisticated, worldly, entertain the likes of Della Wilde? She was a laughing stock, a clown.

'Della.' Alice's voice broke through her downward trajectory. 'Are you here?' Her heels tapped along the cubicles. Eventually a head appeared under the door of hers. 'There you are.'

She couldn't help a small smile at Alice's upside-down face. 'What if it wasn't me?'

'Then I'd be looking rather foolish right now.'

Della emerged. 'You'd be in good company.'

Alice wrapped her arms around her waist and nudged her back into the cubicle. 'I'm sorry about Fliss, she doesn't mean any harm.'

Della shook her head, happy and self-conscious to be in Alice's arms, to be looking up into her face.

Alice brought her lips down to hers. A hint of tobacco mingled with the citrus from the gin on her tongue. Della's nausea further retreated along with her humiliation, replaced by the heady sensation of Alice's touch. The bathroom was silent, not a whisper of activity from the world outside, as if the cubicle existed in its own dimension. It was her and Alice, their bodies hard and taut against each other. With that thought, self-consciousness found her again as she felt the flimsy material of her dress ride up her legs, Alice's fingers between her thighs. She lifted her gaze to the chandelier, unsure what to do or how to act in this moment that was so exquisite and utterly unlike anything she'd known. Then Alice's fingers stilled at the very second she wanted them most.

The door of the bathroom clicked shut and Della realised they were no longer alone.

'Alice, is that you?' Fliss's sharp tone cut through the silence.

Alice put her finger to her lips. 'Yes, it's me.'

Footsteps walked into the cubicle next to theirs. The lock slid shut. 'What happened to your little friend?'

Alice's eyes met Della's, amusement mixed with anxiety. 'She went home.'

Della bit her lip.

'Pretty thing, what I'd give for that bone structure.'

Alice grinned, coiling a strand of Della's hair between her fingers. 'She is rather beautiful.'

Della buried her face in Alice's shoulder to hide her embarrassment. Finally, the toilet was flushed. Fliss exited and washed her hands.

'Are you coming?' Her heels appeared beneath their cubicle door. Della's chest tightened — what if Fliss looked under as Alice had done?

Alice's gaze didn't leave hers. 'I'm feeling rather out of sorts. I might have to call it a night.'

'That's not like you. A bunch of us are going to a club if you fancy coming?'

'Thanks, but you get off. I'll be fine.'

'Probably just as well. I expect Toby will be there, and now he's back on the market . . .'

'I hope he'll be snapped up,' Alice said with a smile.

'Gosh, you're really done. Feel better, darling, and get that little friend of yours some new clothes. She's too delicious to hide away.' The clip of heels and Fliss was gone.

Della blushed at the surprising compliment while they waited in silence, the hum of the city at night puncturing their breath.

'Let's wait a few minutes,' Alice whispered. She stroked Della's face, but it was clear the moment before Fliss interrupted them had been swallowed by mutual fear of discovery.

Through the open window, they heard a motorcar pull up in the street below and toot its horn. The raucous laughter of a rowdy group climbing in, then the car beeped again and drove away.

Alice peeled her body from Della's. 'I think that was Fliss and the others. We should be okay to go back down.'

Della followed Alice from the bathroom, longing to know what would have happened if Fliss hadn't intruded and when she might get another opportunity to find out.

CHAPTER 22

The bar had filled up in their absence. Alice was relieved Fliss and her friends had moved on. Della didn't meet her eye as they returned to their seats. She was shocked too. Shocked how close they'd come to discovery, how far she'd wanted things to go. 'Shall I get us another drink?'

A furtive glance from Della, her lips spreading into a grin. Relief, she was happy. Alice was happy too, ridiculously so.

Della's smile faded. 'I should be getting home.'

'We haven't talked. One final drink and then I'll see you to your door.'

At the bar, Alice couldn't resist studying her muse. Della looked radiant — even Fliss noticed, although Alice didn't think she shared her inclination. Della's bobbed hair swayed as her gaze darted around the room. She longed to put her at ease. Perhaps it had been a mistake to come here. It was a spur-of-the-moment decision. Until this evening, she hadn't understood how unworldly Della was. It unearthed a protective instinct towards her.

She ordered their drinks and was about to return to the table when a man approached Della. Alice sidled up, ready to see him off. He removed his cap. It was Jack Wilde.

He scraped his fingers through his black curls and threw her a nod. Alice glanced at Della, her expression like a stormy sky. She slid into her seat. Jack, uninvited, took the seat opposite.

The waiter appeared with their drinks, setting them on the table and leaving in haste.

'What a charming surprise.' Jack seemed to recover his humour.

'Indeed.' She took a sip of her drink, adjusting to this new situation.

Jack reached for the other glass. 'Shall I have yours, Del? Not a good idea for you to overindulge when you've responsibilities at home.'

Alice put out her hand to stop him. 'I didn't buy it for you.' She met his gaze, challenging him to argue.

He set down the drink and lifted his hands in surrender. 'My mistake.'

Della appeared to have lost the power of speech. Jack drummed his fingers on the table. First Fliss and now Jack. His presence had thoroughly ruined what she'd hoped would be a lovely evening. Alice couldn't work him out, what his angle was. Had she offended him when she'd ignored his flowers and therefore his advances? When both Wildes continued to stew in silence, she decided to take the initiative. 'Surely after a long day at the Ambrose, Della deserves an opportunity to let her hair down?'

Jack smirked. 'There isn't any hair to let down, thanks to you.'

Alice smiled despite herself. Having a conversation with Jack Wilde was like sparring with a fox. She let her index finger glide around the rim of her glass. 'Even so, someone with Della's talent needs to let off steam.'

Jack sat forward. 'Della isn't like you, Miss Winters.'

'So formal. Very well, Mr Wilde . . .' She paused for emphasis. 'What is Della like?' She noticed Della watching the scene unfold with a mixture of horror and interest. Alice wasn't sure where this was going herself, but she was now curious to find out.

'Our mother's ill and our Sam needs a mothering touch — he's only ten.'

She glanced at Della for confirmation. Della flinched at the mention of Sam. Her heart broke for her, and she understood how privileged her life was, free of responsibility. 'I'm sure Sam appreciates his brother too.'

'What do you mean, Ma's ill?' Della broke in. 'She was fine when I left this morning.'

Jack ignored his sister and addressed Alice. 'It's her nerves, you see. Our Ma suffered a great loss in the war. Her husband and two eldest boys. Sam a babe in arms. She didn't speak for weeks. Isn't that right, Del?'

Della met Alice's gaze with liquid eyes and gave a brief nod.

'Me and Della, we're a team,' Jack continued, 'but I can't be expected to carry the household while she passes an evening in a fancy bar.'

Della looked like she might explode. 'How did you find me?'

Jack sat back and folded his arms. 'Eyes everywhere, me.'

Alice studied them side by side. The Wilde siblings. A handsome pair, their features so similar they could be twins. The evening was clearly a bust. Jack had no intention of leaving until he'd successfully delivered Della home. Alice couldn't help feeling there was more to it. If only she could get Della alone, to tell her she understood, that she wanted to help. She attempted to communicate through her eyes, but Della's were clouded with pain.

Her gaze settled on Della's untouched drink and an idea formed. Before she could question it, Alice reached out with the pretence of taking a handful of nuts from the bowl at the table's centre and swept the drink straight into Jack's lap. He shot up.

'Awfully sorry, how clumsy of me.'

Jack scowled, searching around for something to dry off his trousers. Della's face transformed like a light had been switched on.

'They might have towels in the gents,' Alice volunteered.

Jack glanced from her to his sister, weighing up his next move. 'Stay put.' His tone didn't inspire generosity.

The moment he was gone, they snatched up their coats and ran out of the bar as if they'd planned their escape. Neither of them spoke as they raced across the green to the archways of the cathedral. Alice grabbed Della's hand and pulled her into the shadow of the great door. From their vantage point, they watched Jack leave the hotel minutes later, calling Della's name and searching in all directions. He gave up and stalked away.

Alice wrapped Della in her coat and squeezed her hand. 'You're coming home with me.'

Twenty minutes later, she rang the bell at the back of the winter house. Wordlessly, Gillespie let them in.

Jack Wilde had made an enemy that evening.

CHAPTER 23

'I shouldn't be here.' Della picked up the impossibly delicate spoon and stirred the tea for no other reason than to keep her hands busy. She couldn't help thinking running away from Jack had been a mistake, but it was thrilling too. Thrilling to do anything with Alice. Her thoughts drifted to the bathroom cubicle. Should she have reciprocated? Fliss was right, she was green.

'If not here, then where should you be? At home, with that . . .' Alice reached across the table and took her hand.

Della smiled. 'Go on, I don't mind what you call my brother.' She preferred this state of affairs — that Alice actively disliked Jack, when she'd feared the opposite might be true.

Alice looked sheepish. 'I was going to say . . . no, actually, I won't stoop to that level.'

Della took a sip of tea. It was good, the right strength, a dash of milk, not stewed and half cold like the tea on offer in the Wilde household once her brothers were done with it. She cast around the room. An Aga provided warmth, rows of cupboards lined the walls, a large stone sink at one end and copper pans hanging from the ceiling. At the centre, the long pine table at which they sat reminded her of the tables in the

116

Ambrose. Everything put away and organised, a kitchen she could see herself baking in.

'What's so fascinating?' Alice enquired, following her gaze.

'I was thinking what a lovely kitchen this is, how much I'd like to bake in it.'

'I should appreciate it more, but Mrs Drummond, our cook, won't let any family member linger. She rules her kitchen with an iron fist.'

'Quite right too.'

'Do you bake at home?'

Della shrugged. 'I don't get the time, not with meals to prepare, laundry to do, beds to make.'

'Your mother doesn't help?'

'Oh no, she does. Like Jack said, Ma's been ill. On and off since the war, but it's getting worse and . . . blimey.' She shoved back her chair as panic rose. 'What am I thinking, sat here talking when I should be home. They'll be worried and Lord knows what Jack will do and there's Sam . . .'

'You're not going back there if it's not safe.'

'You don't understand. I need to go, Alice. It'll be worse if I don't.'

Alice hesitated. 'Very well, wait here a minute.' She disappeared into the dark back hall through which they'd entered. Della finished her tea, feeling calmer now. She'd get home, face Jack, maybe they'd laugh about it. But she'd humiliated him, and the one thing her brother wouldn't countenance was her of all people making him feel any less of a man.

Alice returned in the same clothes she'd worn that day in the park when Jack mistook her for a boy. 'More suitable clothes for walking you home,' she offered by way of explanation.

Della was touched. 'I'll be fine, you don't need to walk me home. I'll only worry about you getting back.'

Alice beckoned her to the door. 'I won't be alone.'

The butler was waiting for them in the hall. Disconcerted, Della forced a smile, but his face remained passive. Not in a rude way, there was warmth in his demeanour. He was dressed

117

in his butler's uniform and a long greatcoat, his polished shoes shining in the light above the back door. They made their way down the side of the house. He strode ahead, broad shoulders and height giving Della confidence. Not even Jack would attempt to take on such a specimen, not that Jack was much of a fighter. His bark had always been worse than his bite.

Alice took her hand — the advantage of wearing boys' clothes — and they followed Gillespie a few steps behind. Night had blanketed the city, the streets quiet, houses lit from within. Della enjoyed the sensation of their fingers entwined but the chill night air kept her sharp and alert. As they made their descent along Fore Street and the river stretched out like a shimmering serpent ahead, fear of Alice seeing her home inserted itself foremost in her mind.

As if she sensed her anxiety, Alice squeezed her hand. She met her gaze, a smile of reassurance, their conversation stifled by the presence of Gillespie. The thud of his tread carried them over the river, their breath misting the air. Della felt it again, the foreboding, as they left the city behind and approached the railway, the gateway to St Thomas. Her mind worked through possibilities — could they be persuaded to leave her here? The Wildes' street loomed only a few yards ahead in the shadow of the railway line.

'I'll be alright now.' Her voice sounded small and tremulous, not at all convincing.

The butler halted, awaiting Alice's instruction. She took Della's arm and turned them away for privacy. 'Do you think I'm going to let you walk the rest of the way by yourself after your brother's behaviour this evening? Do you think I could go to my bed not knowing you're safe?' Her eyes were blazing. Della felt a rush of love. She mattered to someone. It was a new experience — one she wasn't sure what to do with.

Gillespie clapped his gloved hands against the cold.

'Alright,' Della relented. What was another humiliation when she'd racked up so many that evening? Alice was still here, holding her hand. 'It's left, after the bridge.'

118

Their footsteps echoed along her street. The Wildes' house stood in the middle of the terrace, windows netted against the world. She couldn't stand the thought of Alice seeing the back alley, the outside toilet, the bricked-in yard, but they didn't use the front entrance. The parlour was the place for visitors that never came.

She gestured to the end of the street. Gillespie marched on, his long coat giving him the appearance of death leading them to meet their maker. He stood to one side, letting her precede as they entered the alley. It was dark and ominous, bins stacked up against backyards, debris strewn by a blustery wind. She stopped at their gate, anxious about what she'd find on the other side.

The yard was all shadows, cast by the light from the naked kitchen bulb. Della was relieved to see only Henry and Samuel at the table, no sign of Jack or Ma. She turned to face Alice with Gillespie bringing up the rear. 'I'll be fine. My brothers Henry and Sam are inside, Jack won't bother me with them around.'

Alice walked past her. 'Can I meet them?'

Della ran to catch her up. 'I dunno . . .'

'I'll wait here,' Gillespie said, taking up his post at the gate like a sentry guarding a castle.

Sam jumped down from the table the moment she stepped through the door and ran to her arms. He stopped short at the sight of Alice.

'Who's he?' Sam enquired. The remains of his dinner — baked beans — encircled his lips, lurid orange like a clown's.

Henry glanced up from his book, a kink in his glasses where he'd tried to bend them back into shape. A flush of red found his cheeks as Alice removed her cap.

'She, not he.' Alice pulled out a kitchen chair and plopped herself down. Della couldn't help smiling while simultaneously praying no other Wildes would put in an appearance.

'This is Alice,' she said to Sam, who'd returned to his seat, where he could study their guest with a quizzical frown.

'Why's she dressed like a boy?'

'Why are you dressed like a boy?' Alice countered.

Sam looked down at his grubby vest and shorts. 'Cos I am one, silly.'

'Where's Ma?' Della asked Henry.

He rolled his eyes upwards. No words were necessary — the baked beans, the dishes in the sink were indication enough of the state of things.

'What about Jack?'

Henry shrugged.

'Shouldn't you boys have done the washing-up?' Alice enquired.

They both looked startled. Della bit her lip to hide her smirk.

Henry threw her a puzzled look before pushing his glasses back up his nose and venturing to the sink.

Despite how wonderful Alice was being, Della couldn't shake her desire that she leave. Any minute Jack might materialise and she didn't want to give him further ammunition. They couldn't talk in the kitchen with Henry crashing about at the sink, Sam at his side on a kitchen chair. They couldn't talk outside with Gillespie standing guard, and Della didn't want to take Alice any deeper into Wilde territory. The ramparts were enough for today.

'If you want to . . .' She gestured to the door.

Alice stood. 'Bye, boys.' She waved. Sam offered up his impish grin.

In the yard, Gillespie's form made a shadow much like a tree. He stepped outside the back gate. Alice glanced at the kitchen window, where Henry and Sam were framed in their work. 'I suppose we can't say goodbye properly.'

Della followed her gaze. 'Not really.'

Alice took her hand and kissed it. 'There. I'll see you soon.'

Della stayed where she was, listening to Gillespie's heavy tread on the cobbles and the light tap of Alice's brogues behind. Then the alley fell silent, and with their absence the night closed in.

CHAPTER 24

The events of the evening ricocheted in her thoughts as Alice followed Gillespie along the alley. The Zodiac bar, Fliss's sarcastic laugh. The assignation in the bathroom, Della's lips against hers. Afterwards, Jack. Della in her kitchen, so diminished by her brother. Gillespie, what he'd said to her in the hall when she'd given him a brief appraisal of their evening and asked him to convey Della home. *Are you sure you want me involved, Miss Alice?* She hadn't understood what he'd meant, only that he'd said it out of care, his eyes searching hers for confirmation that his help would be given without reciprocation, but in his own way. Her mind turned to Della's home, the kitchen a quarter of the size of the one at the winter house. No wonder Della envied its generous proportions. Her sweet brothers — not blessed with the same dark looks Della and Jack possessed but lovely in their own way. The evening had sharpened the contrasts between them — her life of privilege and Della's of thankless work. Alice felt the deficit.

It was a relief to leave St Thomas behind and reach the river. Gillespie pressed on until Alice called to him to wait. He lit a cigarette. 'May I?' she asked.

Gillespie eyed her.

'I'm twenty-one and I've been smoking for years.'

He fished out the packet and offered her one, a look of resignation. 'Aye, I know.'

What else did he know? Alice popped the cigarette between her lips. He leaned in with his lighter, a hint of aftershave reminding her of her father. She took the smoke deep in her lungs, then hurried after him. Gillespie — as motionless as a statue or agile as a hare. Never in between.

The river, black as coal, sent a shiver down her spine. They retraced their steps across the bridge, then Fore Street rose ahead, lined with shuttered shops, closed to the night.

'You won't tell my parents about this evening.' Alice flinched at her sharp tone — was she giving him orders? She was more accustomed to discussing tea with this man.

His lips betrayed a small smile. 'I've no wish to relay the events of this evening to your parents.'

'Thank you.'

He nodded.

'They wouldn't understand,' she added, feeling the need to qualify her request. 'It would lead to difficult questions.'

He made no comment.

Alice sighed and stopped walking to regain her breath against his fast pace. 'Mr Gillespie, I thought we were friends?'

He stopped too, throwing her an indulgent look.

She hastened again as he'd already moved on. A few more steps, and he surprised her by breaking the silence. 'I believe they would understand. Your father, certainly.'

Alice tried to shake off a brittle feeling, the reminder of her father and his possible affair. Is that what earned her his understanding, because he was behaving badly too? 'What makes you say that?'

Gillespie looked suddenly defeated. 'I've known him a long time.'

She nodded, unable to dispute what horrors they must have witnessed together during the war.

'He's brave, braver than you'll ever know, but life doesn't always give you the opportunity to prove it.'

Alice frowned — what a puzzling man Gillespie was. She tried to smooth her ruffled feathers and think kindly on his words. 'What about Mummy?'

Gillespie's expression closed. 'She's a saint.' He said it so quietly, she might have misheard. *Mummy, a saint?* That was a new one.

He seemed disinclined to further conversation. She accepted the silence for what it was and switched back to Della, the Zodiac bathroom, what delights they might experience next time — when and where that next time might be. If only they could leave all this behind and follow their dreams to Paris. She pictured them in a garret, perched at the top of one of those elegant Parisian buildings — a bit like the attic at the winter house, she supposed, with a window that opened onto all the beauty Paris could offer. A croquembouche around every corner. The memory made her smile.

* * *

The winter house was cloaked in darkness when they returned, its white walls stark against the night sky. She followed Gillespie through the side gate and down the path to the servants' entrance, lined with potted bay. He stopped abruptly and put his finger to his lips, then pressed himself against the wall, gesturing for her to do the same. She followed his example until the reason for this strange behaviour became apparent.

Jack stood with his back to them, smoking. 'I knew if I waited long enough, you two would show up eventually.' He turned around, his features lit by the crescent moon, and all smugness drained from his face as he took in Gillespie.

'Bloody hell.' Jack coughed and spluttered as Gillespie's arm came around him like a vice.

Alice pulled off her cap. 'You can set him down. This is Jack, Della's brother.'

Gillespie did as he was asked but remained too close to Jack for his comfort.

Jack straightened his collar. 'Where's Della?'

'We've seen her home.'

'You two didn't need to run out on me, you know. I wasn't going to do anything.' He raked his fingers through his curls. 'Della's got responsibilities, she was needed.'

'So you said. What were you doing at the Zodiac? It doesn't strike me as your sort of place.'

'What are you implying?' He took a step forward. Gillespie's arm came down like a draw bridge.

As with all conversations she'd conducted with Jack, she had no idea where this was going, but someone needed to put him in his place.

'I know what you are.' He gestured to her clothes. 'I've heard about women like you. I'm not having you corrupt Della.'

'That's quite enough for one evening.' Gillespie's tone was like a shard of ice.

Jack threw him a furtive glance and addressed Alice. 'My sister doesn't need you filling her head with nonsense.' He stalked away.

Alice waited for him to disappear through the side gate before meeting Gillespie's gaze. 'Thank you.'

He nodded. 'Watch which enemies you make, Miss Alice. I might not always be here.' With that he conveyed her inside, and Alice went to bed wondering what he'd meant.

CHAPTER 25

The Ambrose was busier than ever. It would be Easter soon and the warmer days brought tourists to their door. Ma remained in bed. They couldn't afford a doctor and since there was no obvious malady, Della didn't know what else to do. She hadn't seen hide nor hair of Jack, although Henry assured her he was about. Since running away from him at the Zodiac, she'd been waiting for retribution that hadn't come. It remained in the back of her mind while she made Simnel cakes and dozens of hot cross buns, their tops shiny with glaze.

Sunday shone like a beacon to light the sea of her otherwise choppy life. As if he knew, Jack chose Sunday lunch to make his appearance at the Wilde table. He glanced up from his newspaper, the end of a cigarette smoking between his fingers, when she walked into the kitchen.

'Where's Sam and Henry?' There was nothing forgiving in his tone.

Della masked her anxiety with the rigid set of her jaw. 'Next door. Mrs Phillips invited them for Easter lunch, what with Ma being in bed.'

He eyed her outfit, one of her two decent dresses. 'Where are you going, as if I need to ask?'

Della ignored him and moved to the peg, hoping to retrieve her coat and hat without further interrogation.

'Well?'

'You said you knew where I was going.'

He took a drag on his cigarette. 'You're not to go there.'

'You can't tell me what to do.'

'I can tell folk what you're up to.'

'What am I up to?'

'Filth.' He spat the word. It hit her like a slap.

She took a deep breath and stood her ground. 'I'm not doing anything wrong.'

He stubbed the cigarette out in a saucer and leaned back in his chair regarding her. 'Can't you understand I'm trying to protect you, Del? You wouldn't want your fancy employer finding out.'

Jack knew she was the only one keeping the Wildes fed. As threats go, it had all the depth of a puddle, but still, it was a sobering thought. 'See you later, Jack.'

Her heart clattered in her chest until she'd reached the end of the back alley, proud she hadn't shown him how much he'd got under her skin. What she and Alice did in private wasn't illegal — at least, not yet.

* * *

Gillespie answered the door — his face as serious as always, despite the strange evening they'd shared — and told Della to go straight up. When she reached the attic, there was no sign of Alice. She took a seat on the daybed, the painting calling to her from the easel, hiding under a sheet.

Ten minutes passed and Alice hadn't materialised. Della paced the room, still rattled by Jack and trying to keep her hand from lifting the sheet, but then she was doing just that. First a corner, then the middle until the full portrait was revealed. She gasped and stepped back, forced away by the power of the woman in the image. There was a challenge in her eyes, a defiance in the set of her mouth and luminescent hair that sprang in wild curls like a Medusa.

By the time Alice appeared, Della was seated on the daybed, the portrait covered, but what she'd seen filled the room.

'Sorry.' Alice looked flustered as if she'd been running. 'It was hard to escape. My parents invited guests for Easter lunch and Mummy wanted me to stay for drinks. I don't think she buys my Sunday headaches and need to rest.'

Della nodded, unsure what to make of these domestic arrangements, so unlike her own.

Alice clasped her hands together as if she wasn't sure how to proceed either. All they'd shared had somehow got buried under the weight of daily life. She turned to the easel. 'Did you peep?'

Della couldn't admit it. Alice would ask for her opinion and she was still too unnerved by what she'd seen to form a coherent answer. 'Of course not.'

'I wouldn't have minded, but it's better to wait until its finished.' Alice took a seat beside her on the daybed. 'How are you? Here's me talking nonsense and I haven't asked if there was any fallout with Jack. It's been on my mind all week.'

'I can handle Jack,' she said, determined not to let him infiltrate their time. *Filth* kept coming back to her. Maybe it was filth, but she liked it. This was all so polite, so chaste, when her feelings were anything but.

Alice lifted her chin until their eyes met. 'Something is wrong.'

Della looked away, embarrassed. 'Jack said what we're doing is filth.'

'What do you think?'

She forced her gaze back to Alice, finding a hint of amusement in the crinkle of her eyes. It gave her courage to push Jack's threat to one side. 'I think I'd like to find out what you were going to do, before Fliss interrupted us in the hotel bathroom,' she whispered.

Alice's lips spread into a languorous grin.

There were too many layers to her clothes, Della realised, as Alice freed her from her cardigan then fumbled with the buttons at the back of her dress. Alice's in contrast were loose and fluid, as if they were made for such a moment. Warm hands slid down her camisole, air on her breasts, Alice's lips exploring her skin. Della was so caught up in the pleasure of it, she'd failed to reciprocate. Pushing aside her inhibition, she mimicked Alice, letting her hand glide between Alice's legs, stroking her soft hair, circling her. Alice guided her fingers inside, shifting her thigh between Della's legs, inviting her to open up too. When Alice came, her cries were muted, the arch of her back, the pressure of her body the only indication in the otherwise silent room.

'Now you,' Alice whispered before her lips travelled south, her tongue taking over where her thigh had been.

* * *

A shaft of sunlight crept across the daybed, shifting the slight chill and wrapping them in a warm post-coital cocoon. Della found herself falling asleep in Alice's arms. When she awoke, Alice was dressed and working at the easel. She grabbed for her clothes and pulled them on, embarrassed by her nakedness. For the next hour, she was content to watch Alice create. The sun disappeared behind a cloud, casting the room in shadow by the time she packed up.

'What's that called?' Della asked. 'What you did with your tongue, down there.' She blushed at her innocence.

Alice's eyes flashed. 'Cunnilingus.' She let out a hoot of laughter and slapped her hand across her mouth.

Della snorted and attempted to rein in her emotions. 'Well, I liked it.'

Alice joined her on the daybed again.

The creak of a floorboard on the landing brought them to silence. Their eyes locked in alarm.

'Is that you?' A man's voice. Della hadn't heard it before. It wasn't Gillespie's Scottish brogue. There was a sigh, then footsteps moving away. She glanced at Alice. Desolation replaced the joy on her face.

'Who is it?' Della whispered.

Alice shook her head. 'My father. I think he's having an affair with Martha, my mother's maid.' Tears formed in Alice's eyes. 'It's Mummy I feel sorry for. How humiliating.'

Della threaded her fingers through Alice's, unsure what words of comfort to offer. Abruptly, Alice stood and wiped her eyes. 'No use getting upset. It's their mess.' Her smile seemed forced.

'Alice.'

'I'm fine.'

Della nodded, helpless.

'I'd better see you down.'

At the back door, Alice's expression remained grave. Della wasn't sure if it was their parting or her father that troubled her more.

'I'll see you next week, if not before?' She searched Alice's gaze.

'Yes.' A tremulous smile. 'Let's try to make it before.'

Della started down the path with a sense the scales had tipped again. The happier she and Alice were together, the more their families penetrated that joy. Could either of them muster the strength for the fight ahead? She hoped so — otherwise, what was it all for?

CHAPTER 26

Alice lingered in the dark hall, her mind a muddle of contrasts. Her father's indiscretion parried with the strength of her feeling for Della, no longer just her muse — something much more.

The back door moved open and Martha, face pinched from the cold, appeared before her.

'Miss Alice.' Those large eyes, dilated.

She could only stare at this woman who looked so young, and now found herself reversing her earlier musings. What could Martha possibly see in Father? He was at least forty-five. It didn't bear thinking about. 'Excuse me.' Alice detected her haughty tone, but wasn't she allowed to play the precocious mistress to her subordinate? Feeling somehow wrongfooted, she made for the front of the house.

'Alice.' Her mother's voice from the sitting room. Facing her was the last thing she wanted.

She was sitting on the sofa, the latest Agatha Christie in her hand. A fire crackled in the grate despite the mild weather. 'Do you know if Martha's back?'

'Yes.' Alice winced at her sharp reply.

'Good, she can draw me a bath.'

'I can do it if you like.'

'Martha knows how I like it. Would you be a dear and ring the bell?'

Alice did as she was asked, hating the thought of summoning that woman. Moments later, Martha appeared in her uniform, hair tidied beneath her cap.

'Can I help you, ma'am?'

'A bath please, Martha. Was your grandmother well?'

'Quite well, ma'am, thank you for asking. I'll draw your bath right away.' She bobbed and left the room.

'Such a sweet girl, I'd be lost without her. Her grandmother had a fall last week.'

Alice's mind continued to whirr. Martha evidently failed to inform Father of this development — no wonder he sounded so disheartened by her absence. It appalled her that he stooped to going to the servants' rooms to do his bidding.

'Where's Daddy?' she asked, suddenly wanting to get him in trouble.

'In his study, I expect. I haven't seen him since our guests left, but that's where he usually is.'

Alice joined her on the sofa. 'Don't you wish he'd spend more time with you?'

Her mother set down her novel. 'Daddy and I have never been the sort to live in one another's pockets. We each have our interests. I'll see him at dinner.'

If Della were under the same roof, she wouldn't be able to countenance a separation. Just the knowledge of her presence would require her to seek her out. It made Alice sad for her parents, for her mother especially.

'Did you get some rest?' Mummy's hand came against her forehead. 'I do wonder if we shouldn't have you checked by a doctor. You've been rather under the weather lately.'

'I'm fine, you mustn't worry.'

'What's new with you? I hardly see you these days. Did you patch things up with Toby?'

She shook her head, surprised by the question. 'Toby and I are finished.'

131

Her mother studied her closely. 'There's someone, I can tell.' A smile touched her lips, taking years off her. It's a pity she didn't do it more often, perhaps Father would notice her then. Younger was clearly his preference. Alice pushed the thought away and attempted to conjure a suitably vague answer.

'There are interested parties but no one in particular.'

Her mother cupped her cheek. 'Don't break too many hearts, Alice, especially not your own.'

'I'm fine.' She hoisted a smile and offered her hand. 'I expect your bath is run now.'

Alice noticed too late a streak of black paint on her finger.

'What's that?' her mother enquired, holding her hand aloft.

'I must have brushed against something.'

'It looks like paint to me.' She turned Alice's hands over. 'Goodness, dear, you have it on your nails too.'

She took back her hand. 'Do I? How peculiar. I'd better wash it off.'

Her mother took her hand again. 'Look after these, darling. A man doesn't want an unattractive hand. Come to my room later and we'll have Martha do our nails.' She sounded so happy at the prospect, Alice winced. The idea of that woman touching her nails.

'Alright,' she said without much conviction.

'Good.' Her mother kissed her cheek and left. Alice flopped back on the sofa. She was contemplating returning to the attic, when her father entered the room.

'Ah, there you are, Alice. I was looking for Mummy.' She caught the hint of his aftershave, the same as Gillespie's.

'Martha's run her a bath; she's going to give her a manicure.' She studied her father for signs of guilt at the mention of his lover's name. He merely nodded.

'That will do her good.' He threw her a distracted smile and left.

Alice put her feet up on the ottoman, wondering at her parents' lives. After a few moments with only the tick of the clock on the mantel for company, she made her way up to the attic. With everyone occupied she wanted to be back at the painting, to be in the room where she and Della had made love.

At the attic door, Alice froze. 'I'm in here.' Gillespie's voice from the servants' bathroom. The door drew open. A towel around his waist was all that covered his modesty, his broad, sculpted torso on display. He flinched at the sight of her. 'Miss Alice.'

Alice didn't say a word. She let herself into the attic room and made for the daybed. Who was Gillespie addressing? Surely not her. He was proper to his core. Could he have been expecting Martha? Had she got it all wrong about her father? A moment's relief gave way to more questions. Why then was her father in the attic this afternoon?

Unable to untangle the conundrum, Alice pulled out her sketchbook and rendered Gillespie's form to the page.

CHAPTER 27

'You're not going to make meringue out of those.' Mrs Hastings peered into the bowl of egg whites which Della was supposed to be whipping into stiff peaks.

'Sorry.' She snatched up her whisk.

Hastings shook her head, but her smile was benign. 'You've a great talent. It's been noticed. Don't let whatever boy you're mooning over distract you.'

Della felt her cheeks flame. 'Thanks, Mrs Hastings.'

The cook squeezed her shoulder and went on her way.

Alice, that's who she was mooning over. With the passing of Easter, the Ambrose had settled into a more regular rhythm. At home there was no time to think. Baking provided a little relief and the opportunity for her mind to roam while her hands were engaged in something practical, but Hastings was right, she mustn't let her work suffer.

Two hours later, she pulled the meringues from the oven, stiff white peaks burnished gold. She mopped her brow, the kitchen warm with industry.

'You're wanted upstairs.' William's voice broke through her reverie. He hadn't spoken to her in weeks, not since the cinema debacle. She'd seen him around, sensed his malevolent gaze. He was standing tall, a smirk pulling at his mouth.

'Who by?' Della asked, considering the cooling meringues and the cream filling she still had to make.

Two of her colleagues at a nearby bench slowed their tasks, a sure sign they were listening. Nothing good ever came from a summons upstairs.

'Mr Wilson.'

He was the café manager, responsible for discipline, hiring and firing. She bit her lip and cast around. Mrs Hastings was talking to Leonnard, who had started working with bread since Della pleaded his case.

'I've the cream to make for the meringues and—'

'He said immediately.' Smugness beamed from William's eyes.

'Mrs Hastings?' Her boss looked up, a slight frown. She didn't like being interrupted in the midst of her flow.

'What is it?'

Della left her bench and spoke in a low voice to convey her summons. She held onto a thread of hope that Hastings would intervene, but no one challenged an order from upstairs. 'Very well, you'd better go. You can make the filling when you get back.'

'Yes, Mrs Hastings.'

She removed her cap and overall, folding them on her bench, taking her time, then made her way to the kitchen doors under the eye of her colleagues, the thud of William's tread behind.

'You don't need to escort me,' she said once they were in the corridor outside.

William shrugged. 'I'm going this way too.'

Della wanted to wipe the self-satisfied expression from his face which only added to her unease. Whatever her misdemeanour — and she had no idea what that might be — she couldn't help wondering if William was somehow involved in her capture.

The lift took an eternity to arrive. Della contemplated taking the stairs, rather than be trapped in a confined space with William. What had she been thinking, letting him kiss her at Christmas, taking him home for tea? Fitting in, that's what. Now she had Alice she didn't care about denying who she was, at least to herself.

The lift finally juddered into place. William opened the gate, and Della stepped in. He stood too close as they climbed the next three floors, stealing the air. She kept her eyes to the ground, could see the light reflected in the shine of his black shoes.

At the top floor, he emerged beside her. Was he going to conduct her to Mr Wilson's door like a delinquent child to a headmaster? She forced her feet down the corridor to the administration office. Mrs Bell behind the front desk of the panelled room greeted Della with a smile. *Surely that had to be a good sign?*

'Thank you, William,' Mrs Bell said with a bemused expression.

He looked irritated that his presence was no longer required and backed away. Della enjoyed the fading echo of his tread.

'Take a seat, Della. Mr Wilson will be out directly.'

She lowered herself onto one of the hard wooden chairs unable to shake a sense of foreboding. Mr Wilson rarely ventured into the workings of the café, preferring to let his subordinates deal with the day-to-day of the staff. She eyed the clock on the office wall, its tick disrupting her heartbeat as the minutes passed, then the door drew open and Mr Wilson beckoned her in.

He was a tall, willowy man with a small head outbalanced by toby-jug ears and wispy hair. Della tried to relax as he gestured for her to sit. His desk was positioned in front of the window. Light poured in, giving his crown a celestial glow. He picked up a magazine. She recognised the blue crest of Le Cordon Bleu. Had she been reading it too much or spilled something on one of the staff copies?

Wilson cleared his throat. 'Mr Voisin has recommended you for staff training, Miss Wilde.'

Della sat up a little straighter.

'You may have heard of Le Cordon Bleu? It's a cookery school in Paris.'

'Yes, sir.' She nodded, trying to keep a lid on the fizzing in her stomach.

He set down the magazine and pitched his hands together, studying her over their peaks. 'We pride ourselves at the Ambrose in having some of the best caterers the South West can offer — may I say, to rival London.'

Della felt a little lightheaded.

'Each year, I look at training, budgets and so on. Voisin commends you as a baker of exceptional talent. I'm sure you understand the level of praise he's bestowing?'

'I do, sir.'

He held up his hand. 'I can't promise you'll be chosen, but if we were to put your name forward, would you be interested? The Ambrose would meet the costs in full.'

'I would, sir.' Della worked hard to contain her excitement.

He pushed back his chair, making her jump, and opened the door before Della had even stood. 'Excellent, Miss Wilde. That will be all.'

She floated back to the kitchens, unable to take it all in. Her uniform was just as she'd left it, her meringues still cooling on their rack. The other staff glanced in her direction, but no one approached. She wasn't in tears, so no drama to hear.

Eventually Hastings came to her side, a twinkle in her eye. 'Good news?'

Della grinned. Hastings tapped the side of her nose and went back to Leonnard.

* * *

That evening, the Wilde house was a hive of activity when Della walked in. Jack held court at the head of the table, a new development. He only ever sat in their father's chair when Ma had taken to bed, but there was Ma Wilde, in her usual seat, cheeks ruddy with laughter. Henry sat beside her, his books set aside, and Sam jumped up and down on his chair. Della hung her bag, never more the outsider, and waited for some form of recognition, deciding in that moment not to share her news about Le Cordon Bleu. The Wildes would put an end to it. How would they manage without her? Who would keep an eye on Sam when Ma was sick? Only Alice would understand. She'd come too, Della was certain.

Eventually she caught Henry's eye. He threw her a wave. Jack turned in her direction.

'What's got you lot so excited?' She slid off her coat and hung it on the peg.

'You tell her, Jack,' Ma encouraged, her eyes shining as she looked upon her son.

He leaned back in the chair, letting Della's curiosity play out. 'I had some good news today. We'll be seeing a lot more of each other. I got a job at the Ambrose.'

CHAPTER 28

'Will you keep still,' Alice said as Della fidgeted with her hair for the umpteenth time. The portrait was so close. Really, it was finished, but her inner critic wasn't quite satisfied.

'Sorry.' Della's shoulders slumped. 'I can't think about anything else.'

Recognising the moment had passed, Alice wiped off her brush and joined Della on the daybed, pulling her into her arms. Jack Wilde had a lot to answer for.

'You're not going to be working directly with him though.'

Della fitted into the crook of her arm. 'No, he's in the stores. It's knowing he's there, in the building. I can't explain it.' She lifted her gaze to Alice; there was real pain there. 'It was mine. The Ambrose. One thing I could keep separate from my family. I don't want him to ruin it for me and . . .' She hesitated. 'What if he tells the Ambrose about us?'

Alice stroked a stray curl from Della's face. 'He has no proof, and besides, who'd believe him? You've done such incredible things. Your boss wants to send you to Le Cordon Bleu.'

That smile arrived, lighting up her whole face. They'd talked of nothing but their hopes for Paris since Della delivered both the good and bad news. Alice shared her misgivings about Jack, but she was determined to cling to the good. She and Della in Paris, with more freedom to be themselves. 'I'm so proud of you,' she whispered.

'I'll bake and you'll paint,' Della said, as if tuning directly into her thoughts.

'I'll paint you,' Alice replied, her fingers gliding up Della's leg for the second time that afternoon. The portrait wasn't going to finish itself, and the deadline for the exhibition loomed.

'Shall we get outside?' she suggested, half an hour later when they were decent again.

They descended the servants' stairs, hands entwined, a dreamlike trance in command of Alice's limbs. At the bottom, Della dropped her hand. Alice took a moment to realise Mummy was standing in the dark hallway, her gaze directed at Della.

'Alice, what are you doing creeping about on the back stairs? You didn't tell me you had a friend visiting.' There was a flicker of judgement in her eye. Was it the hand holding or Della's off-the-shelf attire that so appalled her?

Alice gathered herself. 'This is Della. She's visiting Exeter, staying with . . . the Rolands. They asked me to show her the sights.'

'Oh, then you know Toby?'

Della nodded, but her confusion was evident.

'We're going to Northernhay Gardens,' Alice said, before her mother could interrogate further. Why had she said the Rolands of all people when Mummy knew she'd broken things off with Toby?

'Have fun.' A hint of bewilderment in her mother's tone. 'Any idea where your father is? He's not in his study.'

Alice had no idea, but she'd seen Martha leave the house shortly before Della arrived. 'Perhaps he's gone for a walk.' She kissed her mother's cheek, eager to be out the door.

They hurried down the side of the house, Alice's mind frantic with the web of lies she'd started, anxious about what her mother had seen and surmised. How long had she been lurking at the bottom of the back stairs, and why? Did she suspect about Martha and her father? Since Alice's encounter with Gillespie outside the bathroom, she'd tried to put an end to her speculation.

Della was silent too. They reached the gate and stepped into the road. 'Do you want me to go home? I don't want to get you in trouble.'

'Of course not.' Alice checked behind. 'We can't talk here. Let's get to the park.'

Della's stride matched hers as they walked into the city. The trees that lined the street were now wearing their leafy attire; bluebells and primroses brought colour to gardens. She glanced across at Della, her face muddied, capturing something Alice had been trying to render in the portrait — a sort of juxtaposition of emotion that Della often betrayed.

They entered Northernhay Gardens and followed the path to the memorial, putting Alice in mind of the first time she'd met Jack, not an auspicious occasion as it turned out. She followed Della through the Roman arch and along the row of elm trees to a bench at the centre. The earlier poor weather had kept people away but there were one or two walking their dogs in the weak spring sun.

'It's a bit damp.' Della gestured to the seat.

'We'll keep walking.'

'Why did you lie, about who I was?'

'I'm sorry, that was silly. It's just . . .'

'It's alright, I understand. I'm of a lower class. Your mother wouldn't approve. I'm not sure she bought it, you saying I was a friend of the Rolands. I don't look the part.'

Alice grimaced. 'I've made a mess of everything.'

Della's hand brushed hers, a secret signal to say it's alright.

She smiled in gratitude. 'I'm still worried my father is having an affair. When I saw Mummy, I panicked. I felt like I was covering for him and that made me guilty by association, even though I'm not certain.'

141

Della's brow furrowed. 'What about the butler chap, Gillespie. Do you think he knows anything?'

Alice clapped her hand over her mouth, a new idea dawning. 'What is it?'

'Mummy and Gillespie. I joked about him and Martha the other day to myself, but what if Mummy was there because she was going to see Gillespie, and we caught her in the act? Maybe Daddy was up there before to have it out with him or catch them at it.'

'Blimey, Alice, you know how to take one plus one and make three.'

Alice laughed and linked her arm through Della's, grateful for her level-headed thinking. 'You're right, I'm being ridiculous. Mummy would never and she's even older than Daddy — you didn't hear that from me. Gillespie wouldn't be interested, he's so . . . vital.'

Della was studying her with a bemused expression. 'Is he now?'

Alice laughed again. 'I'm not interested, I only desire raven-haired girls with emerald eyes. I'd kiss you now if I could.'

'Alright.' Della blushed, bringing those eyes to life. 'I believe you.'

'But I saw him, the other afternoon coming out of the bathroom. An Adonis.'

They both laughed so loud a passing dog walker threw them a disparaging stare.

'Besides,' Alice said when they'd recovered, 'Gillespie's my friend. He thinks I should enter your portrait in the Royal Academy exhibition.' She slid her hand into her coat pocket, the newspaper cutting still there like a talisman.

'He's seen it?'

Alice shook her head. 'Not yet, but he's seen my other work and thinks I have something.'

'In Paris, you'll take the art world by storm.'

Alice grinned.

'Do you really think we'll go?' Della's eyes widened.

'Of course.'

Della shook her head. 'I'd never have the courage to even consider it if it wasn't for you.'

Alice cast behind and, finding they were alone, cupped Della's face. 'You're braver than you think — look at what you manage at home all the while holding down a job and proving yourself to be a baker extraordinaire. You're a marvel, Della Wilde.'

Della leaned her forehead against Alice's. 'Thank you.'

The desire to kiss her was so strong, Alice almost forgot herself, but Della pulled away, a frown across her face.

'What's wrong?'

'Keep walking,' Della whispered. She now stepped away from Alice, unlinked her arm and retraced their steps.

Alice cast around and hurried after her away from the far side of the park where the railway line crossed into Queen Street station.

'Bloody William,' Della hissed under her breath.

'The waiter?'

'He was watching us from the row of trees.'

Alice glanced back but the path was empty. 'Why should his seeing us matter?'

'He's been annoyed with me ever since I dropped him that day we were going to the cinema. Told me I was weird about you. First him, then Jack. Why can't they keep out of it?'

'He's nothing, a nobody.' Alice could hear the firm tone of reassurance in her voice and maybe she almost believed it, but she wasn't immune to anxiety. She recalled Gillespie's words the other evening. *Be careful what enemies you make, Miss Alice.* She hadn't understood him then, but now she did. She and Della were different, and there were plenty of people who wanted to stand in their way.

A large black bird swooped down so close, they ducked. It settled on the ground a few feet away and fixed her with its gimlet stare. Alice could only stare back. Was this the creature from her street, the one who watched her paint?

'Blimey,' Della whispered.

The bird took flight, circling them once with its ominous caw and flew off to a neighbouring tree, leaving Alice to wonder at its message.

CHAPTER 29

Della said goodbye to Alice at Queen Street with a chaste kiss on the cheek one might bestow on an aunt, and watched her walk away, coat-tails flapping in the breeze. She considered getting a tram, but it was dry, and Della sensed she might have company on the walk home. Not that it was company she welcomed.

His footsteps echoed along the pavement, distinctive in the quiet road. She continued walking until he caught up with her.

'What do you want, William?' They'd dispensed with pleasantries lately. She saw no reason to bother with them now.

'That's a fine way to greet me.'

'You've hardly been cordial. Why are you following me?'

He tapped his pockets for a cigarette and pulled one free. 'Can a man not pay his respects at the memorial in the park he fought for?'

Della smirked at his pomposity. William loved to ruminate on his time at the front, as if no one but him had been touched by the war. Anthony never did elaborate on how William was a hero. She still couldn't picture it, but she'd have to take him at his word. They were lucky to come back and find secure jobs. There were few men who emerged without scars, and those scars leached into their families. The Wildes knew better than most. She sighed, wanting to be rid of this tedious man. 'I didn't know you was fighting for parks. Shouldn't there be a plaque in your honour?' Her gaze remained focused on the junction with the High Street ahead. William struck a match and made a sucking sound as he took his first drag, letting her sarcasm hang.

At the junction, they paused and faced one another. He was wearing a suit that had seen better days, his boots beaten and dusty, betraying their age. It was odd to see him like this, out of context with no smart Ambrose uniform to hide behind. The Ambrose was only a few steps away. She knew William lived beyond Sidwell Street, quite literally at the opposite end of town. The coincidence of their meeting was stark. At what point had he decided to use his Sunday to follow her? Had he been to Alice's? To the Wildes'?

The usually bustling High Street was practically empty, its towering buildings either side of the road creating a silent tunnel. He hovered in her periphery, pulling on his cigarette and looking in both directions, trying to settle on his path. Eventually he broke their stalemate. 'I'll walk you home.'

'Thanks, but it's out of your way and I'd like to be alone.'

'So you can think about her?'

Della shook her head. 'I don't know what your problem is, I've tried to be nice, but—'

'My problem is you.' He drew on his cigarette again. She let the silence play out, scanning the road for escape. 'I love you.' It came out in a stream of smoke.

Della stepped back in shock and tried not to cough.

His features contorted as if he were wrestling with a physical pain. 'Let me save you.'

'Save me?'

'From her.'

'I don't need saving, William.' She'd meant to say it gently, but her words were laced with exasperation.

146

He brought his face close to hers so she could enjoy the full range of his stale breath. 'Don't say I didn't warn you.' With that, he turned and walked away.

Della stared after him, confounded.

She pulled up her coat collar against the chill William had left in his wake and hurried along the High Street for home, not that she'd find comfort there, but distraction would do.

* * *

A thudding hammered through her head as she approached. Sam was in the yard, kicking a football against the back wall.

'Where did you get that?' Della asked, trying to dodge his flailing legs.

'Jack found it.'

She ruffled his hair.

'I'm not a kid, Del,' he said seriously.

'Alright, Mister, no need to take offence. I missed you, that's all.'

'Where've you been?'

'Out with a friend.'

'Della's got a fancy man,' he said in his sing-song voice.

Della chuckled. 'Give over, Samuel Wilde.' She resisted the urge to pull him to her. Sam had developed a strong independent streak recently. Hardly surprising. She went inside.

The kitchen was warm and tidy. A pile of folded mending sat at the end of the table. She hoped this meant Ma was still of their world. Jack's news had had a revitalising effect on their mother, she couldn't deny that.

In need of solitude after her unsettling confrontation with William, she hung her coat and ventured upstairs to her room. Della looked out of the window, misted with condensation, at the rooftops of the surrounding houses and wished they were the rooftops of Paris and that Alice was by her side.

* * *

When Della crept down to the kitchen the following morning, hoping to leave for work before the rest of the house had risen, Jack was waiting for her, dressed in his Sunday best.

'Thought we could walk in together,' he said, a long-absent warmth in his tone.

She pulled on her coat under Jack's watchful eye. He picked up a flask and tin lunch box, no doubt lovingly prepared by Ma, and opened the door, gesturing her to go through.

Della followed him down the alley, unable to shake off a sense of foreboding. Was this to be her life now, escorted to and from work by her brother, spied on by William? They'd have Father Cole around next.

'What time's your shift?' Della asked, attempting to show interest in his new job.

'Six, like you. We can walk in together every day.'

She tried to take the comment as kindly meant, but after their recent interactions, it felt more like a threat.

'It'll be a relief for Ma, to have another wage coming in.' Jack's expression darkened. 'No more Saint Della.'

'I didn't mean it like that.' Why must everything be taken as a slur?

They walked in silence the rest of the way, whether because Jack was nervous or offended, she wasn't sure.

With the Ambrose in her sights, Della quickened her pace, but she was no match for her brother's long stride. It was only when they reached the gates into the backyard that he came to a halt and waited for her to go first.

'Nervous?' She detected a note of mocking in her tone and regretted it. Jack didn't seem to notice. He stood for a moment looking up at the building and she understood. The Ambrose had that effect on her too — the ornate detail in the baroque exterior, the grandeur of the large windows and statuesque columns. It was a building that commanded respect no matter your reason for being within its walls. 'Good luck,' she added.

Jack smirked. 'I make my own luck.' He waltzed across the yard, a swagger in his step as he approached the stores. Della made her way inside, as anxious as if it was her first day on the job. Now she had William and Jack to avoid and an awful lot to lose.

CHAPTER 30

Alice bit her lip rather hard as Gillespie stood before the finished portrait of Della. She couldn't help gazing at it herself, not because she was narcissistic about her talents, but because of the subject. He clasped his hands behind his back. She cleared her throat in a bid to indicate her patience was running out. He glanced at her, his expression giving nothing away.

Eventually he turned to face her. 'It's exceptional.'

She released her lip, now rather sore. 'Really?'

'She shines.'

Alice studied the floor, modesty preventing her from meeting his eye. 'I had a good model to work with.'

'The fact you're in love with her only adds to the luminescence, but it's your talent and skill too that makes it so compelling.'

He said it easily. The fact she was in love with Della slid off his tongue, not in shock, disgust or bemusement, but as fact. It was refreshing, this lack of judgement. She wasn't used to such generosity of spirit and couldn't help being curious about where in his past its origins lay.

'Once you're ready, say the word. I'll pack the portrait up and deliver it for transit to the Royal Academy myself. It would be an honour.'

Alice grinned. 'I want to show Della first.'

'Don't delay too long, the competition closes in less than a week. Ideally, we should send it tomorrow.'

She stared at the painting again, surprised and delighted by how much she liked it. She'd never felt so close to her work.

'I'll leave you in peace.' Gillespie made for the door.

'Thank you, Mr Gillespie, for everything. I'm not sure I'd have had the nerve to see this through if it hadn't been for your encouragement.'

He threw her a brief nod, which for Gillespie was the equivalent of a warm embrace, and left the room.

Once his footsteps died away, Alice settled on the daybed, where she could see the portrait in all its splendour. She wondered what Della was doing at this moment and whether she should meet her from the Ambrose. Gillespie was right, they needed to send the painting without delay.

The bird made its presence known at the window. Alice faced it head on. Its courage had grown. Now perched on the ledge, it stared openly, but it wasn't Alice that captured its eye but the portrait. She walked to the easel and turned it away. The bird chuckled and flew off. Alice watched it go, a tingling down her spine.

In the hall, her mother intercepted her. 'You're not going out?'

Alice reached for her coat. 'I was going to, Mummy.'

'Couldn't you stay in this evening? You haven't told me about your new friend, the one residing with Toby. I must say, I was rather surprised. She didn't look like the sort of girl to mix with the Rolands. Did you notice her coat? The elbows were so thin, she was in danger of poking through. Poor thing. The Rolands would have offered her something better, I'm certain.'

Her mother meant it as a confidence, something for them to exclaim over, an olive branch of sorts, but Alice found it distasteful. She forced a smile, her plans to see Della draining away.

In the sitting room, they settled on the sofa, her mother's face open, expectant. 'Tell me about you. Why are you always hiding away?'

Her back stiffened. 'I'm not hiding away.'

'Is it the break-up with Toby? You mustn't dwell on it.' She stroked Alice's cheek. 'You're very beautiful, darling. Have you considered growing your hair? Some men might find it . . . a little too much.'

Alice suppressed a sigh. This was exactly why she chose her own company over either of her parents. The lack of understanding. Gillespie's words popped into her mind. *Your mother's a saint.* She longed to see her as he did.

'I'm sorry, don't pout. I know short hair is all the rage, I suppose I'm terribly out of touch.' Her face had fallen, her expression so filled with sorrow, Alice realised how unfair she was being. Her mother was trying to find a source of connection in her own indelicate way. She searched for words to put her at ease.

'You're not out of touch, Mummy. I could cut your hair if you like?'

Her mother laughed. 'Oh, Alice, as if I'd allow you anywhere near my hair. I wouldn't even let Martha do it.'

As pleased as she was to have lightened the mood, Alice felt a frisson of hurt. She'd done a good job with Della's hair, but she could hardly tell her mother that.

'Did you know Martha's given her notice? I don't know how I shall manage without her.'

Alice was dragged from her reverie. Martha, leaving? 'Why?'

'She's engaged and her fiancé doesn't like the idea of her working once they're married. It's understandable.'

Such relief to realise her father wasn't having an affair. She squeezed her mother's hand, a rush of affection. 'You'll find someone else.'

'I don't like the idea of getting used to someone new again. Gillespie was talking of leaving too. The whole place will fall apart.'

'What?' Alice stood, recalling another of their conversations. *I might not always be here, Miss Alice.* 'He can't leave.'

'Your father will do his utmost to persuade him to stay.'

152

Alice lowered herself back to the sofa. The fire snapped in the grate, adding to her unease. One thing was certain, her mother's casual tone put paid to any idea that she could be embroiled with Gillespie. Alice had been wrong about both her parents, but that didn't explain why Father visited the attic.

Her mother broke into her thoughts. 'I had no idea you held Gillespie in such high esteem.'

Alice was surprised herself. She'd come to think of him as a confidant over the last few weeks. He knew far more about her interior life than either of her parents. Perhaps they confided in him too, she was sure her father did. That might explain his visit to the attic. She glanced at her mother, who was studying her carefully.

'Oh, Alice, you haven't got a crush, have you? Gillespie's a handsome man, but there are lines we do not cross.'

Alice was horrified. 'Of course not.'

'Good, then we'll say no more. Tell me about the mysterious girl on the back stairs. I don't believe for a second she's anything to do with the Rolands. I know when you're lying, you get a crease between your eyes. And if you've broken up with Toby, why would you be entertaining one of his group?'

Alice tried to muster another story. How she longed to be honest. 'She's not, but she is a good friend. I met her at the Ambrose.' It was the closest to the truth she was prepared to go.

Her mother eyed her. 'She's very striking, cheekbones like cut glass, but what do you know about her?'

'She's the kindest person I've ever met.'

'Well good, bring her to tea sometime, let me get a proper look at her, and for pity's sake, get her another coat. You must have one to spare.'

It wasn't a terrible idea, but Alice feared offending Della with charity.

The clock on the mantel struck seven. Her mother reached for the sherry, the pop as she uncorked the bottle so familiar at the dinner hour it was as if it were an extension of the chime. 'Will you join me, darling?'

Before she'd declined, her father walked in, a weary look on his face. 'Crisis averted,' he said to no one in particular, but his exhaustion suggested he'd reached the end of a long campaign for peace. Gillespie would stay, thank God for that.

'Sherry, Robert?' Mummy proffered the bottle.

'Something stronger.' He rang the bell and Gillespie appeared as if nothing had happened. 'A brandy please, Gillespie.'

'Very good, sir.'

Half an hour later, Alice followed her parents to the dining room, relieved the status quo at the winter house had been restored. Della would be home by now, the portrait would have to be sent without her approval.

CHAPTER 31

Jack was waiting for her when Della emerged from the café, smoking and chatting to one of his colleagues, a casual shoulder pressed against the wall. She wanted to tell him to quit slouching and step away from the hallowed building, to have some respect, but his companion glanced in her direction. She stopped in her tracks — it was William. He stared for a beat, then turned back to Jack, who'd spied her too, leaving her with no choice but to approach.

'There she is — my little sister.' Jack finally straightened. A couple of the other lads in the yard looked up from their work. Della felt like she was the new girl, the usurper, Jack already far too much at home. He thrust a hand at William. 'Good to see you again, mate. You must come to tea sometime, I'm sure Della would like that.' Her brother threw her a sly wink. Her body tensed. William returned his handshake with one eye on Della too.

'What did you say that for?' she asked Jack as they made their way down the High Street.

'Weren't you sweet on him once?'

'You know I wasn't.'

'That's right.' Jack grinned. 'Not your type, but you're definitely his.' He pulled on his cigarette. 'I think I'm going to enjoy working at the Ambrose.'

Della stopped walking. Eventually Jack did too, noticing her pained expression.

His smile faltered. 'Del, I'm joking.'

She moved on, hearing Jack's tread close behind. It might be a joke to him, but she wasn't laughing.

* * *

After an evening of celebration in the Wilde household for Jack's first day, Della was surprised to find the kitchen cold and empty when she came down for work the following morning. As much as she'd begrudged joining in, she couldn't deny the light in Ma's eyes as she listened to Jack recount his day in detail.

The back door was on the latch; Jack had already left. Perhaps he'd sensed her ambivalence and taken offence. She arrived at the Ambrose yard to find him once again enjoying a cigarette with William, his new best friend. They watched her walk past without greeting. Della felt the chill wind of their stares.

In the kitchen, she prepared for the day ahead. The banquet room had been hired for a party that afternoon and she'd been tasked with making the cake as well as dessert for fifty guests. She pulled on her overalls and tucked her hair under her cap. With the required pans laid out in front of her, Della went to the pantry for a new bag of flour. She dragged it halfway across the kitchen floor, cursing its weight and the lack of available help, when Leonnard arrived, rescuing the bag and setting it down at her work bench.

'Thanks.' Della smiled. 'How's it going with Mrs Hastings?'

Leonnard offered up a modest shrug, a twinkle in his working eye. 'I think I have you to thank for my change in fortune.'

Other staff started to arrive. Anthony threw her a wave, William a glare. Leonnard ambled back to his bench.

An hour later, she'd mixed the batter and was pouring it into the prepared tins. The sponges would need forty-five minutes in the oven and then at least an hour to cool if not two before she could assemble the finished cake.

Outside, the city was coming to life, the clop of horses' hooves vying for space on the High Street with trams and motor cars. Della lifted the tins into the oven and returned to clear up the mess before embarking on her next task.

By mid-morning, her hands and arms ached with the amount of butter, sugar and flour she'd worked through her fingers.

William popped his head around the door. 'Your *special* friend's downstairs, Della.' He came to her side, his breath hot against her ear. 'She's with a group of women, quite the party.'

Della kept her eyes on the mixing bowl. His emphasis of the word 'special' hadn't escaped her attention.

'Thought you'd be interested to know.' He smirked and sauntered away.

She was interested, but what could she do? If Alice wanted to see her, she'd seek her out. In the meantime, Della had too much work. She set about pressing the pastry into tart cases. The methodical task failed to provide much distraction, but at least it gave her a focus. Apart from Fliss, she hadn't met Alice's friends. It wasn't as if they mixed in the same circles — another reminder of their differences.

'Whose are these?' Hastings called across from the ovens. She'd pulled out the blackened husks of Della's sponges.

Della slapped her hand to her brow. 'I didn't set the timer.' She'd have to start again.

'It's not like you to forget something so important,' Hastings snapped. 'Carry on with what you're doing. I'll make the cake myself.' She didn't need to express her disappointment — it was there in the cut of her tongue.

A crowd gathered, William among them, drawn out by Hastings' sharp tone and the smoke that perfumed the air.

Della mumbled her apologies and returned to her pastry cases, a river in her vision. She'd let down the Ambrose.

The others dispersed but William lingered in her periphery. She refused to meet his gaze. One thing was certain, news of her humiliation would get back to Jack at the first opportunity.

The morning wore on and no word from Alice. It was foolish to expect it. She eyed the cakes Hastings had left to cool on the next table and could tell by the texture of the sponge, it was a little overbaked — the cake would be dry — but that was no longer her problem.

By late morning, news of her cake disaster had reached the main kitchen. Mr Voisin appeared to inspect Hastings' finished cake. He congratulated her and moved to Della's bench. 'I hear you had a mishap this morning.'

'Sorry, sir, it won't happen again.'

'Make sure it doesn't.' He leaned in, his voice a whisper. 'Now we will serve a mediocre cake, when we would have delivered something exceptional.'

It was a compliment wrapped up in a reprimand. Della allowed his words to lift her spirits.

'Mistakes happen, but the true genius in the kitchen always has a contingency plan. What's yours?'

She met his gaze. He was giving her a chance to make amends. She searched desperately but came up blank.

'Teamwork. The best kitchens thrive on it. Delegate when you need to. Share the load with your colleagues and most important . . . remember to breathe.'

Della's eyes stung with gratitude for his kindness. 'Thank you, sir.'

He nodded. 'You're wanted in the downstairs servery. The MP Robert Winters' daughter requires an audience with you.'

'Oh, but . . .'

He gestured to the door. '*Allez.*'

Della pulled off her cap and made her way at breakneck speed down the back stairs.

CHAPTER 32

Alice waited by the servery doors with one eye on the café, where her mother took tea with a couple of the wives of members of the city council and their daughters — ever the dutiful MP's wife. 'It might be fun,' she'd said when she'd secured Alice's agreement to accompany her the previous evening. Alice couldn't deny she'd only relented because of the opportunity to see Della. It was bad luck they'd been seated in that sly waiter's section. After the park, she no longer trusted him with a message and resorted to using her father's name.

She tapped her foot against the floor, self-conscious, her mind distracted by the portrait, which should now be on its way to London thanks to Mr Gillespie. It was out of her hands, but the guilt she hadn't shown it to Della first was the reason for her visit.

As soon as Della appeared from the kitchens, Alice could tell something was wrong. Della looked exhausted, her skin ashen, eyes downcast. She beckoned Alice to follow her to the yard. No sooner had they stepped through the door than Jack appeared, striding across the concourse in his overcoat, a curious look on his face as he locked eyes with Alice. Della sighed and they returned inside and stood in awkward silence at the back of the bustling servery.

159

'What's happened?' Alice whispered.

Della shook her head. 'We can't talk here.'

'Later then, I'll meet you after work. What time do you finish?'

'I can't, not with Jack watching my every move.' Della cast around. 'Sorry, I'm having a bad morning. What brings you here? William said you were with friends.'

'I bet he did. I'm with my mother, two of her friends and their tiresome daughters.' A nasty thought but absolutely true.

A smile tugged at Della's lips and Alice grinned too, pleased to have lifted her mood.

'Anyway, I couldn't pass up the opportunity to see you and . . .' She hesitated, fearing sharing more bad news. 'I'm afraid I had to send the portrait to the exhibition without you seeing it first. The competition closes at the end of the week.'

Della shook her head. 'You don't need to worry about that. Can't have you missing out on the opportunity to show them London types what an exceptional talent you are.'

Alice blushed. She should never have doubted Della. 'Thank you.'

'I'd better get back, I'm not in Mrs Hastings' good books this morning after I burned a cake.'

'Oh dear, that's not like you.' Alice hated seeing her brought so low.

Della met her gaze with watery eyes. 'No, it ain't. I dunno what's happening, but I feel like Jack getting the job here is going to turn out bad for me and I'm going to lose everything.'

'You won't lose me,' she whispered.

Della smiled but it was weak. 'I'll see you soon.'

Alice watched her go, a forlorn figure in dusty white. She noticed William regarding her from across the servery and returned his hard gaze before hastening back to the café.

'There you are, Alice.' Her mother beamed. 'Did you see your friend?'

Alice slid into her seat. 'I did, thank you. Where are the others?'

'They had to go. Why don't we do some shopping once we've finished here? We haven't treated ourselves in so long.'

All Alice wanted to do was get home and check with Gillespie that the painting was on its way.

'You used to love shopping,' her mother continued. 'I told your father we'd be out for most of the day. We could have a spot of lunch at the Royal Clarence if you like.'

The scene of her assignation with Della, Alice wasn't sure returning so soon was a good idea, but seeing her mother's pleading eyes, she rallied. Gillespie wouldn't let her down. 'Sounds wonderful.'

Her mother's face transformed, filled with a happiness which had been absent for far too long. 'Good, then it's settled.' She signalled for the waiter. William appeared at their table. 'The bill, please.'

'Certainly, Madam. Was everything to your satisfaction?' His eyes met Alice's. There was hatred there.

'Indeed,' her mother replied.

He sloped away with their empty plates. Her mother took her purse from her handbag. 'I need to use the powder room. Take this and pay the bill if I'm not back in time. I'll meet you at the entrance.'

Alice watched her mother leave. She seemed to walk a little taller, more elegant, more her old self. A day of shopping together might do them both good.

William returned to the table with the bill. Alice counted out the money and placed it on the plate under his watchful eye. She begrudged him his tip, but decorum prevented her from being churlish. He picked up the plate and leaned in, his voice low. 'Della will tire of whatever spell you've cast, and when she does, I'll be waiting. I love her you see, Miss Winters, and I'm not going to let you or anyone else stand in my way.'

Alice pushed back her chair. 'There's nothing less attractive than a man who doesn't understand the word no.' She walked away, pleased to have had the last word.

* * *

They arrived back at the winter house laden with bags from Colson's. Mummy had insisted they visit their dressmaker and treated them both to a new wardrobe for spring and summer. Alice couldn't shake the guilt about this, something she'd never experienced before meeting Della.

'Let's have afternoon tea since you didn't eat much at lunch. I'll tell cook.' Her mother's eyes shone with the exertions of the day and something else — joy.

'I'll go, Mummy. You rest. We've been on our feet for hours.'

Her mother untied her silk scarf. 'Alright, dear. I wonder where Gillespie is. I did tell him not to expect us until dinner. Perhaps your father has given him the afternoon off.'

Alice hoped it was because he'd taken her painting. She spoke to Mrs Drummond then took the opportunity to check the attic and ensure the portrait was gone.

A rumble of laughter stopped her outside the servants' rooms. She'd know that laugh anywhere, so rarely was it bestowed by her serious father. It came from Gillespie's bedroom. A sinking sensation travelled through her body as if it reached the obvious conclusion before her mind could catch the thought. Gillespie's voice next. 'Look at the time. I'll be missed downstairs.' The creak of the bed.

A sigh from her father. 'We get so little opportunity to be together.'

Alice wasn't sure she had the stomach for more. It was an intimate conversation, one she didn't want to be party to, but her feet remained rooted to the spot.

'I still think it would be better for everyone if I left.'

'You promised you wouldn't talk of that.'

A hard note in Gillespie's reply. 'You made me care about your family . . .'

The bed creaked again as if they were lying back down. There was no further conversation, only a soft mumbling Alice couldn't discern.

Reality caught up with her now. She turned and ran down the stairs, tears blinding her vision. Gillespie? *Anyone but him.*

CHAPTER 33

Clouds tinged with pink scudded across the darkening sky. Della scrubbed at the pan encrusted with burnt potato from the shepherd's pie they'd had for dinner — a nice bit of mince provided by Jack. Where it came from was anyone's guess. He wouldn't receive his first pay until the end of the week, but if Jack wanted to show off as man of the house, she wasn't about to argue, not when Ma was so happy.

She'd offered to wash up, with a desire for solitude after what had been a troubling day. First the cake, then Alice's visit, William's smug presence and Jack walking her home, boasting about the people he was meeting, the friends he was making, William foremost among them.

'You should give him another chance, Del. He's a decent bloke and you can't really carry on with that Alice, it ain't normal.'

Della pushed the memory away, set the stubborn pan on the sink to drain and dried her wrinkled fingers. She was about to go upstairs when she caught sight of a figure in the yard. She'd seen Jack go out earlier, maybe it was him. A soft knock came against the door. She drew it open, shocked to find Alice on the other side, her face shrouded in shadow, a tremor to her voice.

'We need to talk,' she whispered. 'Somewhere private.'

Della grabbed her jacket from the door and joined her in the yard, leading her away from the house past the privy cloaked in darkness to the wall behind.

'What's happened?' She wrapped her arms around Alice's shaking body. 'You're shivering.'

'It's my father.' Alice took a shuddering breath. 'You know I feared he might be having an affair. Well, it seems I was right.'

'Oh, Alice, with the maid?'

Alice's voice cracked. 'With Gillespie.'

'The butler?'

'Shh, if it got out it could ruin him.'

'Are you certain?'

'I heard them in bed together.'

'Blimey.'

'Quite.'

'I mean, not that its wrong exactly.'

'I'd be a hypocrite to criticise, but it is illegal, and I keep thinking about poor Mummy. What this would do to her.' She buried her head in Della's shoulder.

'Will you confront your father?'

'I don't know what to do. It's strange, but I feel more betrayed by Gillespie. I thought he was my friend. Now perhaps I was an indulgence. A way to bring him closer to Daddy.'

She found Alice's hand and squeezed it. 'Don't make any rash decisions.'

Alice met her gaze. 'It's a relief to tell someone.'

They stood, heads bowed together, shadows in the dark. Della searched her mind for what they could do next, for where they could safely go. Taking Alice into the house would invite intrigue. Her brothers would be sniffing around. Ma, who was in the parlour mending, would put on airs and graces she didn't possess. It was too embarrassing to countenance.

A train rattled by, a screech of brakes, stealing the moment. Alice broke away. 'I'd better get home. Mummy will wonder where I am. We were supposed to be having tea, then I found my father in bed with the butler, and I disappeared like a genie.'

She smoothed Alice's cheek, wet with tears. 'Will you be alright, walking back? It's getting dark.'

Alice sniffed and pulled herself up to her full height, towering above Della. 'I'll be fine.'

Under cover of darkness, Della found her lips. It wasn't much, but to kiss Alice in the boundaries of her home felt at once dangerous and completely natural. 'I'll meet you tomorrow, after work.'

Alice nodded. 'What about Jack?'

'I'll think of something.'

She opened the back gate and listened as Alice's footsteps died away, finding she couldn't judge Gillespie or Alice's father — weren't they doing the same thing? As much as she envied her wealth and home comforts, there was a code people like Alice's family lived by. No one much cared what went on in the houses at the bottom of town. A scandal was dealt with by fists. But gentry, they had certain rules, especially gentry who held positions of power. Della pondered this as she stole across the yard.

A flash from a torch and the privy door creaked open. Jack emerged. She didn't need to ask if he'd heard everything, it was there on his face.

'Well, well, Della Wilde. I never knew a visit to the privy could be so enlightening.'

165

Alice sat with her secret all through the following morning. Father had left for London in the early hours and wouldn't be back until the next day. In the hall after breakfast, Gillespie confirmed to her the portrait had been dispatched. She'd forced a bright smile of thanks in return and hurried away, unable to meet his eye. It was her mother she dreaded. Since their shopping expedition the previous day, Alice felt a renewed connection between them. Despite its large airy rooms spread over four floors, the winter house had never felt so small.

And now the attic room where she loved to paint was lost to her too. She couldn't go there with the same feeling of excitement when it was tainted by what she'd overheard.

After lunch, Alice paced her bedroom, replaying the conversation over and over, attempting to work out her feelings. In a way it struck her as natural. Her father and Gillespie had been thrown together by war, they'd bonded in the face of immense adversity and danger, they'd fallen in love. What were they to do when they returned to England? How could they carry on? She thought about Della, what it would pain her to give her up when their love was so new. But no matter how much she wanted to understand her father's choices, bringing his lover into the very house where his wife resided seemed immeasurably cruel. That was the part she couldn't countenance.

It mustn't come out. She didn't care one jot about her father's career, the potential loss of the winter house. Gillespie would survive, he was resourceful, even if it came to prison. It was her mother she wanted to protect. Her mother who would be ill-equipped to weather the storm, a laughing stock, a thing to be pitied.

'Alice?' Her mother's voice followed by a light tap against the door. 'The latest issue of *Woman's Life* has arrived. We could look together.'

Alice tried not to roll her eyes. She could never relate to the women depicted in *Women's Life*. They all appeared preoccupied with marriage, children and perfecting their domestic skills. She much preferred something focused on fashion, like *Vogue*. Still, it would offer a distraction. She opened the door and plastered a smile across her face. 'Good idea, I'll be right down.'

By afternoon tea, she struggled to contain her agitation. Gillespie served them in the sitting room while they listened to a radio play. Alice studied him as he set down the tray. She recalled their meeting in the kitchen. The brown betty teapot, the sense someone understood her, saw her, the real her. Gillespie caught her eye and fixed her with a curious expression as if he could see the torment in her soul.

Outside, the skies were clearing after what had been a wet morning. Alice stood, sending *Women's Life* from her lap to the floor. Gillespie swooped in to fetch it up. 'Is everything alright, Miss Alice?'

She couldn't look at him. 'Mummy, you don't mind if I pop out for a while? I need some fresh air.'

'I'll come too if we can have tea first.'

'Don't trouble yourself. I thought I'd take my friend one of my coats now that I have some new clothes coming.'

Before her mother could protest, she ran from the room and up the stairs. When she emerged with a coat for Della slung over her arm, Gillespie was waiting for her in the hall with a large cloth bag Mrs Drummond used for shopping. He held it open while Alice folded the coat inside, never more self-conscious of his penetrating gaze.

At the front door, he hovered after she'd stepped outside as if he sensed something was broken between them. At the end of the road, she checked behind. Gillespie was still there.

* * *

With the Ambrose in her sights, Alice made her way through town, the bag slung over one shoulder. She wasn't sure how Della would take this act of charity, but it provided a decent cover with her mother. She waited outside the bank next door, so she could spy Della and separate her from Jack.

Her hopes were crushed as he appeared first, noticing her straight away. 'Miss Winters.' He doffed his cap but looked too pleased with himself for Alice to feel anything but anxious.

'Mr Wilde. I'm waiting for Della.'

'You won't be seeing my sister today.'

Alice frowned. 'What do you mean?' She was about to explain about the coat when Della emerged, a look of hopeless resignation on her face as she took in the scene. Alice made to move but Jack stepped in her path.

He glanced over his shoulder. 'Go home, Della.'

Della mouthed something to her Alice couldn't comprehend. She held the bag aloft. 'This is for you . . .' Della had already turned and hurried away.

Jack took the bag and peered inside then handed it back to her. 'My sister don't take charity.'

'I'd prefer to let Della decide.' She sighed, puzzled by Della's retreating figure. Why was she letting Jack bully her? 'You can't stop us from seeing each other.'

Jack smiled with conceit. 'Shall we go for a drink?'

'I'm not interested in going for a drink with you.'

'I think you might be, once you hear what I've got to say concerning your father and a certain butler.'

A liquid sensation travelled through her limbs. *Jack knew?* Surely Della hadn't told him, but she had run away — *guilty?* Alice didn't want to believe it. She let Jack take her arm, her body defeated, and allowed him to lead her into the Royal Clarence Hotel.

The bar was quiet and they took a corner booth. Jack ordered drinks and sat back, a disingenuous grin on his face. The predator in sight of its prey. He lit a cigarette and offered her one. She took it, grateful to have something to do with her hands.

He leaned in once their drinks had arrived. 'We have an interesting situation.'

Alice could see he intended to take his time, like a cat might taunt a mouse. 'Get to the point, Mr Wilde.'

'I think we can dispense with formalities now that we're, shall we say, of one mind.'

Alice drew on her cigarette and expelled the smoke in his face. 'How did you find out?'

Jack smirked. 'You're not going to deny it?'

She shrugged. 'Deny what?'

'Della didn't tell me. I was tempted to pretend she did, but I realised that wasn't necessary. You won't see my sister again if you want your father's dirty secret to remain out of the press.'

'That's your price for silence. Me to stop seeing Della?'

'That and a little financial incentive wouldn't hurt.'

'I thought you didn't take charity.'

'This is business.'

'Business? Is that what you call blackmail?'

Jack sat back, the smirk on his face indicating how much he was enjoying himself. 'What a thing to suggest.'

Alice took a sip of her drink, aware he held all the cards. The whisky settled her nerves. 'So, how did you find out?' She couldn't help wanting to know.

'I was in the privy when you and my sister had your touching little heart-to-heart. I heard it all. Every single word.'

'What is it about me and Della you find so threatening?'

The smirk slid off his face. 'Threatening? I'm not threatened by you. But you do need putting in your place. There's plenty of men, good men, who deserve to earn a decent wage. You're distracting Della from her proper path. She needs to be married and out of the Ambrose. She's got no business taking a man's wage or spending time with the likes of you.'

'That's the most ridiculous thing I've ever heard. Della deserves the success she's worked hard for.'

'What about the men who fought?'

'Like you?'

His expression darkened. 'Like my father, my brothers.'

'Punishing Della won't bring them back. My father fought, Mr Gillespie too.'

'Yeah, and they came back a pair of pansies, while good men, better men, fell with honour.'

Alice could see she wasn't going to win an argument with this man. His prejudice only made her want to stand up for Gillespie and her father more, but it was her mother she needed to protect. That was the true cost here, not her father's reputation, but her mother's heart.

'State your price.'

Jack's face clouded as if he hadn't believed he'd get this far. 'You stop seeing my sister. No contact.'

Tears pricked her eyes. She gave a brief nod while searching for a way out she couldn't see.

'I want ten pounds.'

Not an insignificant sum, but Alice knew she could get it. 'Alright,' she whispered.

'Meet me here at 5 p.m. tomorrow. Come alone, no funny business.' He downed his drink and walked out of the bar, leaving Alice with the bill.

170

CHAPTER 35

Della stayed in her bedroom after work, telling Ma she had her monthly pain. She sat at the window, looking over the roof tops, face wet with tears.

Jack had gone out the previous evening after he'd overheard Alice's secret. When he returned, stinking of beer, he told her his plan in the dark of the kitchen while the rest of the house slept. How he'd put a stop to Alice and her seeing each other, how he'd make a tidy sum for the Wildes in the process. No more money worries for Ma, food on the table and coal for the stove. Surely Della could see this was the best outcome for everyone. He wouldn't be fulfilling his role as man of the house if he didn't put an end to her carrying on like a queer. This way she'd be free to marry, to make a home and family like a proper girl. To make Ma proud. Della could think only of Alice, of the wound this would inflict, the impossible situation it put her in.

A knock came against the door and Ma entered the room. Della wiped her cheeks free of tears.

'Cheer up, love, I've brought you a cuppa.' She set the mug on a chair Della used as a night table and perched on the edge of the bed. 'Are you sure you won't eat? Jack brought a nice bit of pork home today.'

More meat for the Wilde table, but how was Jack providing it when he hadn't been paid? Della sat up. 'Where did he get it?'

Ma touched her cheek, a rare moment of affection. 'Don't look so worried, he's earning a good wage now. Things are looking up for the Wildes.' Her face bloomed with a pleasure Della hadn't witnessed in far too long, but the news of the meat troubled her. Nothing was ever straightforward where Jack was concerned.

'I'm not hungry,' Della whispered, laying back down and pulling the eiderdown around her.

'Rest up, you deserve it, and you know where we are if you need anything.'

She listened to the creak of Ma's footsteps carrying her back downstairs. The transformation Jack's job had brought about in their mother was remarkable. It was a shame it came at a price only she was required to pay.

* * *

The following morning, Della walked to work under clear blue skies, the sun glinting off the rooftops in direct contrast to her mood. She'd left early on purpose, keen to avoid Jack, knowing he'd met Alice and made his demands. There had to be a way out of this, but for the life of her, she couldn't see it. At the Ambrose, she went straight to the kitchen, made herself tea and carried the mug to the ballroom, the scene of her first meeting with Alice.

The room smelled of Brasso and something woody. The tables had been cleared to the side. Light flooded in at the windows, dust motes danced in lieu of people. Della closed her eyes, trying to conjure the room as it was that evening. Balloons, streamers, women in party frocks, Alice the most vibrant among them marching along the table, an untouchable spectacle. How wrong that first impression had been. It was an act. Della preferred the Alice she knew, the artist with the dry sense of humour whose caring nature left her undone.

Tears engulfed her then, a fear it had all been for nothing, but there was defiance too. She wouldn't be the version of herself Jack and William wanted. She was the woman in the portrait. It was a shock, that someone could see her both inside and out and render it in colour. That's where she'd find her strength — in Alice's version of Della Wilde.

She finished her tea and made her way back to the kitchen. There was pastry to make, cakes to bake, flour to sift, sugar to weigh. Work would claim her focus until the answer came.

Leonnard was the only other baker there when she walked into the kitchen, his head bowed in concentration, his hands engaged in kneading dough. Della put her inhibitions aside and joined him at the table.

'You like making bread?' she ventured.

'It's my favourite. Fancy cakes are nice but bread fresh from the oven is hard to beat.'

'Oi, I make fancy cakes.'

He grinned. 'Best baker at the Ambrose, so I've heard.'

Della blushed. 'I dunno about that. I reckon you're gonna give me a run for my money.'

Leonnard offered a throaty chuckle. The joy that he'd been given this opportunity briefly lifted her spirits as she moved to her bench.

Moments later, more staff spilled into the room. Della kept her head down, her gaze focused on the tasks of the day, but a sinking feeling accompanied her through the rest of the morning as her mind cartwheeled through possibilities. Jack had his faults, but they'd been close once. She'd never have believed he'd stoop so low. When had he made her his enemy?

CHAPTER 36

Alice stood at the attic window, watching the birds fly in and out of the opposite tree. The raven was conspicuous in its absence. She wasn't even sure it was a raven, perhaps all along the bird she associated with Della had been a jackdaw or a common crow. Either way, she missed it. She missed her.

The question over how to raise the money for Jack had plagued her all night. It accompanied her through breakfast, which she took in her room, through lunch with her mother's desperate attempts at conversation, and now as she found herself back in the attic. Despite its painful associations, it offered the best place to hide away from those she wanted to avoid.

Outside, a cab pulled up in front of the house and her father emerged. Gillespie appeared to greet him, but there was nothing about their exchange that would give them away. They played their roles well. Best to give Father time to get settled before making her plea for the money. She wasn't sure she trusted herself in his presence, but since she had no independent financial means beyond a small allowance, all paths led to him.

Half an hour later, Alice knocked at the study door.

A disgruntled throat clearing reached her from the other side. 'Come.'

His focus was engaged in the papers in front of him. Alice waited while his pen scratched along the surface before he set it down and met her gaze.

'Alice, what brings you to my door?' He made an arch with his fingers as he sat back to study her, his expression open and warm, with no idea of the knowledge she held.

Alice took her time — she needed to get this right, to keep the emotion from her voice. She gazed at the shelves lined with books, so familiar and yet unknown, the window overlooking the street outside, the small grate, cleaned of ash. It would remain that way until next autumn now. Her father cleared his throat again, a note of impatience?

She took the chair opposite and conjured her well-rehearsed request. 'I want to get Mummy a gift. We had such a lovely time in town the other day, she treated me to all sorts of things, but I didn't get anything for her. It was so good to see her happy, a little of her old self coming back.'

Her father's expression softened. 'Well, of course you must buy Mummy a gift, how much did you have in mind?' He reached for his cheque-book.

'Is twenty-five pounds awfully extravagant?' Alice bit her lip.

Her father looked taken aback. 'What on earth do you intend on buying her?'

'I don't know yet. Alright, how about twenty?'

He shook his head but scrawled in his cheque-book and tore the sheet from the binding. Rather than handing it to her, he pulled the bell cord.

Gillespie appeared moments later.

'Gillespie, accompany Miss Alice to the bank. She has a cheque to cash in and I don't want her carrying that sort of sum alone.' The cheque was passed into Gillespie's hand.

Alice stood, alarmed. 'Oh no, I'll be alright.'

Her father shook his head. 'Gillespie will accompany you on your shopping expedition too. I'm sure you'll need help carrying whatever extravagant thing you intend to buy. Now, be off. I have much to do.'

Alice glanced at Gillespie. His face betrayed no emotion. She looked from him to her father, head bowed to his desk again. 'Thank you, Daddy,' she whispered, and left the room.

In the hall, Gillespie waited for her instruction. Somehow, she'd have to lose him once the cheque had been cashed at the bank. It wasn't going to be easy. 'I'll fetch my bag.' She offered a thin smile.

'I'll be here,' Gillespie replied, a faint twinkle in his eye.

Ten minutes later they were making their way along the road. All around there were signs of spring merging with summer — gardens resplendent in colour, trees turning to blossom. A sense of renewal and hope. But Alice couldn't find either in the turmoil of her mind.

She searched for something to say to break the ominous drum of their footsteps but each time she glanced at Gillespie, thoughts of him and her father stalled her tongue. It wasn't unusual to avoid conversation. Gillespie was her subordinate, but they'd shared too much for the rules of decorum to stand in their way. She wondered what her mother and Gillespie would do in a similar situation; he'd been known to accompany her to town for the same purpose. Did he feel guilty for his affair with her husband? How did it work?

When Alice couldn't stand the tangle of her mind any longer, she broke the silence. 'When will the painting arrive at the Royal Academy?' Her tone sounded haughty.

'I'm assured I'll receive confirmation. It should be there tomorrow.'

Alice nodded. 'Thank you.'

'You already thanked me, Miss Alice. It was my pleasure. I believe your talent will shine.'

She hated her delight at the compliment and pushed it away. He had no right.

They reached her father's bank, which she'd forgotten was next to the Ambrose. Alice couldn't help looking up at its windows, wondering where Della was within those walls. She followed Gillespie into the bank. She'd agreed to meet Jack at

5 p.m. at the Zodiac — that gave her just over an hour to lose Gillespie, and now she knew exactly how.

'I should like to take tea, Gillespie,' she said as they emerged from the bank, the cash stowed away inside the pocket of his greatcoat.

The hint of a frown touched his eyes.

'You can join me if you like?' His strong sense of correctness would forbid him accepting the invitation.

'I'll wait outside.' He gestured to a bench on the opposite side of the road.

'Better let me look after the money. It will be safer inside the Ambrose rather than out on the street.' She offered her hand.

Gillespie's eyes narrowed. 'Your father insisted I look after the money. Don't fear, it will be safer with me.'

He was right, of course. No one would dare attempt to rob a man the size of Gillespie. Even so, needs must. Alice met his gaze with a cold, hard stare. 'Are you defying my orders?'

'I'm following your father's orders.'

'By making me, his daughter, unhappy. Do you think that would please him?' Her petulance repulsed even her.

'I believe he'd trust my judgement.'

Alice could feel her emotions boiling to the surface. She blinked back tears of fury and checked the clock above the bank.

'What is it, Miss Alice?' Gillespie's tone was gentle. 'Let me help.'

She shook her head, searching her handbag for a hanky, begrudgingly taking the one Gillespie proffered. 'You can't help, damn you.' She blew her nose and it sounded like a trumpet. Her mother would have been appalled.

'Please, Miss Alice, you're distressed. If you'll permit me, I'll accept your offer to join you for tea.' Before she could argue, he'd taken her arm and conveyed her into the café.

The nice waiter who let her ride on the trolley greeted them at the door. He exchanged a whispered word with

Gillespie before seating them at a corner table. As soon as they were alone, Gillespie sat forwards. Alice's resolve melted under his sympathetic gaze.

'Of all the people who could help me, you are the last . . .' Tears engulfed her sentence.

The waiter returned to take their order but backed away at the sight of her distress.

'I'd never intentionally do anything to cause you harm. I hope I've always tried to act—'

'I heard you . . .' She'd have to tell him. 'With Daddy in the attic.'

His face drained of colour.

'Now, do you see?' Her voice hardened. 'I couldn't collude with your secret, so I told Della. I needed to confide in someone. Then her brother Jack found out and now he's blackmailing me.' She let out a long breath as if it were the first she'd taken for hours.

Gillespie looked dismayed. He didn't speak for what felt like an eternity. The waiter — Anthony, she recalled — approached again. Alice rallied and ordered a pot of tea — she certainly had no appetite. Would Anthony mention her presence to Della? She suppressed the thought, no time for that. When Gillespie finally met her gaze, his eyes were liquid.

'I'm sorry,' he whispered.

Alice knew he was, but sorry wouldn't help with Jack Wilde.

'What are his terms?' Gillespie asked, regaining his composure.

She studied him. *No explanation? No attempt to win me round?* This man was straight to business, and in a way, it was a relief. She swallowed to control the tremor in her voice. 'I'm not to see Della again and he wants ten pounds delivered to him today at the Zodiac bar at 5 p.m. Quite a pathetic sum when you think about it.'

Gillespie shook his head. 'And if you don't meet his terms?'

She lowered her voice. 'He'll go to the press with the story that the MP Robert Winters is sleeping with his butler.'

Gillespie blanched as if hearing it out loud was too much to take. It wasn't only the scandal, but they'd be arrested too.

'What's his evidence?' Gillespie asked, recovering.

Alice shrugged. 'Me.'

'But if you deny the story, it's your word against his and the press will believe a young woman from a good family over a scoundrel like Jack Wilde.'

'Will they? These are hard times, Mr Gillespie. Mass unemployment, war-wounded men starving, the government are hardly popular. It will leave a stain even if I deny it.'

He nodded, adding weight to her reasoning.

Anthony appeared with their tea, easing the tension.

When he'd left them alone, Gillespie spoke again. 'Take the money to Jack. I'll deal with him later.'

'You'll make things worse.'

'It can't be worse. I'll not stand by and see you unhappy. Give him his money, let him think he's won until I can work out what to do.'

'And Della?'

Gillespie cast around, his brow furrowed. 'Come here every day for tea. Show her you're waiting for her, that you're not going to give up.'

Alice was surprised by the smile creeping across her lips. 'Do you think it will work?'

'We can but try.' He poured the tea. 'If Jack only wants ten pounds, why did you ask for more?'

Alice added a cube of sugar to hers. 'I need to buy Mummy something, otherwise it would look suspicious.'

'Then we'd better drink these and go shopping or you'll be late. It wouldn't do to keep Jack Wilde waiting.'

They drank in silence. As Alice set down her drained cup, feeling somewhat better than she had an hour ago, her thoughts returned to Gillespie and her father, how angry she should be and yet, she couldn't conjure it.

As if he read her mind, Gillespie fixed her with a quizzical expression. 'You're not going to ask me about it?'

Alice found she didn't want to know, not yet. 'Another time.' She studied her hands, folded in her lap.

'Whenever you're ready.'

She nodded, unsure if she ever would be.

* * *

Outside, the day was fading. Della would be leaving the Ambrose soon. The temptation to linger for a glimpse was strong but she couldn't risk Jack's wrath.

Gillespie handed her the money, sealed in its envelope. 'Ten pounds. I've taken the liberty of keeping the other ten. There's a brooch your mother admired on a shopping trip once. Would you be happy if I made the purchase?'

Alice failed to hide her surprise. 'A brooch?'

'It's my job to pay attention. I'll meet you back here in half an hour. If you don't appear, I will come looking for you.'

'That's both reassuring and quite condescending, Mr Gillespie.'

Alice walked away, puzzled as to why she couldn't help but like this man who'd caused such a fissure in her life.

CHAPTER 37

Anthony peered over her shoulder as she decanted the batter into a waiting cake tin. 'Any left over?'

Della smiled despite her bad mood. 'Go on, then.' She handed him the bowl.

Anthony grinned, taking the spoon and scraping the sides. 'Your friend's having tea downstairs. Damn, this is good.'

A fluttering sensation interrupted her heartbeat. 'What friend?'

'The posh one who came back here on my trolley.'

Della fiddled with a stray curl, attempting to conceal her agitation. 'Did she ask . . .'

'She looked a bit upset,' Anthony added, a streak of batter cresting his lip. 'A big bear of a man was with her wearing a greatcoat from the war. They made an odd pair.'

'Gillespie,' Della whispered. Why would Alice be having tea with Gillespie after what she'd discovered?

'You alright, Del?' Anthony set down the bowl.

Della rallied. 'I'm fine, hang on.' She plucked the corner of her apron and wiped a streak of batter from his cheek.

He grinned. 'Thanks.'

She stepped back at the sight of William approaching, a storm on his face. 'There you are,' he addressed Anthony. 'I can't manage your section as well as mine.'

'Alright, mate, I was on my break. See you later, Del.' He followed William towards the servery.

'What do you mean, see you later?' William asked Anthony in a not particularly friendly manner.

Anthony shrugged. 'It's just something you say. It's alright, you've got no competition, I'm spoken for.' He slapped William's back and chuckled.

Della watched them leave, struggling to contain her disquiet. If only she could go down to the café and see Alice, but if Jack found out . . .

* * *

After her shift, she lingered outside the Ambrose with no desire to hurry home. A displaced thing with no one and nowhere to be.

William trudged to her side. 'What's going on with you and Anthony?'

Della shook her head, in no mood for his pathetic jealousy, and struck out for home. It was preferable to talking to William.

He fell into step beside her. 'Anthony's got a thing for you.'

'He's married and you're insane.'

He grabbed her arm. 'What do you mean?'

'Get off me, William.' She tried to shake free but his hand was like a vice.

A shadow appeared out of the corner of her eye. Gillespie studied William, his expression like stone. 'The lady would like you to unhand her.' His tone was cold, hard, but faultlessly polite.

She could see William weighing up the situation. Gillespie had the advantage in stature and his presence was inviting attention from passers-by. Her arm was released. She shook it free of the ghost of his grip.

They remained as they were, an awkward triangle.

'I'll be off,' William said eventually. He sloped away, every now and then casting a glance over his shoulder, no doubt to ensure Gillespie wasn't following.

When he was out of sight, the butler turned his attention to Della. 'You'll be safe from here.'

Della conjured a smile. 'Thank you.'

He nodded and walked away. She tracked him through the crowds, hoping beyond hope Alice might materialise, but he disappeared into the narrow lane leading to the cathedral. Della decided not to follow. She'd had enough drama for one afternoon.

* * *

She arrived home to find the table set for dinner and her mother sitting in her chair humming, while her deft hands worked the needle and thread. What a shame this change in Ma was down to Jack.

Della pulled off her jacket. 'Shall I start dinner?'

Ma shook her head. 'Jack said this morning he'd be bringing something special home and we was to wait.'

Della frowned. 'Not more meat,' she whispered.

Ma looked up from her sewing. 'What's that, love?'

'Nothing. Where are the others?'

'Henry's reading as usual.' This was said with fond resignation rather than the irritation of old. 'Sam's next door. Mrs Phillips has got a new puppy. How she'll feed it with her Frank out of work and nought to eat, the good Lord only knows. Still, Sam's gone daft over the dog. Keeps him out from under my feet. We'll see what Jack brings. Maybe we can share some of our good fortune.'

Della nodded, both disquieted and touched that her mother might be willing to share. Where had this genial spirit come from?

The back door flew open and Jack walked in, setting a parcel on the table between them. 'Steak,' he said, pointing at the brown package tied with string, discoloured in patches where blood oozed.

Ma squealed with pleasure. 'Oh, Jack, you good boy. I haven't seen a decent bit of steak in far too long.'

Della inspected the package hoping for clues as to its origins, but there was nothing to reveal its former owner.

'What shall we have?' Ma said, hauling herself to stand.

Jack rested a hand on her shoulder. 'You relax, Ma, Della can cook.' He pulled off his jacket. 'Fry it up, we'll have some for supper. It'll do us all good.'

Seeing the expectant look on her mother's face, Della added coal to the stove and pulled out a copper frying pan. Once there was sufficient heat, she added lard and watched it glide across the base like a skater on an ice rink, before collapsing in a puddle of melted snow. Jack unwrapped the meat and dropped it in the pan. The thick fatty sides hissed and spat, causing Della to retreat. She watched her brother roll up his sleeves and add a generous pinch of salt.

He tipped her a wink. 'It's been a good day.'

Della noticed the envelope poking out from the top of his shirt pocket. So, Alice had paid him. She felt tarnished by association with this man she called her kin, but there was hope there too, selfish hope. If Jack had money, maybe he did buy the steak from a reputable source. As the room filled with mouth-watering smells, she glanced at her mother, watching them from the table, her face beatific with pride. Jack had her in a vice, tighter than any grip William could manage.

CHAPTER 38

Alice hurried away from the Royal Clarence Hotel in the direction of town in search of Gillespie. The meeting with Jack had been unpleasant to say the least. She'd never forget the smug look on his face when she slid the envelope across the table.

'It's been a pleasure doing business with you, Miss Winters. Should I find myself short of funds, you'll be hearing from me.'

Alice fizzed with anger. 'You said it would be a one-off payment.'

Jack sipped his drink. 'I said no such thing.' He leaned in, his handsome face marred by the ice in his eyes. 'Times are hard, men have families to feed, there's no work and we have to stand by and watch your kind fritter away your wealth in places like this.' He gestured to the bar. 'A reckoning is coming. You'll see.' He sat back, pleased with his speech.

She stood. 'If that's all, Mr Wilde, I'll be on my way.'

'Remember what I said about Della. She'll forget you soon enough.'

Alice wasn't about to allow that to happen. She walked away. This time, he was the one left with the bill.

Navigating the narrow alleyway that led to the cathedral close, Alice almost collided with Gillespie. They fell into step

185

without a word of greeting. He was carrying a small gift bag, tied with ribbon.

'You got the brooch for Mummy?'

He nodded. 'I trust your meeting went as planned?'

Alice sighed. 'He said he'll want more.'

'I thought as much.'

'What can we do?'

Gillespie didn't answer.

It wasn't until they reached the top of their road that he stopped and turned to face her. 'You don't deserve this. It's your father's problem and mine. I promise I'll fix it. I don't know how yet, but I will.' He walked on without waiting for a response.

Alice hurried to match his stride. At the back of the house, he handed her the gift bag and they separated, each to play the roles they'd been given.

She found her mother in the sitting room, studying a notepad full of French vocabulary. Her lips were moving but making no sound, as if she feared uttering them out loud. She set aside the notepad as soon as she noticed Alice.

'There you are. Daddy said you went shopping with Gillespie. You might have invited me.' The reproach was thinly veiled.

Alice offered the gift bag. 'Then I wouldn't have been able to surprise you with this.'

Her mother's lips spread into a smile. 'Gosh, you are naughty.' She took the bag and untied the bow. Inside was a velvet jewellery box. She undid the clasp and gasped. Alice came to her side to see the brooch Gillespie chose.

'He remembered,' her mother whispered. She lifted the brooch to the light. Jade encased in gold in the shape of a four-leaf clover. 'I thought it was too extravagant, and a bit silly, but I've never forgotten it. Well, I never.' She looked at Alice as if noticing her for the first time. 'Thank you, darling girl.'

Alice studied her shoes. 'Gillespie was the one who chose it.' She also wondered if he'd contributed to the cost from his own pocket. Would ten pounds have been sufficient funds for such a gift?

Her mother laughed. 'I know that, but buying me something was your idea.' She stood and kissed Alice's cheek, the hint of her flowery perfume familiar and comforting. 'I'd better change for dinner. A blue dress with jade isn't going to work.' She hurried from the room with a spring in her step.

Alice flopped in a chair by the hearth, exhausted by the day and her dealings with Jack. How puzzling her family were. Gillespie sleeping with her father but also able to understand and anticipate her mother's every need. What an odd trio they made. She was puzzled by her own reaction too. Had Gillespie put her under a spell? She should be raging at her father. Part of her wanted to, but the layers of stifling propriety stood in her way. What was it about her class that required such a code of behaviour, a levelling of one's passions unless they were conducted out of sight? She thought about Della, her naked emotions always close to the surface, and loved her for it. Such freedom she enjoyed over her conduct but none over her place in life. They were all imprisoned by something.

Alice carried this to her room, where she dressed for dinner and wondered how Gillespie would fix things and what Jack would demand next.

* * *

The Ambrose was bustling when she entered the following morning. Alice craned her neck, hoping to be seated in Anthony's section again. She could see the other waiter, William, working the upper balcony.

Instead of Anthony, a waitress approached. Alice asked for a table on the basement level. The further she was situated from William the better, but she did hope news of her presence might reach Della's ears.

Settling herself, she ordered a pot of Earl Grey without bothering to peruse the menu and contented herself with people-watching. The Ambrose attracted the full spectrum of clientele. There were nannies with charges dandled on their knees. Older women, their hair piled high like her mother's, precarious under elaborate, wide-brimmed hats, passing the day in a flurry of tea, delicate cakes and gossip. Groups of girls her own age, enjoying a restorative breakfast after a night on the town. By lunchtime there would be men in suits, and secretaries. It was fascinating. If only she'd had the foresight to bring her sketchbook.

The tea arrived. Alice regretted not ordering food, feeling the need to have some sort of diversion. She'd have to get used to this if she were going to keep it up every day. The thought of being near Della, of finding some small loophole in Jack's rules, provided a frisson of pleasure.

An hour later, with the tea finished and her bladder pressing with need, Alice asked for the bill. Anthony brought it with his usual genial smile. 'Back again.'

'You can't keep me away.' She placed coins on the plate. Della might hear of her visit after all.

She stood to leave and glanced at the balcony, finding William staring at her like a vengeful God from above. She met his gaze and held it until a customer forced him away.

CHAPTER 39

Della beat softened butter and sugar until they were smooth and light. She coated the base of four tins with the mixture, then arranged pineapple rings around the edge of each. Next came the glacé cherries, vibrant and sticky from their jar. Customers were mad for pineapple upside-down cake.

Mr Voisin came to her side as she sifted the flour for the cake batter. She tensed, an impulse she couldn't control. He cast his critical eye over her work. 'Well done, keep it up.' He popped a glacé cherry in his mouth and went on his way. Her limbs relaxed. At least her job was going well, even if the rest of her life remained a festering pile of horse dung.

'Alright, Del?' She dragged herself from the brink of melancholy to meet Anthony's friendly gaze. He hadn't been around the last few days. 'You were off somewhere, but judging by your expression, it wasn't very nice.'

Della sighed. 'You're right about that. Where have you been hiding?'

Anthony cast around. 'Figured I'd better keep my distance. William got in a right mood when I talked to you the other day.'

189

Della shook her head. 'He gave me a hard time when I was heading home.' She omitted the detail about Gillespie coming to her rescue.

'He's still got it bad.' Anthony winked.

'It's not funny. I've told him I'm not interested, but he won't take no for an answer.'

'William's always been a bit intense. Do you want me to have a word?'

'I don't want to come between you.'

'You're not. William hangs around with your brother these days.'

Della took up her spoon, conscious of time and the need to get the cakes in the oven for afternoon tea. Anthony speaking to William might make things worse. 'Don't worry, I can look after myself.'

He squeezed her shoulder. 'I'm here if you need me.'

His kind words almost brought up the tears that were waiting in the wings.

'By the way, that posh friend of yours has been in every morning for tea. She sits alone, staring into space. Is she alright?'

Della focused on the cake batter. 'I haven't heard from her lately.'

Anthony shrugged. 'Nice to have that sort of time and money.'

'You haven't mentioned it to William, have you, that Alice has been in?'

'No, but like I said, I've been avoiding him. He's probably seen her himself.'

This was true. 'Next time you see Alice, can you tell her thanks from me?'

'Course I will.'

'I'd better crack on. Don't be a stranger.' She offered him a glacé cherry from the jar. He popped it in his mouth and grinned.

'With treats like that, I'll be round every day to see my favourite baker.'

William chose that moment to storm through the kitchen. He paused long enough to throw them a piercing stare. When she turned back to Anthony, he'd gone.

Della spent the next hour preparing the remaining cakes, her mind a muddle. Alice was sending a message which sent her heart soaring with hope, but if William knew then Jack would find out sooner or later. Was antagonising him a good idea? Alice wasn't breaking his terms, but she was pushing the boundaries.

By the time she lifted the cakes into the oven, her elation had faded into fear.

CHAPTER 40

'A letter for you, Miss Alice.' Gillespie caught her in the hall as she was pulling on her coat and offered up a silver platter on which sat a cream envelope, heavy with quality. Her eyes met his, confirming what she already knew — her painting had arrived at the Royal Academy. He bowed and backed away, leaving her to experience the news for herself.

'What's that?' Her mother appeared behind.

Alice slid the envelope inside her coat. 'A party invitation, I expect.' She forced a bright smile. 'I'm off into town.'

'Again. What's his name?' Such hope in her eyes.

It wasn't a terrible idea, to let her think she had a new man, but weren't there enough lies in the winter house? Alice had known for a week now, and although Gillespie shared her secret, she'd never felt more alone.

'Bring him for dinner,' her mother said.

Alice threw her a wave and disappeared out the front door.

* * *

The Ambrose was busy with families and weekend visitors. Alice recalled the envelope in her pocket and ripped it open while she waited for a table. Confirmation her painting had arrived. She folded it away and allowed herself a brief smile, which faded as she was directed to the balcony floor.

William acknowledged her presence but clearly took perverse pleasure in keeping her waiting. She sat for fifteen minutes before he approached with no word of apology. 'What can I get you?' He didn't bother to pull out his notebook. Alice was tempted to make her order long, so he'd be forced to pay her full attention, but she had neither the money nor the appetite.

'Coffee, please.' She threw him a saccharine smile for good measure.

'You won't get to see her, you know.' He muttered the words, almost imperceptible as he cast around the room. 'You're wasting your time.'

Alice's cheek muscles smarted with the effort of maintaining a serene expression. 'I'm not sure what you're talking about. I came in for coffee. Should I request an audience with your superior?' She sounded like one of her mother's friends and wasn't sure she could pull it off.

William's lip curled, he moved away.

Alice sighed and pulled out the novel she'd taken to bringing — her first Agatha Christie, borrowed from her mother, who was quite the fan. It failed to capture her attention, which was hardly Mrs Christie's fault. Alice couldn't keep her mind from straying to Della and the predicament they were in. She was starting to realise her presence was futile, but what good was it to sit at home? Returning the novel to her bag, she retrieved her small sketchbook and pencils, casting around the café for a suitable subject.

Anthony swept past, a loaded tray balanced with precision on his arms. He stopped a few feet from her and circled back. 'Della says thanks for coming,' he whispered and moved on.

Alice smiled with renewed motivation. She was still grinning when William returned with her coffee. He set it before her, deliberately clumsy, causing a little to spill into the saucer. It wasn't until he walked away that she noticed he'd left a note on the table. The paper was small and oblong, torn from a waiter's notebook.

Meet me in the yard at 12, JW

Alice slid the paper into her purse and took a sip of coffee. It fizzed in her anxious stomach. *What now?*

* * *

By the time she stepped outside, the High Street was littered with people, cars and trams. She had an hour to kill until her summons. Part of her wanted to ignore it, to risk Jack's wrath and see if he had the gumption to carry out his threat, but the thought of her mother's heartbreak put paid to that idea. Instead, she walked down street after street, her mind a maze of options, each one reaching a dead end.

He was leaning against the wall, a cigarette dangling from his parted lips. He straightened his tie when he noticed her, a vain man despite himself. A couple of the lads in the yard wolf-whistled. Jack grinned at the attention.

'What now?' Alice was in no mood to linger.

'That's hardly a friendly greeting.' Jack checked behind to make sure his colleagues hadn't heard her disparaging tone.

'We aren't friends.'

'If that's how you want to play it. I'll need another payment. You've got a week, same place, same time.'

'No.' Alice surprised herself. This was a new tactic.

'Alright, then you'll be hearing from the press. Oh, and the police will want to speak with your father on account of the fact he's breaking the law.'

She blanched at the implication. 'How much?'

Jack smirked. 'Didn't put up much of a fight. Another ten. It won't be the last.'

'But . . .'

'You brought this on yourself for breaking the terms of our agreement.'

'I did no such thing.'

'I know your games. You think you're clever, showing up at the Ambrose every day, hoping to see Della. It's sad is what it is, sad and desperate. Just 'cos you're queer, don't mean you can tarnish my sister.'

Alice seethed but bit her tongue for Della's sake. 'Why another ten? Why not ask for more now and get it over with?'

Jack flicked ash to the ground. 'This isn't about greed, it's about redressing an imbalance that's gone on since the war. Ten pounds is nothing to your kind, but for people like me with families to feed, it means the difference between a full or empty larder. Besides, I figure ten is easy enough for a rich girl to go to Daddy for, and maybe I like meeting you, maybe it does my reputation good to be seen in the Zodiac with the likes of Alice Winters.'

'You're a vile creep.' She stormed away, holding in tears until she'd reached the back of the winter house.

She crashed through the door, straight into Gillespie.

CHAPTER 41

A light breeze caused the water to ripple as Della lingered by the river on her way home, in no hurry to spend a stifling evening in the presence of Jack. It was exhausting, keeping up a pretence for Ma, and now she had the meat to worry about too. He'd turned up the previous evening with a glazed ham, just like the ones the Ambrose sold in its deli. Ma was quick to jump to his defence when Della enquired about its origins.

'How about a bit of gratitude to your brother for providing for the family? I thought you of all people would appreciate him taking the load.'

If that was acknowledgement of what Della had been doing for years, making a fuss could send Ma back to her bed. She didn't want that on her conscience.

Ducks and swans glided past, heads bowed for food. She stood at the edge, catching her distorted reflection in the murky mirror. Her hair was growing fast. The plait remained in her chest of drawers, coiled like a snake. A reminder of who she used to be before Alice changed her forever.

The windows in the Wilde kitchen were thick with condensation when Della approached. *They must all be there gathered around the table, dinner bubbling on the stove.* It should be a happy thought, but she paused at the back door, an outsider wanting to savour another second of herself before the mask came down and she lost a sense of who that was.

A billow of steam obscured her vision when she entered. It cleared to reveal Ma at the stove, Jack at the head of the table and next to him, William.

'Here she is, our Della.' Jack threw her a smile, but there was anxiety in the way he raked his fingers through his hair. 'You're late.'

Della shrugged off her coat and hung it up, buying herself time. *Late for what?* Sam intervened, grabbing her arm. 'Jack says we can get a puppy now he's earning a good wage.'

'That's right.' Jack ruffled Sam's hair. 'Aren't you going to greet our guest, Della?' He turned to William. 'I must apologise for my sister.'

William's eyes locked with hers. 'That's alright, Jack, she's worth the wait.'

Her skin came alive. Henry glanced up from his book, smirking from behind his spectacles. Sam pulled a face and made a puking sound.

'What a sweet thing to say.' Ma left the stove and gripped Della by the shoulders, propelling her to the table. Her hold was gentle but firm as she lowered Della into the seat next to William.

'Don't you need my help, Ma?' Della implored.

'All taken care of. Jack got us veal and ham pies. I've boiled some potatoes and there's greens from the market. The Wildes will eat like royalty from now on.' She squeezed Jack's shoulder and smiled with pride.

Della couldn't look at William, but his unwanted presence stole the air from the room. She studied her nails, their moons gleaming where she'd scrubbed them at work free of pastry. A burn from a few days ago had blistered on her finger; she worried at it with her thumb. Around her she was vaguely aware of conversation between Ma, William and Jack. Sam went outside, no doubt to visit next door's puppy, and Henry as ever disappeared into his book. How she wished she could join him in whatever realm he'd entered.

'Are you going to speak?'

Della looked up, startled. Jack was eyeballing her.

'What's that?'

'William asked if you'd like to go for a walk with him after dinner.'

'Oh.' She shook her head. 'I can't.'

Jack sat forward, a strain in his jaw. 'Why, what have you got on this evening?'

She searched for a viable excuse. How about because she didn't want to? Because William made her skin crawl? How about because he made her a little afraid too?

'You're being rude, Della.' Ma's sharp tone tugged her back into the room.

'I'm meeting a friend.' She forced herself to look at William. 'Sorry.' It sounded feeble — she didn't like herself for it.

'Which friend?' Jack pressed.

William's nostrils flared. 'Anthony?'

Jack looked confused. 'But I thought . . . ?'

'Who's Anthony?' Ma asked.

Before Della could correct them, Sam came bounding into the room, dragged by next door's puppy on a piece of rope. She shoved back her chair as the puppy crashed into the table, pulling Sam with it and upending the half-pint of bitter William had been drinking into his lap.

'Christ,' he swore.

Della giggled, an uncontrollable, full-bodied giggle that began in her shoulders and spread through her limbs. Henry joined, then Sam, who'd let go of the puppy and landed on the floor, where it was licking his face. Ma offered William a tea towel.

Only Jack watched on, his expression muddied as if he were trying to unravel a complicated puzzle. Della met his gaze and held it for a beat before detaching herself from the tangle, grabbing her coat and disappearing through the door.

CHAPTER 42

Gillespie's usually serene brow furrowed the further Alice relayed the details of what had passed with Jack. She was too upset to hold any of it in, too angry that she'd been made to suffer for the actions of others. They faced each other in the back hall, Alice still in her coat, certain her make-up was now two streaks down her face.

When she'd finished, she sank onto the bottom step of the back stairs. Gillespie looked drained too, as if all that made him vital had been sucked out like a deflated balloon.

'I won't let this happen again, Miss Alice,' he said eventually. 'This has gone on for too long.'

'What has?'

Gillespie spun around and Alice shot up. They both lost the power of speech as her mother stepped into the dim light of the hall. How long had she been there? How much had she heard?

A flicker of emotion travelled across her face as she took in Alice's appearance. She turned to Gillespie. 'We'll have a pot of tea in my bedroom, please.'

He took a moment to register the request then threw Alice a helpless look and walked away to the kitchen.

'Let's get you out of this coat.' Her mother moved around her, easing the coat from her shoulders. She slung it over the bottom of the banister and offered her hand. Alice took it as if in a trance.

Mummy's bedroom was the finest in the house with a large bay window offering views over the landscaped back garden. Alice sank onto the bed, soothed by the soft eiderdown, calling her to sleep. She was a child exhausted by the game she'd been forced to play with Jack.

Her gaze took in the room, the epitome of comfort and style. 'Don't touch, Alice,' she'd been scolded when she was young, but how could one not want to touch such beautiful things? Alice understood now, the ruin her small self might have wrought. Back then it seemed cruel, a deprivation, a closed door on a grown-up world she didn't understand.

Her mother sat beside her, a soft flannel in her hand. She smoothed away Alice's tears with her thumb, then used the flannel to clean her cheeks free of make-up. It was a lovely feeling, to be cared for. It helped Alice slowly come back to herself until she remembered why she was there.

A light knock came against the door. Her mother took the tray from Gillespie. Alice detected the strain in his voice even at a low murmur. The door was closed behind him, the tray placed on the dressing table.

She watched her mother pour tea, take the sugar prongs and drop one cube into a cup. It was brought to her, on the bed, a breaking of the old rules.

Her mother sat opposite, slipping off her shoes and crossing her legs with the agility of a ballerina. 'You're going to tell me what's going on, Alice, and you're not going to leave out a single detail. You think it might cause me pain, but it causes me more to feel shut out. Shall I start by telling you what I think this is about?'

Alice crossed her legs, mirroring her mother, now curious as to what she might have gleaned.

'It's something to do with the girl in the coat.'

Alice wiped a stray tear from her face. She nodded.

'You care about this girl, yes?'

Again, she nodded.

'But something has happened. Something to do with this house. Something to do with Daddy and Gillespie?'

Alice recoiled. 'How . . . ?'

'Honestly, sometimes I think you all assume I'm an idiot. Gillespie attempts to hand in his notice, and I'm not supposed to question it? The last time he tried to leave was when I found out about the two of them. I knew if he was doing so again, another member of the household had either discovered their secret or was close to it. Who else but you?'

'You know?'

'I've known almost since the day your father brought him here.'

'And you don't mind?'

'I wouldn't say that exactly. If you'd seen what your father was like when he came home from the war, you might not be so quick to judge. It was hell.' Her face crumpled. She reached for Alice's teacup and took a sip. 'Do you really want to hear it?'

'I think I need to.'

Her mother returned the cup to its saucer and stared out of the window as if searching for a way to begin. Alice waited, somewhat impatient but all too aware this was her mother's story, and it would be told in her own time. Eventually, her gaze returned to Alice. 'I sensed something about Daddy, even before the war. He did his best to be a caring and attentive husband, but there was an element missing, a sense he was playing a role, keeping something of himself back. It would occasionally descend like a black cloud, taking him further out of reach. One had to let it pass.'

Alice thought about Della, what she'd said about her mother's dark moods.

'Whenever he came home on leave, it was as if he was behind a glass panel watching us, even interacting with us, but

201

not actually there. I tried not to read too much into it. We'd been apart after all, we had to get to know one another again.'

Alice frowned. 'I don't remember. I suppose I was too young.'

'You idolised him.'

She couldn't help being surprised by this, it felt like years since she'd spent any time with her father.

'When the war ended, I thought, *Thank God, he's safe. He'll come back, we'll have more children, life will resume.*' She shook her head. 'He could barely look at me.'

Alice watched a tear slide down her mother's cheek. She offered her a hanky, realising too late it was the one Gillespie had given her and she hadn't returned. Her mother didn't seem to register the embroidered initials *EG* as she dried her eyes. Alice wondered what the E stood for. How odd not to know Gillespie's Christian name.

'Months went by, he slipped further away, then a letter arrived. I know now it was from Gillespie, but at the time I had no idea. It transformed your father. I didn't question it. My husband was back, except he wasn't. Not really. He said he had a friend from the war, he wanted to find him a job. Our butler had retired the previous year. With your father away I hadn't bothered to replace him. Now he wanted to give this friend the role. His eyes came alive at the very idea. I saw no reason to deny what clearly made him so happy.'

She lay back on the bed, her expression now somewhere else. Outside, anthracite clouds had gathered, darkening the room. Alice considered switching on a lamp, but she didn't want to disturb the delicate balance of the moment.

'I was struck at once how young Gillespie was, how tall, how broad. I'll admit, I found him attractive despite our distance in years. It had been a lonely war.'

Alice bit her lip, unsure if she wanted to hear more.

'There's no need to look so scandalised.' A brief smile from her mother, but it faded. 'It took me a long time to understand what was happening. The bond they'd found in the trenches went beyond the fealty of a master and his subordinate. What they'd been through together, the pain they'd witnessed, well of course I felt shut out. How could I comprehend such an experience? I could only empathise, but my empathy wasn't wanted. I tried to deny it for as long as I could. I refused to see what was before my eyes. I liked Gillespie, I welcomed his tranquil presence in my home, even if my husband no longer embraced me beyond a chaste kiss when decorum required. I chose that over the storm. The clouds had cleared. It was bearable until . . .'

'What?' Alice whispered.

'I found them together, not in a passionate embrace, but talking in the most intimate manner. The tenderness on your father's face. It took my breath away and I knew.'

'Did you confront him?'

She shook her head. 'Not at first, I didn't want to believe it. I tried to speak to Granny, but she was appalled — not with Daddy but the fact I was so upset. Told me to shut up and put up. You know how she could be.'

Alice took her mother's hand. Her grandmother had died three years ago, a stalwart of the Victorian age. 'You must have felt so alone.'

'I had you, but then there was school and . . .'

'Why did you send me away? I could have gone to school here.'

'That wasn't only my choice. We wanted you to have the best education, the best of everything.'

Alice flinched, disgust for the conceited way of her class. *The best of everything.* She couldn't accept it, not when she considered Della and her struggles.

'What have I said to upset you?' Her mother sat up.

Alice recovered. There was no point raking over something that couldn't be changed. 'It doesn't matter.'

Her mother took another sip of tea before resuming. 'It was Gillespie who came to me offering to resign. I'll remember it as one of the most insightful and painful conversations of my life. That man has far more emotional understanding than your father. He knew I knew, and he hated himself for it. I refused to accept his resignation because without Gillespie your father would disintegrate, and maybe by then I needed him too.' She was staring into the distance, as if she'd taken a leave of absence and put herself back there in that conversation. Slowly, she brought her gaze to Alice.

They were silent for a moment, sitting under the weight of painful words. Her mother squeezed her hand. 'Now you've heard my confession, are you ready to give me yours? There's nothing you can't tell me, Alice.'

Where and how to begin? With Della, the painting, the blackmail? What a story she had to tell.

A sharp knock came against the door, dispersing her thoughts. Her father walked in, startling at the sight of the two of them and their grave expressions.

'You already know?'

'Know what, Robert?' Mummy replied.

He wrung his hands together. 'It's Gillespie. He's gone.'

CHAPTER 43

Della didn't know where she was going or what it would achieve, but she'd chosen it. Chosen not to do Jack's bidding. Despite the clattering in her chest, no footsteps echoed behind. At the end of the alley, she struck out for town, wanting to be anonymous, wrapped in her city. The further she walked, the safer she felt, but as she climbed Fore Street past shuttered shops, a sense of abandonment settled on her. People were heading home, a place of security, while she had nowhere to be, and no one to be there with.

The Ambrose was lit for the evening, a port in a storm, but tonight it could offer no comfort. She scanned the High Street, unsure where to go. The answer was right in front of her. The Empire Electric. An evening at the cinema without the burden of William's unwanted attention. She checked her pockets for the admission fee and joined the queue.

'Della,' a familiar voice called from the crowd. Anthony waved and pushed his way through the queue to join her, a woman of about Della's height with a pixie face, cropped brown hair and matching brown eyes on his arm. 'This is Mrs Anthony Riley,' he said with pride.

'You daft man,' Mrs Riley scolded with a smile in her eyes. 'I'm Kath.' She offered her hand.

205

Della shook it, glad to put a name and face to the woman who shared her friend's world. 'It's lovely to meet you.'

Anthony slid his arm around his wife. 'Della makes the best cakes in Exeter.'

Kath's eyes widened. 'Got any with you? I could murder a custard tart.'

Della raised her hands. 'I'm all out but I'll save one for you, next batch I make.'

'I like her, Anthony,' Kath said with a grin. 'Do you want to join us? We're here for the Chaplin.'

'I don't want to impose on your evening.'

'Kath doesn't believe in public displays of affection. We'll be as chaste as nuns during the film.'

Kath hit Anthony with her handbag. Della chuckled, her dark mood fading. 'If you're sure.'

She followed them inside, protested when Anthony paid for her ticket and sat on the other side to Kath in the middle of the cinema, glad to escape her troubles and the unpleasant recriminations awaiting at home. Her cheeks ached from laughing by the time the credits rolled. It was worth the faint tinge of body odour that perfumed the darkened hall.

As they emerged into the chill night air, Della now saw her folly. The long walk home in the dark, the threat that could be waiting when she arrived.

'You alright, Del?' Anthony asked as he helped Kath into her coat.

She rallied. 'I'm fine. Thanks for a lovely evening.'

Kath wriggled free of his grip. 'She's worried about walking home and quite right too. Where do you live?'

'I'll be okay, I'm in St Thomas.'

Kath glanced at her husband.

'I was already planning on offering to walk Della home, once I've seen you back first.' He patted his stomach. 'You can't say I don't get enough exercise.'

'I don't want to put you out of your way,' Della said, while praying he'd still take her.

'It's no trouble. Kath's got to get home to relieve our neighbour who's looking after the kids, but I can see you back.' His face was open, kind eyes smiling.

'Thanks.'

Della tried not to intrude as they headed along the High Street then cut across town in the direction of St Leonards, which made her think of Alice. Passing her road was like a sharp stab in the chest. Kath kept pulling her into conversation, asking questions, drawing her out. They continued, away from the grand mansions, towards Heavitree. She realised how far out of his way Anthony was going to have to walk, but now she didn't really know where she was, and the dark night only added to her confusion.

'Nearly there,' Kath said as if sensing her anxiety.

'I'm sorry you're going to have such a long walk.'

'Stop apologising. It'll do him good. I know all about the cake batter he eats when he's at work.'

Anthony protested but they all knew it was true. Outside a narrow terrace, Kath said goodbye, giving Della a peck on the cheek and insisting they must have tea soon.

'She's lovely, your missus,' Della said as she and Anthony retraced their steps.

Anthony smiled. 'Yeah, I lucked out there. Kath and I have known each other since we were kids. She waited for me to return from the war. Put me back together afterwards, if I'm honest.'

'You're restoring my faith in humanity.'

They talked about work, about Hastings' sharp tongue, about why Mr Voisin had recently shaved off his moustache. Anthony reckoned he'd met a woman. Eventually they got to the subject they'd been skirting around. Their mutual friend.

'I tried to have a word with William, told him maybe he needed to back off.'

Della frowned — clearly it hadn't worked. 'He was at my house for tea this evening. That's why I left because they were all conspiring to make something happen.'

'Blimey, you ran out on him?'

'Am I terrible person?'

'Course not, if you've told him no and he isn't listening, well, that's his problem. There's keen and there's harassment.'

'I think you're ahead of your time.'

Anthony chuckled. 'That's Kath, she doesn't let me indulge any wayward opinions.'

'I like her.'

'She likes you, I can tell. Will you have tea with her? She doesn't get out much, what with the kids. I'd like to see her make a good friend.'

Della smiled. 'Course I will.'

They passed the grand Victorian red-brick facade of the Exeter Eye Infirmary, skirting the edge of the city centre.

'That girl, Alice . . .'

Della swallowed. 'What about her?'

'Why doesn't William like her being your friend?'

'He don't seem to like anyone getting close to me.'

'Yeah, but surely that's only men, unless . . .'

The inference hung between them. Having found this burgeoning connection with Anthony, she wasn't keen to lose it.

'I've got this aunt,' Anthony continued when Della remained silent. 'She lives with a friend, has done for years.' He stopped walking and faced her. 'They're happy and they aren't hurting anyone.'

'I know what you're trying to say, Anthony, but I can't talk about it, not yet.'

'Fair enough, and if I'm barking up the wrong tree, tell me to mind my own business, but I wanted you to know, if that's the way things are, well, it wouldn't bother me.'

Della's eyes filled with tears at his understanding, his kindness. 'Thank you,' she managed, grateful for the dark to mask her emotion.

He put his arm around her shoulder and gave it a squeeze.

They reached the Wilde back alley. Della insisted he leave. She couldn't stand the thought of him being seen and risking Jack's wrath. Anthony obliged, but swore he'd watch her to the gate. She didn't see how he'd know, the dark was so thick.

'Shout when you're there,' he said.

'Alright, and thank you — for everything.'

'Night, Del. I'll need a double helping of batter tomorrow after all this exercise, my shoes are worn to the pavement.'

'Don't make me feel any worse than I do.'

'You made our evening, now get off or I'll never get home.'

Della entered the alley, a tunnel of doom. At the gate she called goodnight. Anthony called back and she stepped into the yard. The house was cloaked in darkness. Was Jack in bed or lying in wait? She used the privy, trying to ignore the sounds outside, the ones her fearful mind conjured. Scuffles, footsteps, the crash of a bin, most likely a fox or a cat. When she emerged, the yard was empty. There was nothing but her own fear lurking in the shadows.

CHAPTER 44

Alice watched her father slump onto the bed, his shoulders hunched, all sense of dignity disappearing as her mother enfolded him in her arms. It was a destabilising sight, to see one's parent undone.

She slipped away, feeling like an intruder. In truth, she welcomed the moment to ingest what her mother had said. The attic called to her, both a place of escape and discovery. She hesitated outside Gillespie's door, the handle still warm as if his hand had only just been there. The room was sparse, no sign of its former occupant, as empty as Martha's down the corridor. *Martha*, how wrong she'd read that situation.

Retreating to the attic room, Alice sat on the daybed. How could Gillespie abandon her like that? What would she do about Jack without his help? Her watery gaze swept to the easel. The Royal Academy couldn't be further from her mind. It was then she noticed an envelope resting on the easel shelf. She knew who it was from and slid her finger along the seal.

Dear Miss Alice,
    Forgive me for leaving, know that you're not alone. I'm working on a solution. Don't give Wilde another penny.
    Yours, G

He was as succinct on paper as he was in life. Alice folded the letter and put it back inside the envelope, feeling the weight of his pain in every word. Whatever he was up to, she owed it to her parents to tell them what was going on. Maybe it was finally time for a reckoning, not on Jack Wilde's terms but her own. If she could somehow subvert his blackmail . . .

'Alice?' Her mother's voice from the other side of the attic door. She pulled it open and her parents filled the frame.

Her mother stepped into the room, her eyes casting over the space. 'This is where you hide.' She took in the easel, the box of paints, the envelope in Alice's hand.

Her father was slower to follow, his gaze more bewildered, understanding dawning at what Alice could have — indeed had — heard. His eyes found hers, it was all there.

'This was Granny's,' her mother said from the daybed. 'I'd forgotten it was here. Where did you get the easel?'

That was her question? Where did Alice procure an easel? 'I ordered it with some birthday money and carried it here myself from town. It was in a box,' she added, curious as to why it mattered.

'What do you paint?'

She shrugged. 'Portraits mostly.'

'Can I see?'

'Maybe later.' She glanced at her father, whose gaze had been arrested by the letter in her hand. No doubt he knew Gillespie's handwriting. She held it aloft. 'This is from Mr Gillespie to me.'

Her father frowned. 'Why would Gillespie write to you?'

Her mother patted the daybed. 'Join us, Robert. I think Alice has some things she'd like to say and we're going to hear her out without interruption.'

A look of defeat returned, but he sat in the space her mother made. Alice pulled up a chair, the one she'd used for Della's portrait. It was bizarre, to sit in the gloom of the attic under her parents' scrutiny, as they waited to be educated like children before a schoolmistress. She let the letter remain in her lap.

'It all started on my birthday when I met a girl called Della Wilde.'

* * *

'Good God,' Father muttered, one of several utterances he'd made during her confession. Alice saw him then not as her austere, intelligent father but a fallible man, his emotions close to the surface.

Mummy patted his knee. 'Alright, Robert.'

His hand enveloped her mother's. Alice still couldn't fathom it, this thing they called a marriage.

He glanced at his wife. 'This will ruin us.'

'Only if we let it,' her mother said, but she looked worried too. 'When does this Jack want the next instalment?'

'One week.' Alice glanced at the letter. 'Gillespie says not to give him another penny.'

'May I read it?' Her father's tone was a little desperate.

Alice handed it over, there was no reason now to keep him in the dark. He scanned it several times as if searching for some hidden meaning from his lover.

Eventually he folded it in two. 'If Gillespie says to wait, we wait.' Alice watched him slip the letter into his jacket pocket. It was his now. Her part was done.

CHAPTER 45

Della crept out of the house past the spoils of the previous evening's feast littering the kitchen table. An exile in her own home. She wondered if William had stayed for dinner or if he'd made his excuses. When would he get the message she wasn't interested and leave her alone?

The sun was up, casting shadows of the buildings as Della climbed Fore Street into the city. She mulled over the pies, the glazed ham and the meat. If Jack was stealing them from the Ambrose, how was he doing it? He had access to the stores, but everything was made fresh in the kitchens and sent straight to the deli or servery. Jack had no business in either location — unless he had an accomplice? She pushed the thought away, guilty of jumping to conclusions, motivated by the wounds Jack had wrought. He had money now, and plenty of it thanks to Alice. A fresh burst of anger pulsed through her body, unable to find a release beyond tears and a clenched fist.

Leonnard was the only other baker in when Della entered the Ambrose kitchen. She paused at his bench, keen to see what he was working on. His deft hands kneaded a ball of dough. Della watched, mesmerised as he worked it back and forth in methodical sweeps. Making bread had always been considered one of the lower tasks of the bakery, but with Leonnard's skills, she could see it was an art form in itself.

'Do you want to try?' he asked.

Della nodded, taking the soft dough between her fingers. She worked it as Leonnard had done, her palm pushing hard, her fingers pulling it back, finding relief in the repetitive action. A channel for her frustration. After a few minutes he stopped her and placed the dough in a large bowl, which he covered with a damp towel. 'Now, we let it prove.'

'Thanks, that was fun.'

'Your turn,' Leonnard said, gesturing to her bench. 'What are you making today?'

'Apple pies for the deli.' The deli made her think of Jack. 'Can you show me?'

'Course I can.' Della reached for the mixing bowl, pleased to have a focus. Leonnard weighed the flour under her instruction while she went to get butter from the pantry. Ten minutes later, they were rubbing flour and butter through their fingers to achieve a breadcrumb texture. Leonnard had long fingers with squared-off short nails, impeccably clean. She glanced up to find him studying her with his single eye and blushed.

'The others will be here soon,' she said for something to distract them.

'Mrs Hastings will be pleased to see us working like this. She's told me you're the one to learn from in the Ambrose bakery.'

Della smiled, grateful for the compliment.

'I think that waiter William might not be so pleased though,' Leonnard continued. 'He watches you all day.'

She reached for a jug to fill with water, disconcerted even Leonnard had noticed.

'You don't like his attention much?'

She shrugged. 'Not really.' Leonnard was certainly perceptive.

'I might only have one eye, but it doesn't mean I don't notice things. People see the patch and not the person. William watches you, he doesn't notice me watching him.'

Della frowned. 'What do you see?'

'Morning, you two.' Hastings bustled in, stealing the opportunity for further conversation.

'Leonnard was kind enough to show me about kneading bread this morning, so I'm letting him into my pastry-making secrets.'

Hastings threw them an indulgent smile. 'I hate to drag you away, but Leonnard, can you bring a couple of sacks of flour up from stores, please?'

'Right away, Mrs Hastings.' He nodded at Della and disappeared through the doors.

'He's a lovely lad, but don't go getting his hopes up. A lad with a single eye is never going to make a skilled pâtissier like you. Better to leave him to bread.'

Della was about to argue when Hastings hurried away to speak to Mr Voisin, who'd entered the kitchen.

Finding herself alone, she finished making the pastry, allowing her mind to roam to the previous evening, how kind Anthony and his wife had been. She wanted to do something nice in return. Perhaps Mrs Hastings would agree to her staying late so she could make them a batch of custard tarts. They were Anthony's favourite and Kath had expressed a liking for them too.

She was chopping apples for the pie filling when Mrs Hastings pulled her focus. 'Have you heard? Anthony was set upon in the street. He's pretty bruised, won't be back for a while, poor lad.'

Della almost dropped her knife. 'When did this happen?'

'Last night down by the river. His wife said he saw a friend home after the cinema, and it happened on his way back. He came limping in, looking a fright. Could hardly breathe, the pain he was in. Shocking.'

Her eyes filled with tears. It had to be William. Jack didn't know about her friendship with Anthony. No, this had William written all over it.

'There now, love.' Hastings rubbed her back. 'I know you and Anthony are close.'

215

She wiped away her tears with her cuff. 'Is he at home?'

'Aye, nought much to be done but wait for his bruises to heal.'

'Is it alright if I make him some custard tarts? I'll pay for the ingredients,' Della said. 'I could take them this evening.'

'You're a sweet girl and no need to pay just this once.'

'Thanks. Is William in?' she asked, hoping to sound both interested and disinterested.

'Rang in sick, apparently. Not like him.'

Della returned to her work. That news was confirmation enough.

* * *

That evening, she struck out for Heavitree, a box of custard tarts in her arms. A boy of about six answered the door, putting her in mind of Sam when he was that age.

'Ma!' the kid hollered when he saw Della.

Kath appeared, the strain showing in her face.

'I'm so sorry. I heard what happened. I feel responsible,' Della said before Kath could open her mouth.

'It's not your fault, so don't go wasting time thinking it is. He was unlucky. Come in.'

She followed Kath through a narrow hallway to the kitchen at the back, where three children were huddled around a table. 'Do you want a cuppa?'

'You're busy. I brought Anthony these. Custard tarts.' She offered the box.

'His favourite. Hang on, I'll check he's decent and you can go up.'

'I don't want to be a bother.'

'He'll be glad to see a friend.'

Della hovered in the kitchen, where the children eyed her from the table. She searched for something to say, relieved when Kath returned.

'You can go up but only let him have one of those tarts. Leave him the box and they'll be gone in a flash.'

Della smiled, glad to be out of the stifling room.

'First door at the top of the stairs,' Kath called after her.

The stairs creaked under her tread, the wall adorned with family photos Della was too self-conscious to study. She gave a brief knock and entered, almost dropping the box at the sight of Anthony propped up in bed. Her free hand flew to her mouth.

'That bad?' he said with a brief chuckle before his smile slid into a grimace and he gripped his side.

Della perched on the end of the bed. 'It's all my fault.'

'It was you who beat me up? Crikey, what did I do wrong?'

'Stop joking about, Anthony. I know who it was.'

'How'd you figure that, if I didn't even get a good look at the bugger?'

'Why are you covering for him?'

He lowered his voice, a note of warning. 'Drop it, Del. If Kath hears . . .'

'But . . .'

'He thought I was messing with you. Didn't give me a chance to explain. There's no other witnesses, my word against his. I don't want either of us getting in trouble.'

'He rang in sick today. It all adds up.'

'William and I go way back. When we were at the front together, he got me out of a tight spot. I owe him. So please, just drop it.'

Della stared out of the window over the rooftops of Heavitree. The bloody war got into everything, even now, all these years later.

'What's in the box?' Anthony asked.

'I made you custard tarts.'

His eyes lit up. 'A woman after my own heart.'

'The woman who has your heart says you're only allowed one.'

He smiled. 'Fair enough.'

They were quiet while he ate, emitting the occasional groan. Della wasn't sure if it was with pleasure for the custard tart or pain from the effort of eating.

When he'd finished, he dusted his fingers. 'Promise me one thing?'

'What's that?'

'Look after yourself. Stay out of William's way. I dunno what's got into him, but I'm worried about you.'

'I'll be alright,' she said with a confidence she didn't feel. She wasn't alright. Forbidden from seeing Alice because of Jack, another friend injured by association because of William. Della Wilde had become bad news to all those she loved. Maybe she was the one who needed to disappear.

* * *

Three days later, Anthony's words played on her mind as Della made her way home along Fore Street with a sense she wasn't alone. William was conspicuous in his absence at work and ever since Anthony warned her to take extra care, Della had been on edge. It was exhausting at work and exhausting at home, where she continued to avoid Jack.

The footsteps came heavier now, raising the hairs on the back of her neck. She pulled her collar up, too nervous to glance behind, and scanned the street ahead. Enough people were walking in the same direction as her. There was no rational need to fear an attack and yet she did. A man's throat cleared. A flood of adrenaline, her instinct was to run, but then he spoke.

Gillespie.

'Sorry, Miss Wilde.' He scanned the street too. 'I didn't mean to scare you, but we need to talk.'

Della took a moment to recover. 'Where do you suggest?'

He gestured to a hostelry a little further down the road, the Devonport Inn, a pub with a reputation for flouting the licencing laws. It wasn't the sort of place she'd usually frequent, but despite his size and perhaps because of it, Gillespie made her feel safe. Alice trusted him and Jack despised him, that was reference enough. She followed him inside.

It was a spit-and-sawdust pub with a mixed clientele, but they were more from her world and Della felt instantly relaxed.

Gillespie conveyed her to a table. 'Drink?'

'Ginger beer, please.'

He went to the bar and returned with her drink and a pint for himself. He looked tired, worn down. His eyes, as he set them on her, spoke of regret. 'I gather you're aware of the situation with . . .' He appeared unable to utter it. Instead, he cast around the pub and took a sip of his pint.

'It's alright.' Della hoped she sounded reassuring. 'I know what's going on and I'm sorry for it. Sorry my brother is such a louse.'

Gillespie's face remained passive. 'He's asked Miss Winters for more money.'

Shame burned her cheeks. 'I dunno what to say.'

'You're not responsible for your brother's actions. In fact, you and Miss Winters are the innocents in this. The question is, how are we going to get you both out of it and what do you want?'

'Want?'

'What for you would be a happy outcome?'

Della was bewildered. She'd never been asked such a simple question. The answer played on her tongue, but could she say it? How much did Gillespie know about her and Alice? She took a sip of her drink to buy a little time and met his gaze, finding nothing but kindness there. Still, she couldn't conjure the words.

As if attuned to her discomfort, he lowered his voice. 'You don't have to be explicit. You know my secrets and Miss Winters has confided the depth of her feelings for you. I'm not here to comment, I'm trying to ascertain if you share those feelings.'

'I do,' Della jumped in. 'I want to be with her, and I want to train as a proper chef, hopefully specialising in patisserie at Le Cordon Bleu in Paris. I've been recommended, but what with this business with Jack and him maybe stealing from the Ambrose and William acting like I'm his property, I'm scared it's all going to come crashing down. I've lost Alice. Way things are going, I'll lose my job too.' She took another steadying drink, aware she was gabbling.

'Paris,' Gillespie whispered.

'Alice was going to paint, and I was going to do my training and—'

'Tell me about the stealing, and who is William?'

Della cast her gaze over the pub, but their table was far enough away for her to speak without being overheard. Even so, she kept her voice low as she unburdened her soul. It was like being in the confessional, but it brought far more relief than the practised speech she made to Father Cole on the rare occasions Ma dragged them to Mass.

When she'd reached the end, Gillespie downed what was left of his pint. 'Thank you, Miss Wilde, you've been most helpful. Are you happy for me to act independently to bring this matter to a satisfactory conclusion?'

She studied his earnest face. 'You ain't gonna do anything, you know, violent?' As angry as she was with Jack, he was her brother, and that counted for something.

He fixed her with a level expression. 'I'm not going to add assault or murder to my list of sins, if that's what's worrying you.'

She had no idea of his plan but again she thought about the trust Alice placed in this man. What did they have to lose? 'Alright, Mr Gillespie. You do what you must.'

He stood. 'If you need to contact me, leave word at the Royal Clarence Hotel.'

Della suppressed her surprise that a butler could afford such an address.

He held open the door.

'Is Alice okay?'

'She's well.'

'Does she know about our meeting?'

'No.'

Della nodded.

Outside, she lingered a while watching Gillespie make his way up Fore Street. What a peculiar man. Heeding his warning and darkening skies, Della pulled up her collar and made for home, walking a little taller than she had in a long time.

CHAPTER 46

Gillespie's absence was heavily felt in the winter house over the following days. Alice noticed a change in all of them. Without the butler to underpin the household, they moved around like ghosts in a sort of purgatory. Father was more attentive, his gratitude that his secret had been absorbed into the family apparent. Mummy appeared to blossom in her role as indulgent wife. Alice couldn't understand what was happening, and if there was more, her mother wasn't telling her.

On the fourth day post Gillespie, they were startled by the doorbell during breakfast. 'I'll go,' Alice offered. It was ridiculous to think they'd forgotten how to answer their own door.

Mrs Drummond hovered in the hall. Her demeanour suggested she shared her employer's bewilderment, no longer sure of her role.

'Thank you, Mrs Drummond, I'm going.'

The postman was on the other side. He blanched a little at Gillespie's absence, but quickly recovered. 'Letter for you, Miss.' He passed a cream envelope into her hand.

She closed the door, noticing the London postmark, the address printed in her name.

Her father appeared in the hall. 'Who was it?'

'The postman.'

He waited, assuming the letter was for him.

'It's for me,' Alice added.

'Not from . . .' He couldn't meet her eye, but it was clear he was thinking of Gillespie.

'No, Daddy.'

He nodded and returned to the dining room.

Alice left breakfast to her parents' no doubt questioning looks and hurried to the attic, ripping open the seal as she took the servants' stairs. The heavy type on the embossed paper informed her she'd been selected for the Royal Academy exhibition. She gasped with delight, crashing through the attic door and twirling around the small space, disrupting the dust motes. But her reverie didn't last long. The two people she wanted to share this news with were out of her reach.

She went to the window, seeking Della's raven. Or crow. Whatever it was, she hadn't seen it lately. The tree opposite remained empty, new growth obscuring her vision of every branch. She couldn't sit tight and wait for Gillespie as her parents had suggested. If Jack wanted the money, he wouldn't act against her until it was in his hands. Why then shouldn't she go to the Ambrose?

In the hall, her mother intercepted her. 'Where are you going?'

Alice pulled on her coat. 'The Ambrose.'

Her father joined them. 'Is that wise?'

'I have some news to share with Della. I can't sit around waiting to hear from Gillespie.'

'What news?' her mother asked.

Alice handed her the letter. She scanned the page and looked at Alice, her eyes shining. 'That's wonderful. Look, Robert.'

He studied the letter too. 'Congratulations.' His eyes betrayed genuine pride.

'I wouldn't have entered without Gillespie's encouragement, and Della's my muse. I need to share this and she's the only one whose whereabouts I know.'

Her mother reached for her coat. 'You're right, we mustn't be bullied, and you deserve this. Come, Robert, we're going to celebrate our daughter's success.'

Without question, her father pulled on his coat too. She followed her parents from the house, an awkward trio navigating this confusing new world.

* * *

As they entered the Ambrose and were directed to a table, Alice had to remind herself that they weren't doing anything wrong. No one yet knew her father's scandalous secret and even Jack couldn't forbid her having tea with her parents. He could try. Still, it felt like the walls were alive with whispers. She could see her parents thinking the same thing, the stress showing in their faces. Alice scanned the café for the nice waiter, but not even the nasty one was around today.

'What will you have?' Mummy gazed at the menu.

Alice tried to focus. 'I'm not terribly hungry.'

'We must order. Didn't you say your friend makes cakes? We'll choose something decadent and ask to give our compliments to the chef afterwards.'

Alice regarded her mother with surprise. *An opportunity to see Della?*

'What about you, Robert? I've never known you to turn down a chocolate éclair.'

'Very well.' Father closed the menu and checked his pocket watch. Alice wasn't sure if it was a self-conscious act or because he wanted to leave.

A waitress took their order and they waited, like actors about to rehearse a play. Every so often an acquaintance of her mother or father would approach to exchange pleasantries. Alice could see what was at stake for them. This world of respectability they'd worked so hard to maintain would crumble in an instant if Jack had his way.

Despite the difficult circumstances, the éclairs were fault-less. The pastry sweet, the chocolate ganache rich and the cream piping the perfect accompaniment to the two, bringing out a smile of appreciation even from her father. If this was Della's work, Alice couldn't help beaming with pride.

'We haven't toasted you, Alice.' Mummy raised her tea-cup and they gently clinked china. 'We must go to the exhibition. When is it?'

Taken aback, Alice checked the letter, still in her coat pocket. 'It runs from May to August.'

'We'll go as soon as it opens, won't we, Robert?'

Father, who had been looking around the café, brought his gaze back to theirs. He gave a nod which neither confirmed he was listening nor that he intended to go to the exhibition.

'A few days in London will do us good,' her mother added.

Alice hoisted a smile. As much as she appreciated her parents' support, she wanted to go with Della. In that moment, the need to see her was unbearable. She cast around the café wondering again how to make it happen and thought about her mother's idea, to give their compliments to the chef. She pushed back her chair. 'I'm going to see if we can request an audience with Della.' Without waiting for her parents' agreement, she made for the stairs.

The trouble with the Ambrose was their desire to keep the patrons from seeing what went on behind the scenes. Every effort was made to present a seamless operation. Eventually, after several wrong turns, Alice arrived at the door she'd been hoping to find, the one where she'd talked to Della for the first time after her ludicrous escape on the cake trolley.

She darted out of the way as the door swung open and a waiter and two waitresses walked through, their arms full of dishes to be conveyed to customers. Alice slipped inside and found herself in a different world.

Another waiter appeared with a tray, dodging her deftly and moving on. She could see the kitchen doors beyond the servery and realised this was her chance to sneak by unnoticed in the bustling room.

'Mademoiselle, are you lost?' A heavily accented voice.

Alice spun around to see a compact man with a tall chef's hat. The same man who'd brought Della to her on a previous occasion. 'We wanted to thank the chef for our éclairs. They were perfection.'

His expression softened. 'Many thanks for your compliments, Mademoiselle. I will convey your message.'

'Oh, but couldn't I deliver it myself?'

He frowned.

Alice knew she'd have to use her father's name. For how much longer would it open doors? 'I'm here with my parents, Robert and Mary Winters. We'd love to thank Della ourselves.'

As she had known it would, his expression changed, although to one of puzzlement and then clarity. 'Of course. Della's skills precede her. I'll have her report to your table.'

'Thank you.'

She returned to her seat. 'Della's going to come to our table.'

'Splendid.' Her mother poured the dregs of the tea while her father checked his watch again. It irritated her that, given the circumstances, he was the architect of this disaster.

She wasn't ready when Della appeared. Her hair had grown but it remained vibrant, the curls bouncing as she walked across the café to their table. She was wearing an overall, cinched at the waist, her cap in her hand, the chef from the servery in her wake. Della's eyes were saucers as she took in Alice.

'Florian Voisin.' Mummy was on her feet, greeting the chef with kisses on both cheeks as if he were an old friend, while her father looked on bemused.

'Madame Winters, what a lovely surprise.' Mr Voisin unhanded her mother and turned his attention to her father. They shook hands before all eyes swivelled to Della.

The chef took Della by the shoulders. 'Here she is, our pâtissier extraordinaire.'

Della blushed at the compliment, but her eyes held a thousand questions.

How Alice wished she could answer them. She could hear her mother talking, exclaiming over the éclairs, but Alice had lost the ability to speak.

It was over before it started. Della was being conveyed away. Alice shoved back her chair and ran after her, catching her as she was about to disappear through the servery doors. The chef threw Della a baffled expression and left them to it.

'It's in the exhibition,' Alice blurted, knowing they had no time at all.

'The portrait?'

'Of course the portrait. You're going to be hanging in the Royal Academy in London.'

Della grinned. Alice wanted to hug her. They stood as stiff as skittles, staring at each other.

'I saw him, your butler, Gillespie.' Della checked behind. 'He said he was going to sort it all out.'

'When was this?'

'Yesterday, after work.'

'How did he seem?' Alice was desperate for every detail.

Della shrugged. 'A bit weary. Do you really think he'll sort it? I agreed, but I'm not sure what to.'

'I hope so.' Her hand twitched to take Della's.

'It's so good to see you. Anthony said you'd been in, but now he's laid up I didn't know.'

'Laid up?'

'I can't explain.' A waiter walked past, throwing them a disgruntled look as they moved out of his way. 'I'd better go, or Mr Voisin will have my hide.'

'Alright. I'm here. I'm always going to be here.'

Della smiled at that, and Alice did too. It was enough.

She returned to find her parents in their coats, and her mother helped her into hers. 'Della's lovely,' she whispered. 'Florian speaks very highly of her.'

Alice pulled on her hat, delighted by the compliment. 'How do you know him?'

Her mother took her arm but didn't elaborate.

CHAPTER 47

Della walked home that evening, her steps like the light, a little brighter. Seeing Alice, coupled with her discussion with Mr Gillespie and William's continued absence, gave her hope.

Sam was standing on an upturned bin in the yard, straining to see over the fence into next door's garden. She could hear the puppy yapping from the other side.

'Get down from there, Sam.'

He glanced in her direction. 'I thought you was Jack. He's promised me a puppy.'

Della wasn't convinced this puppy would materialise but there was no use disappointing Sam. That responsibility lay at Jack's door. 'Come in all the same, tea will be ready soon.'

Sam jumped down and ran for the kitchen. Inside, Ma scrubbed the flagstones around the stove. She looked up. Della witnessed a shadow of disappointment on her face.

'Jack not with you?'

'I'm sure he'll be along in a minute. We work in different departments. I'm not his keeper.'

Ma stopped scrubbing and set down the brush. 'I'm surprised you two don't walk home together. Mind you, after your rudeness the other evening when that nice boy William was here, I don't think you're in Jack's good books.'

Jack wasn't in hers.

'I hope he's got my puppy.' Sam, relentless in his quest.

Ma shook her head and returned to her scrubbing. Della hung her bag. 'Shall I start dinner?'

'We'll wait for Jack.'

When he hadn't materialised an hour later and Henry joined them in the kitchen in search of food, Ma finally accepted the cherished son wouldn't be providing that evening's meal. She made a simple supper of potatoes, bully beef and baked beans. Sam grinned with delight and Della was grateful to know the provenance of the food she was eating.

She was clearing the plates when Jack finally burst in, no meat or jovial greeting. In fact, her brother looked worn out.

'You're late, Jack. Everything alright?' Ma asked from her mending.

Jack checked over his shoulder at the darkening yard and pulled off his jacket. 'Fine.' He hung it on the peg and muttered something under his breath.

'I saved you some dinner. Bully beef and spuds, I'm afraid.' There was a hint of anxiety in Ma's tone. She didn't like this version of Jack. None of them did.

'Did you see the bloke about getting a puppy?' Sam asked.

'Leave your brother alone,' Ma scolded. 'Let him have his dinner.' She fussed around and Jack let her.

Della could tell something was bothering him. She focused on rinsing the dishes, appreciating her view of the yard and wondering what or who had made Jack so jumpy.

Half an hour later with the rest of the house dispersed, he came to her side with his empty plate. 'You needn't look so pleased with yourself.'

Della frowned. 'I'm just washing up.'

Jack studied her. 'It won't work.'

'What won't work?'

He didn't answer, instead his gaze slid to the yard.

'Someone out there?'

He lit a cigarette. 'You shouldn't have run out on William.'

'You shouldn't have brought him here when you knew I wasn't interested.'

Jack drew on his cigarette, a hint of conciliation in his tone. 'Give him a chance. Don't ask me why, but he's mad about you. For all our sakes, go out with him again.'

She considered his desperate face. 'What's in it for you? Why do you care so much whether or not I go out with William?'

Jack blanched. 'He's a mate.'

True, but that wasn't enough. Jack was close to begging. Realisation dawned. William had some sort of hold over her brother, and she was the prize. She couldn't believe it but everything about Jack's expression told her it was true. Maybe he'd even got Jack the job at the Ambrose. *Could it be that simple?* She shook her head with a sense part of the puzzle was missing.

'What?' Jack's voice betrayed a note of anxiety.

Della dried her hands. 'I'm not going out with William — not now, not ever. Whatever he has over you, you'll have to accept it.'

Outside a dustbin clattered in the alleyway. Jack jumped ten feet in the air, dropping the cigarette in the sink. It sizzled as it hit the suds. She watched his face drain of colour.

CHAPTER 48

Alice stepped back from the easel, set down her brush and cracked her aching shoulders. A terrible habit but one she couldn't resist when her body was stiff from adopting a single position. It felt good to be painting again, shame her chosen subject made that simple joy somewhat ambiguous. Gillespie eyed her from the canvas. She'd used the sketches she'd made after catching him from the bath all those weeks ago. Of course, now Alice realised it was her father he'd called to.

For whom was she painting this portrait? Certainly not her father, although he might be the one to appreciate it. No, this was for her, the rendering of a beautiful subject made all the more compelling by its complexity.

A soft knock came against the door and her mother entered. Alice panicked — the paint was too wet for her to sling a cover over the easel.

Mummy's eyes lit up. 'Can I see?'

Alice blocked her path. 'I'd rather you didn't.'

She looked abashed. 'Very well, I understand. You artists and your delicate temperaments. I'm glad you've found your muse again.'

Alice's face fell. If only her muse were here with her now. Tomorrow was Jack's deadline and not a word from Gillespie.

231

She turned the easel to obscure the canvas from view as her mother made her way to the daybed and patted the seat beside her.

'I've been thinking about London. Couldn't we just go? Your exhibition opens next week. We could have a summer trip, get away from all this.'

'What about Jack, Gillespie and Daddy?'

Her mother's brow furrowed. 'I rather think this is their mess to clean up.'

Surprised, Alice agreed, but she couldn't leave Della even if it was impossible to see her.

Her mother read her mind. 'You don't want to leave Della?'

Alice shook her head, finding her eyes wet with tears.

'Darling girl.' She took her in her arms.

'Why do you stay with Daddy?' The question had bothered Alice ever since she found out the truth.

She felt her mother's embrace slacken. 'I don't think you'd understand.'

'You care about Daddy, and you wanted to stay for my sake, but what about you? What do you get out of it?'

Her mother pulled back. 'There have been times when I've resented their relationship. Society thinks women my age are done with passion once we've borne children, but I can tell you, we're not. We still want passion in our lives. Daddy has it with Gillespie and I don't. It isn't fair, but denying him the man he loves wouldn't change anything. He still wouldn't have wanted me, and we'd all be miserable. It may sound strange but when I found out about your father and Gillespie, it brought us closer together. Everything your father had buried about himself could breathe. I got to know the real version of my husband and I liked what I found. As the wounds healed, we agreed, so long as I was discreet, I could carry out my own love affairs. In truth, it was harder than I imagined. How could an MP's wife, someone in the public eye, pursue another man while keeping such a secret? I suppose I lost motivation, but perhaps now is the time to explore other options.' She blushed. 'One in particular.'

Alice's jaw dropped. 'Who?'

Her mother laughed at her scandalised face. 'Never mind. Know that I'm okay and be happy for me.'

She nodded, curious but willing to let it go for now. They'd all kept their secrets, didn't her mother deserve her own?

'So, what about London?'

'I'm supposed to meet Jack tomorrow and pay the next instalment.'

'That's true. Your father is going mad not hearing from Gillespie.'

Alice sighed. 'Frankly, so am I. We have to give him a chance.'

'But what if he doesn't come through?'

'He will.' Father was standing in the open doorway. 'Gillespie's never failed me.' He walked into the room, shoulders slumped with the weight of their predicament. He made no attempt to peer at the easel, instead squeezing himself between them on the daybed and looking at them each in turn. 'If I may, I should like to make my confession.'

Alice glanced at her mother, who returned her look of surprise.

* * *

'I'd been at the front for about six months when Gillespie joined us. That made me an old hand. I thought I'd become immune to everything the war could conjure. Men stretchered out, their senses consumed by monstrous fear, limbs lost to bodies, brains blown to mulch. There was nothing the war could throw at me that I hadn't already seen, until Gillespie. I remember his arrival like it was yesterday. I was seated in the dugout with Rodgers, playing cards and drinking cheap rum. A standard pastime to while away the hours, waiting for whatever suicide mission HQ would come up with next. Do you know they used to dish rum out before we went over the top? Only way they could get some of the men to do it. A little oil for the nerves.' He shook his head, despairing at the insanity all these years later.

'HQ had let us know another man would be joining after he'd lost most of his regiment. We pondered over whether this was bad luck, having a chap carrying that kind of burden. Still, he'd survived where his comrades hadn't so he must be made of something, and how true that was. The dugout seemed to fill to the rafters from the moment Gillespie crouched to descend the steps. We'd offered him the worst bunk, as was customary in such circumstances. I could see it would be an ill fit, his build and weight bringing him close to the floor and the rats. I wasn't about to offer to swap, despite my admiration.'

His gaze flickered to Alice with a sad smile. 'Gillespie's Scottish accent was even thicker back then, but he said little and what he did say was considered and impactful, as if words were a commodity too precious to waste. I suppose you could say he rationed them like food. He had a way of communicating with his eyes. I'd asked Rodgers to show him the ropes that first evening, but when he stood to undertake the task, I found myself putting my hand on his shoulder and telling him to relax. I'd take Gillespie along the trench and show him our world.

'It was a cold, quiet night, the air misting with our breath as we whispered. We could hear the distant hum of the Germans in their trenches no more than three hundred yards away, doing much as we'd been doing. Chatting, drinking, passing the time, their boots as filled with mud and water as ours, clothes so damp they made a second skin. Gillespie took it all in with his silent appraisal. Something about him made me feel safe and very, very afraid.

'You see, I recognised it instantly, what I'd been trying to keep a lid on. What I'd suppressed through school at Blundells, up at Cambridge and when I met and married the kindest, loveliest woman a man could hope for.' He reached for her mother's hand and kissed it. 'Gillespie brought it all roaring to the surface. I knew I was forever changed. It took a year, side by side, experiencing some of the most horrific things a man can see, for us to admit how we felt.

'When I returned, I was lost, not just from what I'd been through but lost without him to tell me how to live. We'd agreed it couldn't go on. Tried to put a brave face on our parting, but it was agony. I wrote to him every day. Long rambling letters begging him to join me here. I was selfish, thoughtless and utterly consumed. My campaign took four months, harder won than any general election.'

He fell silent. Alice waited in case there was more. Her father looked miserable, sitting there with his hand in her mother's, burdened by his own story and the depth of his fear over losing the man he loved. She couldn't judge him, in fact quite the opposite. Alice felt closer to him than she had since she was a child. When he continued to remain silent, she moved to put a sheet over the canvas, realising that perhaps she was painting it for her father after all.

CHAPTER 49

That night, Della didn't sleep, her mind chewing over her argument with Jack, studying it from every angle, seeing things with fresh eyes. The sense she was missing something important bothered her as she walked into work. William and her brother hadn't known each other until that disastrous day she'd brought William home for tea after the Christmas party, but what if they'd continued an acquaintance without her knowledge? What if all of this stemmed from William and not Jack? He'd witnessed her brother's jealousy over her job, maybe she'd even mentioned it. He'd seen the scarcity of food at the Wilde table. Could he have capitalised on this, told Jack a job was his at the Ambrose if he could deliver Della? It seemed a bizarre length to go to, and how did blackmailing Alice fit into the picture?

She hadn't found the answer by the time she arrived in the Ambrose kitchen. Anthony was there, his eye still bruised but his smile as wide as ever. The group around him slowly dispersed once Della said hello.

'You alright to be back?' she asked, concerned as Anthony winced lifting a tray.

'Not really but I was going mad cooped up at home. Kath couldn't wait to see the back of me.'

236

'Don't take any risks.'

'I'll be fine.' He touched her arm. 'Listen, William's back today too. He came to see me to apologise, and I agreed I wouldn't let on. He's got no idea you suspect, so please don't go confronting him. He's genuinely sorry and I'd rather put it down to a bloke losing his head over a beautiful girl.'

She bit her lip. It wasn't okay. Why should men like William get away with bad behaviour?

'Please, Del?' he pressed when she didn't reply.

She sighed. 'Alright, but only for you.'

'You're a star.'

Della checked behind to make sure they were out of ear-shot. 'Did William get Jack the job here, do you know?'

Anthony shrugged and looked like he regretted it. 'Could have done, I suppose. They've been mates for a while, and I know your brother was keen. I thought William was only tolerating him to get closer to you.'

Della nodded, now seeing the truth in that. 'Thanks, take care of yourself today.'

* * *

Ten minutes later she was in the pantry gathering supplies, when through the small window she spied Jack and William in the yard. She studied their interaction with curiosity. Having assumed in the past that Jack was the lord and master, she now noticed how he had trouble meeting William's eye. How William towered above him, how her brother raked his fingers through his hair — a nervous tic.

She managed to avoid William for the rest of the morning, but after the lunchtime rush he came into the kitchen for a cup of tea, Anthony at his side, his face strained. Della wasn't sure if it was the pain of his injury or working hard to keep William happy that made him look so fatigued. Anthony barely acknowledged her as they passed.

'Here comes trouble.' Mrs Hastings dusted her hands on her apron. 'It's good to see the pair of you boys back.'

237

'Thanks, Mrs H,' Anthony said. William made no comment but glanced at Della. He didn't look well either, his skin a little pallid, his shoulders sloped. She returned to her work, not wishing to invite interaction, but it was too late — his brogues squeaked on the flour-dusted linoleum at her side.

'Aren't you going to welcome me back?'

Della turned to face him. 'Welcome back.'

'That's it?'

'What was wrong with you anyway?'

He shrugged. 'Caught sommat.'

'Not like poor Anthony, then. Scum, whoever set upon him.'

William shifted. 'I'd like to give them what for.'

She forced her gaze to meet his. 'What would you say, to the spineless creep who beat him up?'

He puffed out his chest. 'They wouldn't get the chance to speak again if I had anything to do with it.'

Della noticed Leonnard across the room, watching their interaction. Something in his benign expression gave her strength. 'Punch them, would you?'

William didn't move but his eyes held a hint of fear.

'Beat them to a pulp? Give them what they deserved for setting on an innocent man — and from behind too, so I heard.'

William's mouth twitched. He leaned in, his lips close to her ear. 'If I were you, I'd shut up.'

Anthony reappeared carrying two mugs of tea. 'Here you go, mate.'

William dragged his gaze from hers. 'Della here's got lots of theories about your attacker. Reckons they must be a spineless creep.'

Anthony's laugh was nervous. He threw Della a warning look.

'You know me,' Della recovered. 'Always barking up the wrong tree. Good to see you both back.'

She turned to her bowl and let the flour calm her shaking hands. But she wasn't barking up the wrong tree. She now realised she needed to see Gillespie and tell him they'd got the wrong man. What use was it dealing with the puppet when the puppeteer was still at large?

* * *

The Royal Clarence Hotel was no place for the likes of her, but Della smoothed down her hair and marched in, attempting to look like she belonged when it was obvious she didn't. Being back there brought her to Alice, what they'd done in the bathroom and how Jack had managed to ruin it all. But not quite. She still had Alice, her job, her hopes and dreams. Gillespie had reminded her of that.

The receptionist gave her the once-over when Della made her request, before disappearing through a door behind the desk. Della had expected her to send a porter to fetch Gillespie from his room. She cast around the sumptuous lobby, all plush red carpet and bronze. The receptionist returned, a pinched expression on her face as she told Della to follow.

On the other side of the door existed another world. A small office where a clerk in half-moon spectacles sat hunched over a ledger. A laundry room filled with steam, followed by a kitchen bustling with life, making Della feel instantly more at home. The receptionist's heels clicked at a pace, preventing Della from lingering. Suddenly they were outside in a small forecourt where a car was being polished by a tall man in a chauffeur's uniform, and there, as he lifted his gaze, was Gillespie.

'Thank you, Miss Sparrow.' His expression inscrutable as ever.

The receptionist offered him a smile which went unacknowledged before she turned on her heels and clipped away.

Gillespie's face softened for Della. Not quite a smile but certainly the idea of one. 'You have some information for me, Miss Wilde?'

'Is there somewhere we can talk?'

He gestured to the garage.

239

It was a cavernous space with two other motor cars gleaming with polish. Gillespie directed Della to a wooden chair at the back of the room. 'Would you like tea?'

She nodded, grateful for the time this brought her to get the information she wanted to convey in the right order. He disappeared in the direction of the hotel kitchen and returned moments later with two steaming mugs.

He leaned against the wall, waiting for her to begin.

'We've got the wrong man,' Della blurted.

Gillespie didn't look particularly surprised.

'I know Jack's the one blackmailing Alice and I haven't worked that bit out yet, but I think this all stems from William, the waiter you saved me from outside the Ambrose.'

Gillespie blew on his tea. 'You'd better start at the beginning.'

Della relayed it all, how William was sweet on her, how he'd pressured her into taking him home for tea but then she'd broken it off. How he'd been jealous, beating up Anthony because he saw him as competition, somehow pressing Jack to persuade her to court him. Telling her she was weird for her friendship with Alice.

Gillespie listened intently, and when she'd finished and downed her tea, he fixed his eyes on hers. 'You said your brother's been bringing home food, food you're concerned he's stolen from the Ambrose.'

Della nodded, a little ashamed at the accusation.

'Could William be involved?'

'I dunno. I mean, as a waiter, he's got more opportunity, but Jack works in the stores.'

'But not the deli. You said some of the food was cooked — pies, a glazed ham — surely the food from there is prepared on site. It would arrive in its raw state.'

This was true, and Jack couldn't march into the deli and help himself. 'I suppose William would have more access,' she said, still puzzled as to his motive.

'If William saw Miss Winters as a threat he wanted Jack to alleviate, could your brother have used the information he

240

gleaned from you as an opportunity to ensure Miss Winters stayed out of your way?'

'That makes sense, but it don't explain the money. Also, Jack said he thinks we're weird. William said that too.'

Gillespie raised an eyebrow. They both fell quiet. Della could see his face clouded in thought, and her own head ached with the effort of working this out. It felt like they were missing something, but they couldn't see it.

'Have I wasted your time? Got it all wrong?' Della asked, feeling a little foolish.

Gillespie shook his head. 'The theory's sound. I'm grateful you brought it to my attention. What we need now is a motive. If William is hell-bent on securing your affections, although I can't help questioning his methods, and Jack is doing his bidding, what hold does William have over Jack?'

Della shrugged. 'I honestly don't know.'

'Then maybe we need to ask the puppet.' Mr Gillespie straightened. 'Would you be willing to meet me here tomorrow to talk to your brother when he's expecting Miss Winters and her payment?'

Della was surprised, but what did she have to lose? 'Alright.'

He nodded, a satisfied look on his face. 'If you'll permit me, I'll need to share this information with Miss Winters directly. Is there a message you'd like me to convey?'

Della blushed. 'Tell her I'm not going to give up.'

'Neither is she.' He offered his hand. 'Thank you, Miss Wilde.'

Outside, he accompanied her to an iron gate which led onto a narrow alleyway. 'Meet me here tomorrow at 5 p.m. If you follow the alley, you'll find yourself in the cathedral close.'

Della thanked him and went on her way, relieved to be back in the hubbub of Exeter and a little excited to have instigated this plan. Was she trying to save Jack? To redeem her brother because it lessened her own burden? She just hoped Jack would offer up what they needed.

Either way, her brother was in for a shock.

CHAPTER 50

Raised voices coming from the study alerted Alice to Gillespie's reappearance in the winter house. She found her mother in the hall, not bothering to hide the fact she was listening, although the conversation was hardly conducted in whispers.

'I only said I'd stay if we weren't causing more pain. We've done damage, Robert, we have to face up to that.' Gillespie's accent was stronger when it contained emotion.

'You can't avoid pain, living is pain.'

'Aye, but you can choose not to carry on inflicting the same wound over and over again.'

'Even if it causes a greater one?'

'To us, maybe. We have to live with that.'

'You're talking in riddles.'

'Robert, it's simple. We've lived together at the cost of your marriage. Your wife might tolerate it, but we can't deny that hurt. Now a reckoning has come and I'm grateful for it. A chance to set things right, to release others from facing the same burden, from making the same mistakes. I'm talking about your daughter.'

Alice felt her mother's hand on her shoulder. 'I think we should leave them to it,' she whispered.

In the sitting room they passed half an hour flicking through old copies of *Women's Life* and pacing, while muffled voices drifted through the open doorway. Finally, the study door flew open. Father emerged — his face ghostly white. He didn't glance in their direction, but his heavy tread could be heard on the stairs and then in the room above. Gillespie stood in the hallway, watching him go. Slowly, he brought his gaze to theirs.

'I'll go to your father.' Mummy left the room, pausing to give Gillespie a hug.

Once she'd released him with a kiss on the cheek, Gillespie made his approach. 'Miss Alice.'

'Hello, Mr Gillespie.' It was a formal greeting, considering what had just passed.

He closed the door and gestured for her to sit. She noticed he was wearing a chauffeur's uniform with the crest of the Royal Clarence Hotel and realised, with a stab of pain, nothing would be as it was in the winter house again.

'I've just had a meeting with Miss Wilde.'

'Della? What did she say?'

'She's a clever woman, your Miss Wilde. She saw what I failed to. She puts up with much and expects little, and yet her generosity is boundless.'

Alice smiled despite the gravity of the situation. She couldn't have formed such a succinct description, but she was absurdly pleased to have Gillespie reach that opinion independently. What on earth had passed between them?

'Tomorrow, if you're agreeable, Miss Wilde and I will meet with Jack. She no longer believes her brother is acting alone.'

'But who . . . ?'

'You're not the only one to have recognised her exceptional qualities. Another interested party has found your friendship with her extremely frustrating to his own pursuit. He's keen to see you off in no uncertain terms, but a gentleman, and I use that term liberally, cannot act with a lady as he would with another man, where fists might settle the score.'

Alice untangled his words. 'Are you talking about William?'

Gillespie nodded, eyes now blazing. 'It's our belief that William has some sort of hold over Jack and is using him to do his bidding. It isn't yet clear what that hold is, which is why we hope by meeting Jack tomorrow, we can fill those gaps.'

'So, you don't need me?'

'I don't believe we will.'

'But isn't it risky? What if Jack doesn't give up William? Won't he go to the press with the story about you and Daddy?'

'It is a risk, but one your father and I must face. I've done everything I can to lessen the blow, removing myself from the house, seeking other employment.' He gestured to his clothes.

'That's why you've let Daddy think you're ending things, so he can deny the story?'

Gillespie looked pained. 'It's for the best.'

'Do you really believe that?'

He didn't answer. Instead, he cleared his throat, as if to clear the tremor that was there in his eyes. 'I believe congratulations are in order.'

Alice frowned before realising he was talking about the exhibition. 'Thank you, I honestly wouldn't have entered if it hadn't been for your encouragement.'

'Your talent speaks for itself, and your mother mentioned she'd like to take you to London for the opening. I think that's a good idea while this blows over.'

Alice felt her eyes well up. 'What about Della, when will I see her?'

'One thing at a time, Miss Alice. Have faith.'

CHAPTER 51

On the day of their meeting with Jack, time passed in its own dimension. One moment the Ambrose kitchen clock appeared to cease its tick, the next it was as if it had been pushed forwards several hours. By the end of the day, a fist of anxiety had formed in Della's stomach.

She filed out of the Ambrose with the other staff, Jack a few people ahead. At the corner of the building, she lingered, watching her brother's confident gait as he made his way along the High Street. How would they continue to live under the same roof if the confrontation turned out bad for her?

When he was sufficiently far ahead, Della followed, glancing behind a couple of times, fearful of William.

Gillespie met her at the gate, as he'd promised. They made their way to the back of the hotel. 'I've asked to be informed by reception when Jack enters the bar,' Gillespie said, his eyes alive with interest. 'I'm happy to do most of the talking, but if you want to take the lead, please do so.'

Della nodded, unsure what she'd say but comforted by his solid presence.

After a moment, a different lady from reception emerged from the hotel, signalling to Gillespie. He waved his thanks and turned to Della. 'Ready?'

Delay was futile. With a swift nod, she followed him inside. He gestured for her to enter the bar first and she did so, her gaze searching out Jack. He was in a booth at the far end, smoking, an agitation in the way he drummed his fingers on the table surface. His eyes met hers. Shock quickly gave way to anger until he took in Gillespie and the anger drained into fear. Della was surprised by a stab of pity for him.

He stubbed out his cigarette and stood to leave.

'Hello, Jack.'

He didn't look at her. 'Whatever this is, you've made a big mistake.'

'Please take a seat, Mr Wilde, your sister wishes to speak with you.'

'Where's Alice?'

'She's not coming. Your blackmail hasn't worked,' Della replied.

He rubbed his stubble, his gaze shifting to the exit, but the wall of Gillespie stood in his way.

'Talk to me, Jack.' Della slid into the booth next to him. 'We can sort this out.'

Gillespie took the other side. A waitress came to their table and left when Gillespie gave an almost imperceptible shake of the head.

Jack fidgeted with a beer mat, tracing its edges through his fingers. 'What do you want?'

Della touched his arm in an attempt to calm his distress. 'The truth.'

He dropped the beer mat and sat back. 'Why don't you tell me what you think the truth is?'

'Because you'll twist it to your advantage. I know you're not working alone. You might dislike me, but I'm your sister, surely that counts for something? Or at least, it used to.' She held his gaze, daring him to look away. If he did, she'd know their relationship was irrecoverably lost. A lump formed in her throat as Jack glanced at the beer mat, but then he lifted his gaze to her again, his eyes softening.

Neither of them seemed to know what to say next. Gillespie was silent too, perhaps appreciating the weight of this moment that felt to Della like a precipice.

'What happened to us, Jack?' she asked, a last-ditch attempt to reach her brother. 'We used to be a team, I only wanted to make you proud but instead, you resent me as if everything's my fault — Ma being sick, your struggle to find work. I know it's been hard, it's hard for everyone, but I'm not to blame. I don't deserve to be treated like this.' Tears filled her eyes and she cast around the room.

The barman was polishing glasses, lifting each one to the light and checking for smudges. It helped her regain her composure, then Jack's hand found hers under the table, giving it a brief squeeze and letting go. It was a small gesture but one that gave her hope. When she met his gaze, his eyes were watery too.

'Of course I don't dislike you, Del.' His voice was thick with emotion and his brow furrowed. 'If only you'd let him court you.'

He rubbed his face with his hands and let out a long sigh before facing her once more. 'That time you brought William home for tea, it was obvious you weren't keen. I don't know why the daft bloke couldn't see it for himself. I found it amusing, I suppose — you squirming while he chatted to Ma about what a lovely girl you were. After you'd said goodbye, not even giving the poor bastard a peck on the cheek, I saw him out. It seemed like the decent thing to do. He asked if I fancied a pint, he was buying, so we went to the pub on Cowick Street.

'In the pub he told me how much he liked you, how if things went his way, he could help the Wildes along, maybe even get me a job at the Ambrose, but only if I had a quiet word with you, encouraged you to keep seeing him.' Jack shook his head. 'It smacked of desperation. As much as I wanted the job, I told him no — it was up to you who you saw. Della's stubborn, I said, she won't listen to me. He didn't like that, but he honoured his word and paid for our drinks. I thought that was the end of it until Ma got sick.

'As the weeks passed and Ma kept to her bed, I got to thinking about William's offer. I couldn't stand seeing Ma like that. I'm the man of the house, I'm supposed to provide, and you was off with fancy Alice.' He glanced at Gillespie. 'I mean Miss Winters.' Jack fished out another cigarette and lit it. 'I tried it on with her, figured her money might help but she only had eyes for you.'

Della kept her features in check, despite her pleasure at this news.

'If I was going to agree to William's terms, I needed Alice out of the way, but she wasn't easy to shift. She really complicated things. I didn't realise how much until I saw you both here in the bar.'

'So that's why you blackmailed her, to clear the path for William?' Della couldn't believe she'd been treated like this, a commodity to be passed around.

Jack winced. 'I was desperate, so I told him I'd do it, that I could handle Alice. He got me the job at the Ambrose the very next day. When I overheard your conversation with Alice about . . .' He glanced at Gillespie again and decided not to elaborate. 'I saw my chance to break the pair of you up.'

'How could you do that? You practically sold me to William.' She couldn't keep the hurt from her voice.

Jack shifted in his seat. 'I thought Alice had put you under some sort of spell. If I could get you away from her, there was a chance you might go out with him. I mean, he's alright looking, got a good job, his own home. A war hero, so he claims.'

'Except I'm not attracted to men,' she whispered.

Jack's expression darkened. 'Alright, you don't need to spell it out.'

'I'm sick of hiding who I am.' Della folded her arms, staring down her brother until he looked away. 'Why did you ask Alice for more money?'

He studied the table. 'You saw Ma's face, all of them fancy bits of food I brought home. It made her so happy, but they didn't come cheap. William arranged a staff discount, or so I thought. He started to pile on the pressure after Alice kept turning up at the Ambrose for tea. It was then he told me he'd stolen the meat and if I didn't hurry up and deliver on my promise, he'd frame me for the theft.'

No wonder Jack was desperate. William knew exactly where to strike. 'Did you know William beat up Anthony?'

Jack shook his head. 'Not until he boasted about it the day he came back. Said I'd end up with more than a few bruises if I didn't fulfil my end of the bargain.'

'So, what now?' Della glanced at Gillespie.

He brought his hands together. 'Where did you intend to go from here, Mr Wilde, if Miss Winters had turned up with the money?'

Jack took a drag on his cigarette. 'I was probably going to ask for more. The longer I could keep Della and Miss Winters apart, the more time I bought myself. Every penny would go on improving things for Ma.'

It was a weak defence, but she could see his predicament.

Della addressed Mr Gillespie. 'If we can persuade Anthony to accuse William of beating him up, couldn't we get him fired?'

'It won't work,' Jack cut in. 'William's got something on Anthony too, something to do with the war.'

Gillespie looked intrigued. 'What regiment did they serve in?'

Jack shrugged. 'No idea.'

'Could you find out?'

'I can try, but William doesn't exactly let me lead the conversation.'

'Anthony might tell me,' Della added.

Gillespie nodded. 'Do we have your agreement you won't carry out your blackmail threat?'

'You have my word. I didn't know who I'd tell. Who's going to believe a nobody like me against an MP? Thing is, I can't speak for William.'

Gillespie's face fell. Della couldn't believe what she was hearing. If William knew about Gillespie and Mr Winters, he held the trump card.

'How could you tell him, Jack?'

Her brother looked miserable. 'The blackmail was his idea.'

'You can't let on to William we know all this.'

'I know and I'm sorry.' His gaze was sincere as it met hers. 'I didn't know what he was like.'

'It's never one's prerogative to make a commodity of someone's heart.' Gillespie's tone was hard, his face grave. 'Miss Wilde, I'll leave you to some time with your brother. There are other matters we need to discuss. Perhaps we could meet in an hour, at the pub on Fore Street?'

Della nodded.

'If you don't turn up, I will come looking.' He directed his gaze at Jack.

'I'll be there, Mr Gillespie.' She sensed this had to do with Alice. She wouldn't miss it for all the world.

CHAPTER 52

Raindrops splashed against the car windscreen, the wipers going full pelt as her father drove away from the city of Salisbury, where they'd stopped for lunch. Alice had hardly touched her food — her mind remained in Exeter, her focus absorbed by the meeting with Jack. It could be days before she learned of its outcome.

She stretched her limbs, stiff from sitting in one position. It was almost five hours since they'd left the winter house. They'd be in London by now if they'd taken the train. It was her father's idea he drive them. Perhaps he wanted time to think. If the worst happened and the story broke, a family trip might be just the thing to quash any rumours before they'd begun. But it could also suggest they were running away.

Alice glanced at her mother, sitting beside her in the back, gaze focused on the passing countryside. They'd exhausted small talk by Dorchester and the car had been silent since save for the clatter of the engine, the pitter-patter of rain.

Three hours later, an endless landscape of trees and fields gave way to the suburbs of Twickenham and Richmond. Alice hoped it wouldn't be too much further, her bladder had been pressing with need for nearly an hour. As five o'clock came and went, she tried to distract herself with the emerging sights and sounds of the city. Buses, trams and every kind of motor car or horse-drawn vehicle vied for space on London's hectic streets. It was an engrossing sight, but she couldn't enjoy it while Della was facing Jack. The not knowing was going to drive her up the wall.

'Alice, look,' her mother seemed to exclaim and point every few seconds, so Alice had little choice but to interact and allow her focus to be pulled into the feast before them.

Her father entered Piccadilly and ground to a halt outside the Ritz.

'Robert,' her mother said. 'You didn't.'

For the first time in a very long time, a small smile tugged beneath his moustache. 'What better opportunity to spoil my family?'

A porter met them and summoned a second to park the car. They were ushered up the hotel steps before their cases had been unloaded. Alice couldn't take it all in, the opulence in every direction. In the vast domed reception, her father made enquiries at the desk, then they were accompanied to their suite of adjoining rooms. As if by magic, their luggage preceded them.

Once they were alone, her father disappeared into his room, leaving Alice with her mother, who continued to exclaim over every detail. Alice wished she could share her childlike wonder, but all she could think about was Della and how wrong being here felt.

'It's his way of showing he cares.' Her mother noticed her apathy.

'It's not that.'

'You're worried about Della and Gillespie meeting with Jack?'

Alice studied the carpeted floor. 'It doesn't seem fair, that she has to be there, sorting out this mess while we all escape. Della doesn't have anyone.'

Her mother gently lifted her chin so their eyes met. 'She has you, darling girl.'

'What good am I here? It's all wrong, not just this situation but all of it. How rich people live at the expense of the poor. It suits us to keep the lower class down. Della's helped me to see all that — and Gillespie too, I suppose. How do we make it better?'

'Gosh, this is a conversation for your father, although I'm not sure he'd see it in quite those terms.'

'Then he's part of the problem.'

'Are you complaining about your privilege?'

'Not exactly, I'm just stating it to be true.' This conversation wasn't going to get anywhere, Alice could tell. Her mother hadn't seen what she'd seen.

'I don't doubt the sincerity of your feelings or the truth in your words, but we're not going to be able to take on the unfairness of the world today.'

Alice realised she didn't want to live in that world, even more convinced there was another way, a way she and Della would find together in Paris. She looked at her mother's concerned face. Hadn't she put up with enough without a miserable daughter for company? 'Sorry, I'll stop trying to put the world to rights. What do you want to do this evening?'

Her mother smiled. 'You can put the world to rights, but not tonight. I'm going to have a luxurious soak in that ridiculous bath to wash the drive off me and then we'll see what trouble we can find.'

* * *

With the bedroom to herself, Alice slipped off her shoes, the thick pile carpet soft beneath her feet. Settling on the Chesterfield positioned in front of the window, she tucked her legs beneath her and cast around the room. Thick navy curtains topped by a pelmet hung in folds either side. Gossamer nets kept the noise of Piccadilly to a minimum, ensuring guests optimum privacy from the buildings opposite. A royal-blue counterpane covered the expansive bed she'd share with her mother later. Plump white pillows were placed with precision, the crisp points of their cases making perfect right-angles. Such luxury, and yet the result was austere rather than inviting. A bed to slip into and lie beneath its cold, starched sheets, undisturbed by passion. If Della were here, they'd throw back the counterpane and soften the starch.

A light knock came against the door and her father entered, dressed for dinner. His wiry frame was such a contrast to Gillespie's solidity it was hard to picture them as a couple. Judging by the slight frown furrowing his brow, his earlier enthusiasm for the hotel had worn off. There was pain there too. She realised his suffering echoed hers. They were both in love with people for whom society would damn them to hell. It should be a source of closeness. Not that her parents hadn't treated the news of her affair with Della with the utmost compassion. She couldn't have asked for better support, but the mess unfolding in Exeter had travelled with them to London and left its mark.

He nodded in greeting and checked his pocket watch. Alice now realised this was perhaps a nervous habit and not intended as a slight.

'Mummy's having a bath,' she ventured by way of breaking the tension. 'It's a beautiful room, you really didn't need to go to such extravagance . . .' She was gabbling. After all they'd shared, it was still a struggle to be herself.

He surprised her by sitting next to her on the sofa, studying his hands folded in his lap, then with a sudden movement he looked directly into her face. She wasn't ready for it, or the tears that swam in his eyes.

'I'm sorry, Alice. I've caused a great deal of pain.'

She wanted to put him at ease but couldn't deny the truth in his words.

'On the drive up I've had time to evaluate how I've conducted my life, the trials I've put your mother through, and now you. It's a difficult path, the one you've joined me on. To love against society, against religious morality. I'm only grateful that you seem to have understood and accepted who you are far more readily than I did. Despite the hurt I've caused your mother, I love her very much. I will never regret marrying her and by extension being a father to you. I'm immensely proud to call you my daughter and yet I've failed to show it. You've opened my eyes to the lie I've been living, to the confusion I caused and the distance it created between us.' He rested his hand on her knee. 'I want to close that gap, Alice.'

She wrapped her fingers around his and let her head drop to his shoulder. His moustache tickled as he kissed her brow. 'Thank you,' she whispered, understanding that his thoughts and hopes were back in Exeter too. Whatever came next, she was grateful he'd given her the gift of knowing she was loved as her true self. For now, that was enough.

CHAPTER 53

With Gillespie's departure, Della felt out of place at the Zodiac. She glanced at her brother, shrunken into his seat, made smaller by his confession. As angry as she was with him, she couldn't help feeling relieved his actions stemmed from a perverse need to please Ma. Even so, the wound he'd inflicted ran deep. It would take her a long time to trust him again.

He lifted his gaze to hers, all the fight drained from his eyes. He looked away, worked the beer mat between his fingers. 'I'm truly sorry, Del.'

She nodded. It would do for now. 'What will you tell William?'

Jack shrugged.

'What will he do when he learns you haven't persuaded me to agree to his courtship?'

He shrugged again. 'Get me sacked?'

She thought so too. William was clever, he could frame Jack for the stealing and take Della down in one swoop. Anthony was the only one who could besmirch William's character, but would it be enough?

'Have you got any mates in the stores who might back you up?'

Jack dropped the beer mat. 'Not really. They're a closed bunch.'

'What about the foreman?'

'He's the one who gave me the job after William's reference. He's probably got something on him too. That's how William operates.'

Della agreed. She sighed, her mind searching for a way out of their predicament. 'I'd better meet Mr Gillespie.'

'What's his deal?' Jack asked as they left the bar together.

'What do you mean?'

'I don't get him. He could have laid me out, left me for pulp.'

'Not everyone settles things with their fists.' The comment made her think of William. 'Watch yourself with William, okay?'

Jack nodded. 'Shall I get Ma to keep dinner for you?'

'What's on the menu?' Della couldn't help smiling.

Jack blanched. 'Nothing dodgy, I swear.' He raised his hands to prove they were clean.

'In that case, count me in. I won't be long.'

'I'll walk you to the pub, can't have you getting into any trouble.'

'Care about me now, do you?'

He stopped and faced her. 'I always have.'

Della wasn't entirely convinced. When they reached the Devonport, she lingered outside, watching her brother disappear down the hill.

Gillespie was already there nursing a pint, a ginger beer waiting for her. He looked relieved when she appeared. It was nice to matter, to know someone cared.

He pulled out a chair for her. Della thanked him for the drink.

'I trust you sorted things out with your brother?'

'I'm sorry for his behaviour.'

Gillespie sipped his pint. 'You take too much on your shoulders.'

257

'This whole thing is ridiculous. I can't fathom why William would go to such great lengths to court me.' She sipped her drink too, providing cover from her blush.

'Many a crime has been fuelled by passion.'

'Not over people like me.'

'You underestimate yourself, Miss Wilde.'

'Give over calling me Miss Wilde and Alice Miss Winters. I can't keep track.'

Gillespie grinned. She hadn't seen it before. No wonder Mr Winters found him worth risking his career for. That smile would have anyone offering up their soul, so rarely was it bestowed. Maybe Gillespie had a point. What was his Christian name, she wondered.

'I'll do my best,' he replied in answer to her question. 'So, what next?'

Della was taken aback, she assumed he'd have all the answers. 'I suppose I need to make things right at work. I can't risk William getting Jack in trouble and me by association. I need that reference for Le Cordon Bleu, or Alice and I will never get to Paris.'

'You mentioned another man who might be able to help?'

'Anthony.'

'If you can find out what William has on him from the war, I could do a little digging of my own.'

'It'll take a batch of custard tarts.'

'Whatever methods you have at your disposal, Miss Wil— I mean Della. Alice is keen for you to see the portrait. If we could clear up matters soon, I should like to drive you to London myself.'

Della's stomach flipped. *London?* She'd never been. Before meeting Alice, she'd only allowed herself to dream of such places, now they were becoming a tantalising reality. She glanced at Gillespie, patiently awaiting her answer. 'I'd like that, Mr Gillespie. I'd like that very much.'

* * *

The following morning, Jack was waiting for her when she arrived downstairs. He'd made toast and offered her a mug of coffee, something of his old self in his demeanour.

'What's brought this on?' She took a sip, the aroma waking up her senses.

Jack shrugged. 'It's a relief, to have it all out in the open. Not to be on opposite sides anymore.'

Della felt it too, but they had further hurdles to clear before they could relax. She munched through her toast, her stomach too nervous to enjoy it, and pulled on her coat. 'We'd better get in.'

'You need a new coat, those elbows are worn down to nothing.'

She glanced at her sleeves and hung it back on the peg. Maybe it was a bit embarrassing.

Jack removed his own jacket and offered it to her. 'Warm enough not to need it today.'

Surprised, she let him help her put it on.

'Alice has a coat for you. Ask her about it.'

'What do you mean?'

Jack looked sheepish. 'She brought it with her that day she came to meet you and I . . .'

'Blackmailed her?'

He grimaced. 'I told her you didn't need charity.'

'Blimey, Jack.'

'I know and I'm sorry.'

'What other awful things did you say?'

'I'm sure she'll give you all the gory details. She must really like you, Del. William too. What do you do to these people?'

Della shook her head — she had no idea.

* * *

The Ambrose kitchen was full of whispers when Della walked in. She'd left Jack in the yard with promises to keep out of William's way.

Mrs Hastings approached. 'Della, love, can I have a word?' She gestured to the pantry. Della followed her inside, regretting

259

the toast and coffee which sloshed around in her anxious stomach. Mrs Hastings looked dismayed. 'There's been a serious allegation.'

Della could see it all, the Ambrose had discovered the missing meat and Jack had been accused. She waited for the inevitable, her mind whirring as to how she might defend him. William worked fast.

'You've been accused of stealing.'

Her jaw dropped. 'Me?'

'You and your brother. Now, I know he's more likely behind it. I said that to Mr Voisin. Della wouldn't do this unless she was forced. Times are hard, but this is serious.'

'I'd never steal.' Her eyes filled with tears.

'Your brother's been seen leaving with things in his satchel, things he wouldn't have access to, but you would.'

'It wasn't me, Mrs Hastings, I swear.'

She squeezed Della's arm, whether because she believed her or out of sympathy, Della wasn't sure.

Mr Voisin's voice carried into the room.

Hastings' gaze met hers. 'You'll be wanted upstairs.'

Della felt sick as she followed her boss back into the kitchen. Leonnard waved from his workbench as if to catch her attention, but Mr Voisin stole her focus, a look of such disappointment on his face she couldn't stand to see it. 'Miss Wilde.' He gestured to the door. She followed him through, her legs like dough.

As they passed the servery, she saw William loading a tray, a smirk on his lips. Anthony was behind him with a furrowed brow. Della held her head high. She wasn't going to accept this without a fight.

'We'll take the stairs,' Voisin said. 'Did Mrs Hastings tell you what this is about?'

'Yes, sir.' Her mouth felt like sandpaper.

'A serious accusation, one I hope is baseless.'

'It is, sir.'

He fixed her with an inquisitive stare. 'Good, you have three floors to tell me everything.'

CHAPTER 54

Alice pressed her forehead against the vast bedroom window, watching the hectic comings and goings along Piccadilly below, while she waited for her parents to return from breakfast.

'Won't you eat something?' her mother had implored. 'It's not every day one gets to breakfast at the Ritz.' This was true, but in her current state of mind such luxuries would be wasted on her.

She was about to turn away when a large black bird flew into view, settling on the window ledge of the building opposite. It was probably a jackdaw or a crow, but Alice indulged the notion it was Della's raven, come from Exeter to wish her well. The bird took flight as a bus trundled past, leaving an acute loneliness in its wake. Whatever the consequences of Della's meeting with Jack, they would have played out by now. What if the bird was a warning, an omen?

Her mother burst into the room, preventing her from further considering that thought.

'Alice, you missed out.' Her face was glowing, and she patted her flat stomach. 'I haven't eaten so much for decades.'

Her father came behind, his countenance a little lighter too. 'It was incredible.'

'I'm glad you enjoyed it. Shall we go?'

Her mother cupped her chin. 'Oh, darling, what are we to do with you?'

'I'm fine, I just want to see the exhibition.'

'Very well. Come on, Robert.' Her mother took her arm.

Ten minutes later the three of them were striding along Piccadilly, the five-minute walk passing in a whisper as they contemplated the Palladian magnificence of the Royal Academy of Arts. Alice couldn't believe her eyes. Despite the early hour, people were already flocking through the elaborate cast-iron gates to the entrance. She felt it then, the missing person by her side.

'I can't go in.'

Her mother looked horrified. 'What? Alice, it's going to be wonderful.'

'It's not that. Della should be here. It won't be the same, seeing it without her. If it wasn't for her, I would never have found the inspiration. For that matter, Mr Gillespie should be here too.'

Her father's pained expression met her gaze.

'It was Gillespie who encouraged me to paint, to see Della, to follow my muse.' She backed away. 'You two carry on. I'm going back to Exeter.' Alice felt it in her bones, it was the right thing to do.

'Alice, please.' Her mother's entreating tone threatened her resolve.

'I need to do this. Please understand.'

Her father reached into his jacket. 'You'll need money for the train and keys to the house. I gave Mrs Drummond the week off.' He pulled out his wallet and beckoned her to the side so he could discreetly hand her the cash.

'Really, Robert, is this a good idea?' Her mother's voice hit a shrill note.

His gaze held Alice's. 'She's right.' He turned to his wife. 'She's braver than me.'

'Thank you.' Alice flung herself into his arms. He returned her embrace without hesitation.

'Bring them back with you,' he whispered into her hair.

Once he'd released her, she hugged her mother, now more bewildered than upset. 'We love you, darling girl.'

Alice gathered her reserves and hailed a taxi.

CHAPTER 55

'Della isn't involved,' Jack said to their accusers. 'She doesn't need to be here, she's innocent. This is all on me.'

Della couldn't meet her brother's eye, but if she had she'd have wanted to convey her thanks. He was ready to sacrifice himself, and maybe that's what he deserved, but it made her blood boil that the real culprit would walk free.

Mr Wilson studied them both. 'That's an honourable sentiment, but we know you got that food from someone who works inside the Ambrose. The foreman, Mr Smythe, said nothing has gone missing from stores and the other men corroborate his assertion.'

'Please, let Della go. I'll tell you everything, I swear, but let her go.'

Della had never seen her brother plead like that before, brought so low. It made her realise Jack did care about her. Even if it meant taking a blow to his pride, his need to put things right was genuine.

'It's also my firm belief Della is innocent,' Mr Voisin added.

She'd kept her answer vague when he'd interrogated her as they walked up the stairs, revealing only that Jack had purchased the items from another member of staff in good faith.

Voisin had asked the inevitable. 'And who is this mysterious member of staff?'

She'd held her tongue. With no hard evidence it was William, how could she accuse him when he knew Gillespie's secret? Alice would never forgive her if she brought her father down.

Voisin's narrowed eyebrows had communicated his exasperation and yet here he was, protesting her innocence.

Mr Wilson nodded. 'Very well, Della, you may return to your duties.'

Della gave her brother one last glance. He met her gaze, his eyes watery with regret, and nodded, ready to accept his fate.

With legs like jelly, she left the office, Mr Voisin in her wake. She could see it all now, William liked to take out insurance policies against people. He visited the Wilde house, witnessed their straitened means. Jack probably talked about how hard things were, how he needed work, and William saw his chance. It was cunning. He had them in a bind.

Once they were alone, Mr Voisin spoke. 'I know you're innocent, I've always known. I suspect your brother is innocent too. Why won't he give him up, the perpetrator?'

'Because the person behind this will cause great pain to another if Jack snitches.'

'I'm sorry this has happened. It saddens me to tell you the board approved their support for your application to Le Cordon Bleu, but with this hanging over you . . .'

Della's eyes welled up. 'I understand, sir.'

'I'm still recommending you, but I can't guarantee Mr Wilson will authorise it.'

'What will happen to Jack?'

'If he won't give up the perpetrator, he'll be fired, without a reference.'

And so, it would start again. Ma in bed, Jack resentful, the Wildes back to square one.

Della nodded. 'Thank you for your support.' She made her way down the stairs, grateful he'd go back to Mr Wilson and plead her case.

In the kitchen, her colleagues did little to hide the fact they'd been talking about her. Della went straight to her bench, wanting to disappear in a cloud of flour. She worked through tea break and her lunch break too, using the time to make a batch of custard tarts for Anthony, which she'd pay for out of her wages. She may well need to use them.

After the rush of afternoon tea, Leonnard came to her side. 'I heard what happened. Why don't you tell them who it is that's stealing?'

Della studied him. 'You know?'

Leonnard checked behind. 'I told you, I see things people don't expect me to.'

'He could hurt people I care about.'

Before Della could elaborate further, Hastings interrupted. 'You look like a ghost, Della Wilde. For my sake, eat something and get some fresh air. We can't have you fainting over the cakes. Leonnard, back to your bench.'

Leonnard threw her a helpless look and sloped away.

Della forced a smile. She still wasn't hungry, but some fresh air after the stifling heat of the ovens would certainly be welcome.

She made her way to the back of the building, no sign of her brother and no one to ask what had happened. Della could only assume he'd been sent on his way. Ma would be devastated. She stepped outside into the warmth of an early summer afternoon, the faint scent of food wafting from the air vents behind the kitchens, and closed her eyes.

She knew he was there from the weight of his breath. 'What do you want, William?'

'Just came to offer my condolences. He was a good mate, your brother. It's a shame things didn't work out differently.'

Della opened her eyes, squinting against the sun casting shadows across the building. 'I know exactly what you've done and I'm going to clear Jack's name, one way or another.'

William smirked. 'The thing you need to realise is, this is all your fault. Before I realised what you were, I'd have done anything to make you happy. Now, I wouldn't offer my hand if you were drowning.'

'Good to know where I stand. What am I?'

'A queer, or at least that Alice has made you think you are.'

She rounded on him, no longer afraid. He could do worse to her yet, but she wouldn't bow to his bullying. 'You really hate me, don't you?'

He sneered and looked away.

'I feel sorry for you.' She was about to say more when Anthony stuck his head out the door.

'What are you two up to?' He took a cigarette from his pocket and offered William one.

'William here was telling me he wouldn't save me if I was drowning.'

William kicked at a stone and walked away.

Anthony lit up. 'Please don't antagonise him. I heard about what happened to Jack.'

'Jack wasn't stealing.'

Anthony frowned. 'Who was?'

Della cocked her head to William's retreating back. 'Framed him, tried to take me down too. Still might.' She looked at Anthony's troubled face. 'If only someone would speak up about what he's really like.'

'I can't, you know that.'

She sighed. 'I made you some custard tarts. I should have told you that first. I'm not very good at blackmail.'

Anthony winced. 'They're good, very good, but I still can't give up a mate.' He leaned in, voice low. 'In the war, he saved my life.'

Della understood, this code between men who'd faced that darkness together. She couldn't compete. 'It's okay, Anthony.' She closed her eyes again, listened as his footsteps retreated, appreciated the sun on her face, hating that William had won. As if custard tarts could save the day. The thought gave her an idea, and she opened her eyes.

The last thing she expected to see was Alice marching across the yard. It was everything she wanted and a total disaster.

CHAPTER 56

Alice registered the exhaustion in Della's eyes, the light of happiness and the wariness of fear. She wanted to hold her tight, let her know she wasn't alone, but the open yard provided nothing but a rapt audience, as if they were standing on a theatre stage.

'I thought you'd gone to London?' Della asked once she'd regained her composure.

Alice clocked the interested parties watching, William and that nice waiter among them. This was a bad idea — she was making things worse.

'I was, but I'm here because I couldn't leave you to face it alone. Come to the Clarence after work. I'm going there now, to see Gillespie.'

'Alright, but I can't be long. Jack's been fired.'

'Fired?' Alice was desperate to know the full story. Her gaze flickered to their audience, the rigid set of William's jaw. 'I'll see you later.'

Della nodded and turned inside.

* * *

Alice hurried along the High Street, ducking into the narrow lane leading to the Cathedral Green. The grime of the train journey lingered on her clothes and in her skin, but she couldn't face the empty shell of the winter house until she knew what was happening. She laughed now at the fantasies she'd carried home with her. The passionate reunion with Della, the hope she might spend the night at the winter house, that they could return to London together.

'He's out driving a client,' the hotel receptionist explained. 'Won't be back for a while.'

'I'll wait.' Alice gestured to the bar.

She ordered an Old Fashioned and perched on a stall, keen to keep one eye on the door. The alcohol slid down her throat too easily. It got to work in her empty stomach, relaxing her tense limbs. She sucked on the cherry, calling it lunch and made idle conversation with the barman, trying to resist the temptation to have another. Before she met Della one was rarely enough. Another drink, a laugh. New friends made and lost in an evening.

Gillespie appeared, saving her from herself as he always did. It was offensive, how handsome he looked in his uniform.

She slid off the stall with an urge to hug him. It had been a long day. The receptionist threw her a look of derision as she followed him to the back of the building. 'You haven't eaten,' he said. Her wan complexion hadn't escaped Gillespie's keen eye. He stopped in the kitchen and asked for a sandwich and a flask of tea.

'You're quite at home here,' Alice said, irritated with this fact as he directed her to a seat at the back of a garage and thrust the sandwich into her lap. What if he didn't return to the winter house?

'Do your parents know where you are?' His tone wasn't rude, but it wasn't friendly.

Alice nodded. 'I couldn't skip off to London and see the exhibition without knowing what was happening. Besides, I

270

want Della there and, well, you — but not if you're going to be grumpy.'

His expression softened. 'It would be an honour.'

Alice waved her hand. 'Enough of that. Tell me what's going on. I went to the Ambrose to see Della. She said Jack's been fired.'

Gillespie's brow furrowed. 'That was fast.' He rubbed his chin and glanced at her untouched food. 'Eat, then I'll talk.'

Alice lifted the sandwich to her lips, now acknowledging her hunger. The Old Fashioned had made her lightheaded. 'Alright, but I can eat and listen. Spill it.'

* * *

When the receptionist brought news of Della's arrival almost an hour later, Alice had been brought up to speed.

'I'll leave you two to get reunited while I try to save my job,' Gillespie said in his wry manner. He closed the door, the crunch of his footsteps receding as he ran after the receptionist, who Alice already knew would be putty in his hands.

She and Della stared at each other across the bonnet of a Rolls Royce, before overcoming their shyness and meeting at the hood, where the Spirit of Ecstasy gleamed with polish. Alice cupped Della's face, bringing her lips tentatively to hers. Weeks apart and the fear of discovery made her self-conscious, but Della's lips yielded and there was no thought of breaking apart.

When Gillespie cleared his throat a judicious ten minutes later, they were leaning against the Rolls Royce, grinning like fools.

'Watch the polish on that one. I haven't finished her yet.' He ran his hand along the wooden surround, a hint of pride in his eye.

'Who owns these cars?' Alice asked.

'The guests. We keep them here in case they want to take a drive. Sometimes I drive them myself.' There was a lightness

271

in his voice. He was enjoying it, playing chauffeur. Alice felt a stab of resentment.

'Where do you sleep?' It was an intimate question. Della looked a little shocked.

'There's a modest flat above the garage. One room with a sink and a small stove. I can keep to myself, although my meals are included.'

'Quite the set-up.' She regretted the childish note in her tone. The winter house wouldn't be the same without him.

He met her gaze with a disarming look. 'Things change, Miss Alice. You'll leave soon, for Paris I hear.'

She felt colour bleed into her cheeks and glanced at Della, who was also battling with embarrassment. Had she told Gillespie their plans?

Della's expression changed. 'My approval came through for Le Cordon Bleu, but the Ambrose might withdraw their support because of Jack.'

Alice squeezed her hand and returned her attention to Gillespie. 'And what about you and my parents? William wants to cause maximum pain. He'll use the story and then you'll be . . .' She didn't want to say it.

Gillespie's poker face wavered for a beat. 'Do we know yet, what William has on Anthony?'

'Saved his life, apparently. I don't know the details, but I've had an idea how I can get them,' Della said, her eyes shining.

'I feared that might be it. The highest debt to hold.' Gillespie shook his head.

'What's your idea?' Alice asked.

Della smiled. 'A visit to a new friend and another box of custard tarts.'

CHAPTER 57

'I'm going to be alone this evening,' Alice said. They were standing in the alleyway behind the Clarence. 'Just me, in the house. No servants, no parents . . .' A smile crept across her lips, a question in her eyes.

Della wanted nothing more, but she had to go home and see for herself the fallout from Jack's news. 'I'd love to, but I've got to check on Sam and the others. If Ma's taken ill . . .'

'I understand. When will you see Anthony's wife?'

This was the problem. She needed to speak to Kath alone, when Anthony wasn't around. His loyalty to William had to be challenged, he was their only hope. 'I don't know yet.'

'I'll be here if you need me.'

Della wished they could kiss goodbye, like other couples.

They parted on the High Street, Alice to the mansions of St Leonards, Della to Fore Street and the ascent into St Thomas. As she walked, she pondered what to do about Kath. The custard tarts she'd made that afternoon were in her satchel.

All appeared normal in the Wilde house. Ma was working her way through a stack of mending. Sam could be heard from next door's yard, playing with the puppy, and Henry was no

273

doubt upstairs with his nose in a book. Ma glanced up. 'You're late, any idea where Jack's got to?'

Della shook her head, unsure what to say next. Jack clearly hadn't returned to share his news. Perhaps he was out searching for another job.

Ma set down her mending, a pair of trousers she was taking up. 'He'll be home soon enough.'

Della felt the strain of the knowledge she couldn't share. She hung her bag and joined her mother. 'Anything I can do for dinner?'

'It's only the usual. I was hoping Jack would bring something.'

There it was again, like a prelude to a sombre song. 'He can't be expected to bring something every day.'

'Aye, I know,' Ma snapped.

Della had no wish to linger in the atmosphere. 'I'll get changed.'

In her room, she sat on the bed, looking over the roof-tops, waiting for Jack and trying to work out what to do about Kath. Sam's laughter as he played with the puppy drifted in through the window. Jack wouldn't be able to fulfil his prom-ise now, but maybe she could. Her plait was still in the drawer along with the money Alice had paid in those early weeks she was her model. She could use the money to get Sam his puppy. *Another mouth to feed?* It all felt so desolate.

Her gaze returned to the window, Jack at last coming in through the gate. Her stomach clenched — William was with him.

Della leaped from the bed, darting down the stairs and into the boys' room below, Henry predictably curled in a heap, reading. 'Shh,' she hissed as he was about to speak. She went to the window — they were at the back door. 'You hav-en't seen me,' she said to her bewildered brother.

Fearing being caught in the entrance hall while she wres-tled with the heavy bolt on the front door, Della slipped into Ma's bedroom, heaved open the sash and peered out. The front porch was a drop of almost four feet. Della perched on the windowsill, her legs dangling above the pitched roof, and closed her eyes, aware of the potential for a bruising fall. Lowering herself, her feet hit something solid. Using the drainpipe, she slid the rest of the way. Her skirt snagged on the leading at the top. She tugged it free with a rip and landed on her feet.

Gathering together the torn material, Della ran up the road. At the busy thoroughfare of Cowick Street, she stopped to assess the damage. The tear ran from just below her knee to her midthigh. There was nothing to be done. She had a long walk ahead with no custard tarts to sweeten the bitter pill when she reached her destination.

* * *

Anthony answered the door, still in his Ambrose uniform, the shirt open at the neck and his braces dangling from his waist.

'Della.' He stepped outside, and his gaze flickered to her ripped skirt. 'What's happened?'

'I need your help. I know you don't want to get involved and I forgot the bloody custard tarts, but this is serious, Anthony.'

'What's William done?'

'Tony, who is it?' Kath hollered from within the house.

'Nothing important.'

Della blanched. *Nothing important?*

He noticed her expression. 'I didn't mean . . . I want to keep Kath out of it.'

His hopes were crushed as Kath pushed her way through the door, noticing Della's dishevelled state. 'What happened to you, love?' She looked at her husband. 'Not important? Have you gone soft?' Kath offered her hand to Della. 'Ignore him, come inside.'

Anthony's eyes pleaded as Della stepped into the house.

In the narrow hall, Kath turned to her husband. 'Dinner's done. Get the kids and you fed, me and Della here are going to have a private chat.'

He was about to protest, but his shoulders deflated. Della wasn't sure she'd argue with Kath either. For a small woman, she had one hell of a commanding voice.

She switched her steely gaze to Della, her eyes softening, and directed her into a small front room. The set-up was much like the Wilde house only nicer, more cared for. There was pride in the way the room was arranged.

Kath beckoned her to sit. 'Where are my manners, do you want a cuppa?'

'Don't worry about me, you've got enough to contend with.' She wanted to get on with it, but with Anthony in the house, it felt like a betrayal.

Kath fixed her with a curious expression as if her mind were busy working on something. 'This is about Anthony being attacked. You know who done it?'

Della nodded. 'Anthony won't accuse him, and I need him to because this person has got my brother in trouble and me by association.'

'I didn't buy it either, someone setting on him like that. I mean, there are nasty types out there, but they usually have a motive. Whoever it was didn't steal a thing, not his wallet, not his grandad's watch.'

Della didn't comment, Kath was putting it together.

'The other thing I found strange is that whatever scum attacked my Anthony, they knew exactly where his bullet wound was — his weakest spot. As far as I know, there's only one other person who has that knowledge. William.'

Della's jaw dropped.

'I'm right.' Kath looked pleased for a second, then her face fell. 'Haven't you heard the story of how William saved Anthony's life? Saved it, then made sure he never forgot. Tony!' Kath hollered. Moments later, he stuck his head round the door. His face bore witness to the trouble he knew was coming his way. 'You need to listen to Della.' Kath stood, offering her husband her chair. When he didn't move, she squeezed his shoulder and looked into his eyes. 'Enough.' She stroked away a lock of his hair from his forehead and kissed him. Della averted her eyes from this intimate display.

When they were alone, Anthony hovered at the mantel, adorned with photographs of generations of his family. Della came to his side. 'I'm sorry, I don't want to cause you trouble, but William's framed Jack for stealing when he didn't. We can't afford to lose his wage and I won't get to go to Le Cordon Bleu when Mr Voisin recommended me. I know William beat you up. You're my only hope.'

'Le Cordon Bleu? Del, that's incredible. You never told me.'

'Didn't want to jinx it, did I?' She offered a humourless laugh.

Anthony studied a photo of him and Kath at their wedding. He was in uniform. They looked so young.

'Must have been hard, going to war, leaving Kath.'

'Worst thing to ever happen. Sometimes I can't believe I made it back when so many didn't.'

'I lost my dad and two brothers.' Della thought about Ma, the wound that couldn't be cauterised running through the Wilde house.

'I'm sorry. I don't think I knew that.'

She shrugged. 'There's not a soul who wasn't touched by it in some way.'

'Where did they fall?'

'Dad at the Somme, Thomas at Passchendaele and George succumbed to the flu on his way home.'

'Blimey, I really was one of the lucky ones. Passchendaele was a hellhole — or a mud hole, more like. I still can't walk in a muddy field without thinking it's going to suck me under. It had a viscous quality, stuck to everything. I saw a horse go down in it, a few feet away. Couldn't stop it. The kindest thing was to put a bullet in its skull.'

Della was glad she'd forgotten the custard tarts, hated herself for her gesture, which now felt trite in the face of what Anthony described. Custard tarts weren't going to fix this.

'What happened, with William? How did he save your life?'

Anthony winced.

Della realised she was moving too fast.

CHAPTER 58

Alice let herself into the winter house, feeling its cavernous proportions like never before. Her tread echoed on her way to the stairs then the trill of the telephone punctured the stillness and snatched her breath.

Minutes later, she coiled the wire through her fingers. 'I'm fine, Mummy, you mustn't worry about me.'

'I hate thinking of you there alone. Daddy and I were so in awe of your painting, we're desperate to see you and celebrate. Can't you come back tomorrow?'

Alice felt a frisson of pride. 'I don't know yet. How's Daddy?' She still couldn't believe he'd paid her fare and agreed to her returning by herself. She owed it to him to get Gillespie to the gallery too.

'He's at Westminster, he has work to do. It's fine, I have people to catch up with, but I'd rather be celebrating my daughter.'

'Soon, I promise.'

'Alice, I don't think you understand how proud we are. You're immensely talented and I wish you hadn't felt the need to hide it from us. I don't know when we gave you the impression you couldn't be yourself, but I'm sorry for it.'

Tears stung her eyes. 'Thank you. Now go and have fun and stop worrying about me.'

She hung up the phone and wiped her cheek, casting around the vast hall. The whole winter house to herself and nobody to share it with.

In the upstairs bathroom she turned on the hot tap, eager to clean away the grime of what had been a long day, but the water quickly cooled. With no idea how to work the boiler, she stepped into a tepid bath and washed in haste. Her mind conjured the previous evening, the luxurious tub at the Ritz, the endless supply of hot water and scented bottles of lotion. A distant knocking from the back of the house pulled her focus. She tugged on her robe, rushed downstairs and opened the door, hoping Della would be on the other side.

Jack stepped forwards, but he wasn't alone.

'We're looking for Della.' His expression betrayed a hint of desperation. Alice tried to shut the door, but William pushed himself against the frame, forcing her back.

'Della's not here.' She hated the tremor in her voice.

William slammed the door, enclosing them in the dark hall. His gaze travelled from her bare feet to the open neck of the flimsy robe and regarded her with glittering eyes. 'We'll search the house.' He shoved Alice forward.

'Go easy,' Jack hissed. It wasn't natural to cast him in the role of friend, but she supposed now he was.

William laughed. 'She's not got that big fairy to protect her today.'

Alice could only assume he was referring to Gillespie. She followed Jack through the kitchen and into the dining room, all too aware of William's hot breath behind.

He cast over her home with a curled lip. As they reached the sitting room, he brought his face close to hers, a mix of pomade, sweat and tobacco. 'Fancy place, shame your father's going to lose it when I report him as a dirty fucking pansy.'

A bead of his spittle landed on her cheek. She rubbed it away, determined not to show her distress despite the cold sweat that pooled at the base of her spine. He walked to the hearth, taking up a family portrait, the three of them posing stiffly outside the winter house on Christmas day. He slid it from the frame and tucked it in his jacket pocket. 'The press will want a photo to go with the story.'

She glanced at Jack. He briefly met her eye — it was all there, his regret, the guilt. She hoped he had a plan, but his expression didn't inspire much faith.

They entered her father's study, a place so private she would never dream of trespassing in his absence. William didn't seem interested in rifling through his things. Alice was grateful for that.

'What do you hope to gain from this?' she asked, attempting to take back some control as they marched her up the stairs.

'People like you and your father need putting in their place.' William poked her shoulder to keep moving. 'You have all this, the big house, the money, and it's still not enough, you have to be perverted too. Men like me fought for a better country. What did we get in return? Mass unemployment, hunger, veterans on the streets, begging for food. People like your father make me sick.'

Alice knew there was some truth in his words, but that didn't mean he could come into her home and frighten her. She remained silent as they checked her father's bedroom and then her mother's. In her own, he opened the wardrobe as if he expected to find Della hiding inside. Next, he rifled through her drawers, his fingers gliding over her underwear as if searching for evidence. 'Look at this, Jack.' He offered up a delicate lace camisole. 'I told you she was a dirty whore.'

'Della's not here, William,' Jack said, a feeble attempt to stop him.

William gesticulated to her with the camisole scrunched in his fist. 'You're not going to take my Della down with your filth. She isn't like you. My Della's pure and innocent.' His eyes glazed over. 'Or at least, she was until she met you.'

Alice squared up to him, her chest rattling with fear. 'Is that your plan? To humiliate my family and rescue Della from my depravity? She doesn't want you, William. She said no.'

Again, his face crowded hers. 'You put her up to it. Della made a grave mistake getting that blind boy to say I was

281

stealing, but I'll forgive her, if she comes with me. I'll even get Jack another job. That's all she wants, is to know her family are secure. I can do that for her. I own Jack, I own the Wildes and I'll own you too.'

'Like you own Anthony?' They spun around, Della was standing at the open door. 'You like to own people, don't you, William?'

She looked magnificent, eyes blazing.

'Blimey, Del,' Jack said under his breath.

William could only stare.

Anthony appeared next. Gillespie brought up the rear.

'This is charming,' William said, dropping the camisole, the wobble in his voice doing his credibility a disservice. He swallowed, the bob of his Adam's apple standing out in his taut neck. 'Can't you see what she's done to you, Della?' He jabbed his finger at Alice. 'She's bewitched you with her fancy ways and her immoral behaviour. You never would have got that stupid blind boy with his dough to bleat to Voisin otherwise. You're blind too, blind to her foul ways. Now you're even trying to turn my best mate against me.'

Della's brow furrowed. 'Leonnard told Voisin it was you?'

'Don't play innocent, I know you put him up to it.'

A smile spread across her lips. 'Well, at least that's one problem dealt with.'

William attempted to leave but Anthony stepped in his path.

'I can't believe you tried to frame Jack and Della, that you beat me up, put Della in danger and now you've stooped to blackmail. What's got into you, mate?'

'You don't understand. Your life is perfect — the wife, the kids, the war wound. You came back and everything fell into place. What about me? You owe me. All I want is what you have. I saved your bloody life. You gave me nothing in return.'

Anthony looked crestfallen. 'You can't force someone to be with you, William. It doesn't work like that.'

'Della wanted me until that bitch got in the way.'

Alice blanched at his mouth, twisted with hatred.

Anthony shook his head. 'So, you got me to the field hospital and I'm always going to be grateful, but that's what we did over there — looked out for each other. I shouldn't be held in your debt. That's the thing I finally realised this evening. Once you've seen something you want, you don't care who you tread on to get it. Even beating me up because you thought I was after Della. Never mind I wouldn't do that. Never mind I'm happily married. This ends now. I haven't reported you for assault, but if you go to the press with the story about Mr Winters, I won't hesitate.'

William smirked. 'You didn't report me straight away and now your wounds are healed and there weren't any witnesses. It's your word against mine.'

Alice's gaze met Della's. The disappointment in her eyes said it all. William had a point.

'Who says there weren't any witnesses?' Jack stepped forward. 'You were in such a temper that night, after you left I went looking for Della.' He glanced at his sister. 'I was worried about her. Funny, until this moment I'd forgotten I saw you beat up Anthony down by the river.'

William sneered. 'You're lying, and you didn't report it either.'

'How could I, when you were threatening to frame me for a crime you've now been proved guilty of? I'm sure the police would understand my reluctance, given the circumstances.'

William clenched his fists, but as his gaze took in the faces around the room, his shoulders deflated. He snatched the family photo he'd stolen from his pocket, tore it in two and threw it to the floor, then stormed out, shoving past Gillespie in the doorway. His footsteps crashed down the polished stairs. The front door slammed. A collective sigh whispered through the house.

CHAPTER 59

'Gillespie's going to drive us to London.' Alice played with Della's curls, coiling them between her fingers.

Della didn't want them to move, the bed was so comfortable. Luxury she'd never known, and Alice's limbs entwined with hers. But she was going to have to inflict a wound, a small one. 'I can't come to London, not today.'

Alice's fingers stilled. She propped herself up. 'But the portrait, I want you there to see it by my side.'

Della turned to face her. 'I will see it, but I can't just leave. There are things I need to put right.' The list was endless, her reference for Le Cordon Bleu for one — would the Ambrose require her to work her notice? Would Jack get his job back? What would become of the Wildes without her income?

'I'll wait.' Alice rested her head against her shoulder.

'Don't. Your parents are expecting you and Mr Gillespie. They need you and your painting. You've knitted them together, given them a reason to feel mutual pride — a connection. Don't dismiss it.'

Alice sighed. 'When did you get so wise?'

She shrugged. 'I think I've spent too much time with Mr Gillespie.'

Alice laughed. 'He's hardly got things figured out either. Look at him, in his chauffeur's uniform cleaning cars. He's still hiding behind something respectable.'

'The world isn't ready for him. He knows that.' She cupped Alice's chin. 'Let him take you to London, see what his protégé achieved.'

'Very well, but I'm going to send him straight back for you.'

Della smiled. 'Alright.'

* * *

An hour later, she was back in the Ambrose kitchen, her hands covered in flour, the buzz of bakers at work. Della knew a summons was coming, she just didn't know when. She tried to focus on the task in hand but saying goodbye to Alice had left her bereft. It was hard to believe there might be a life for the two of them away from all this.

Leonnard hadn't materialised all morning. Anxiety pitched her stomach. Surely William wouldn't exact his revenge?

'What are you making?' Anthony made her jump.

'Not custard tarts.'

He grinned. 'You did promise me some.'

Della set down her bowl of batter and faced him. 'I can't thank you enough, Anthony.'

'You've got nothing to thank me for. I should have acted sooner.'

'How was Kath when you got home?'

He smiled. 'Proud of me, which makes a change.'

'Don't give me that. You know she worships the ground you walk on.'

'The other way round, more like.'

'Have you seen William?'

'No, I doubt I will now. I'll keep my promise, if he puts a foot wrong . . .'

'Thanks.' Della cast around the kitchen again. 'Have you seen Leonnard?'

'I saw him go upstairs with Mr Voisin a while ago. Your brother was with them.'

'Really?' She still couldn't believe Jack had offered himself as a fake witness. It was the icing on the cake.

'I'd better get back. Don't disappear on me, Del. Say goodbye. You're going to take Paris by storm.'

'If I ever get there.'

He folded her in a hug. 'It won't be the same without you.'

Della felt her eyes well up. 'Do you know something I don't?'

'Right on cue.' Anthony stepped away as Mr Voisin appeared at their side.

'Della, might I have a word?'

She threw Anthony a nervous smile and followed the chef from the kitchen.

'You needn't look so anxious,' he said with a twinkle in his eye as they took the stairs. 'Good things are coming your way.' He left her at the office door with a nod.

Mr Wilson was seated behind his desk, a folder with the Le Cordon Bleu trademark adorning the front. 'Miss Wilde, please have a seat.'

Della sat down, a mixture of excitement and fear crashing in her stomach.

'I'm pleased to inform you that you've been accepted on the trainee pastry chef course at Le Cordon Bleu in Paris. The course begins in September. The Ambrose would appreciate it if you would agree to stay on for one month to train up your temporary replacement.'

'Temporary?'

'The Ambrose would like to express our desire to employ you in the future, if that would suit your needs. In short, Miss Wilde, a job will always be here for you.'

Della grinned. 'Thank you, Mr Wilson.'

'Mr Voisin and Mrs Hastings have both sung your praises. Their good opinion is hard won, yet you've managed to retain it.' He passed her the folder. 'Good luck.'

Della stood to leave. 'There is one thing . . . could I take this weekend off, please? I have somewhere I need to be.'

'Check with Mrs Hastings. You're owed holiday, I can't see there being a problem.'

Della left the office as if she were floating on a cloud of flour. By the time she reached the kitchen, the grin was still plastered to her face.

'There she is.' Mrs Hastings beamed. 'Your trainee has been waiting for you.'

Leonnard poked his head out from behind Hastings' generous back.

'Where have you been?' Della asked, eager to grill him for every detail about William.

Leonnard glanced at their boss.

'You two take five minutes outside. I'll be keeping an eye on the clock.'

They didn't waste their time in reaching the yard.

'Leonnard, I owe you a huge thank you,' Della said before he could utter a word.

'I wasn't going to let an innocent man take the fall when I'd seen what William was up to with my own little eye.' He grinned at his joke.

Della smiled. 'You've got that eye on my job too.'

He looked abashed. 'You're a tough act to follow.'

'Don't you forget it.'

'Did you hear, your brother's starting back tomorrow? He seems like a decent bloke.'

Jack had been once, and he would be again. The relief for the Wildes was palpable. Was she really free to go?

CHAPTER 60

Alice bit her lip, waiting for Gillespie's reaction. He'd been standing before the portrait of Della for about ten minutes. Of course, he'd seen it in the tight confines of the winter house attic, but not here in a gallery where it could breathe. Della looked out from a central wall over the entire room, but the talent around her was remarkable. Alice couldn't help feeling lost in a sea of better artists. Her anxiety scaled the vaulted glass ceiling.

Still, Gillespie remained silent. He was torturing her — why, she wasn't sure.

He took a step back and folded his arms.

'For God's sake, say something.' She hated how childish she sounded.

His gaze flickered in her direction then returned to the portrait.

'I only did all this because of you. You do realise that? I would never have dared to get this far, so the least you can do—'

'I'm speechless.'

Alice held her tongue. 'But you just spoke.'

'Only to stop you wittering on. People are staring.'

She cast around the room. It was true, she was drawing attention to herself. How did he know, when his gaze hadn't left the portrait? She studied her nails, adjusted the strap on her handbag, ran her fingers through her hair. Anything to keep her tongue in check.

The click of heels echoed through the gallery. Alice turned to see her parents weaving their way towards them. Her mother, arms outstretched. 'Why didn't you come to the hotel?' She embraced Alice in a cloud of perfume.

'Gillespie wanted to see the portrait, the one he hasn't commented on since.'

To her surprise, her father chuckled and stood next to his man. 'It's rather magnificent.'

Gillespie nodded. 'She has your skill.'

Alice frowned as her father shooshed him with a sharp look.

'What do you mean?'

Gillespie finally paid them attention. 'He used to sketch us in the trenches to while away the time. He's very good.'

'They're mere cartoons compared to this.'

'I didn't say you were as talented as your daughter, only that her skills come from you.'

Alice's jaw dropped. She glanced at her mother. 'Did you know?'

'Oh yes, he used to sketch me before the war, until he found a new muse.' She winked at Gillespie, whose face held the suggestion of a blush. 'Where shall we go for supper?'

'Hang on. I'm not moving an inch until Mr Gillespie tells me what he thinks of the portrait.' Alice stamped her foot for emphasis.

Gillespie fixed her with his inscrutable expression. 'It's without a doubt the prize jewel in the Royal Academy's exhibition crown. None can come close to capturing the essence of its subject. Your painting, Miss Alice, is beyond reproach. Will that suffice?'

A tear crested her lashes. 'Thank you, Mr Gillespie.'

* * *

The four of them sat down to dinner at the Savoy. It was the most relaxed Alice had ever seen either of her parents and Gillespie was quite transformed, cracking jokes and paying the staff compliments that made them blush. Only a trained eye would notice the sparkle that existed between him and her father. She regarded her mother for signs of hurt but she appeared as genial as the others.

'Your father and I have been discussing some changes to our lives in the coming months,' her mother said, once they'd ordered dessert.

Alice took a sip of her champagne, curious about what was coming next.

'Since you'll be in Paris with Della, we thought we'd close up the house and put it to a better use. It could provide a home for local men who fought in the war but can't earn a living due to their injuries.'

Her father cleared his throat and Alice readied herself for one of his speeches.

'I got into politics with the naive hope of making a difference. Lloyd George promised a country fit for heroes to live in. I wanted to be part of that.' He gave a bitter laugh. 'Difficult times are coming. The government's meagre efforts to address the hardships of the men I stood alongside, who sacrificed everything for this country, are beyond the pale. Now more than ever, I need to take up their plight.'

Surprised and impressed, Alice returned her attention to her mother.

'But where will you both live?'

'Daddy's going to take a flat in London, close to Westminster, and I've been offered a cottage by the sister of a friend while she goes travelling. It will provide a base for when your father needs to be in Exeter.'

'Which friend?'

'The one who teaches me French. Just think, I might be fluent when I visit you in Paris.'

Puzzled, Alice looked at Gillespie. 'And what will you be doing? Cleaning cars at the Royal Clarence?'

'I shall need a valet.' Her father and Gillespie stared at one another for a moment too long.

'Right.' Alice let her gaze drop to the starched tablecloth, confused by her tears when her parents' philanthropy was everything she could have hoped for.

'Oh, Alice.' Her mother reached across the table for her hand. 'You'll always have a home with us, but we can't carry on as we have been. It's you that started all this. We'd been sleeping for years. You woke us up.'

Her father rested his hand on top of her mother's, so they made a stack. 'It's true, darling girl.'

She wiped her eyes, studying the bloom of happiness in all their faces, realising how childish she was being expecting them to stay the same while she moved on. 'I'm sorry, I think your idea for the house is wonderful. It was a shock, that's all.'

* * *

An hour later, they walked tipsily to the hotel. Gillespie hung back to tie his shoelace. Alice hung back too. 'Are you really going to be Daddy's valet? Will that be enough for you?'

He fixed her with his benign smile. 'It's the best we can hope for until the world catches up.'

Alice nodded. He was right, of course.

'I thought I might take a drive this evening.'

'Isn't it a bit late?'

'If I leave directly, I believe I can have Della back here by tomorrow lunchtime.'

She grinned but her smile slowly faded. 'What if she can't come?' Gillespie was persuasive, but if Della had family commitments . . .

'Have faith, Miss Alice. You'll find Paris a more tolerant place, but you'll still need to be discreet.'

'I know.'

'The portrait will sell. It should make you a tidy sum.'

'I'm not sure I want to part with it.'

'You won't always feel that way about your art. I believe your next portrait will make your fortune.'

Alice frowned. 'Next portrait?'

'The one that sits on your easel. A handsome subject.'

She laughed. 'When did you see it?'

'When I visited my old room after the confrontation with William.'

'I rather thought Daddy might like it.'

'If he does, make sure he pays you a fair price.'

Alice laughed again and linked her arm through his.

* * *

'Are you awake?' her mother whispered from the pillow beside her.

Alice rolled onto her side. 'I am.'

'Are you thinking about Della?'

She blushed, grateful for the dark room. 'I was.'

Her mother's hand found hers under the covers.

'Who teaches you French, Mummy?'

'I rather feared you were going to ask that. I can't wait for you to meet him again.'

Alice propped herself up and switched on the bedside lamp. 'Again?'

Her mother squinted before propping herself up too. 'You met him at the Ambrose.'

She searched her mind and came up blank.

'He speaks very highly of Della.'

She gasped. 'Della's boss?'

Her mother laughed. 'Florian Voisin.'

'How long?'

'It's early days.'

'Does Daddy know?'

'He does. Be happy for me, darling, and for Daddy and Edward too. We're all exactly where we should be.'

Alice lay back and smiled. So that was his name. Edward Gillespie.

CHAPTER 61

The gate creaked on tired hinges as Della entered the yard, the evening sun casting her long shadow. Through the kitchen window she could see Ma scrubbing potatoes at the sink, her face serene. Behind, Jack and Henry were at the table, one with a cigarette and the paper, the other with a book and a distant smile. On the other side of the fence, Sam chatted to the puppy who wouldn't be a puppy for much longer. She closed her eyes, taking a moment to drink it all in, this feeling they'd be okay without her.

'There she is.' Ma offered a smile. 'Salad for dinner. I got some lovely early potatoes at the market.'

Della hung her bag and reached for her apron. 'What can I do?'

'Actually, Del, have you got a minute?' Jack stubbed out his cigarette and stood.

She followed him into the yard and leaned against the wall, the sun warming her face. Jack appeared nervous, raking his fingers through his hair as if searching for the correct way to begin.

'I heard you got your job back?' She decided to break the ice.

Jack nodded. 'I wanted to say sorry, properly. While I'm not sure I understand your thing with Alice, I should never have treated you like a . . .'

'Commodity?' She echoed Gillespie's words.

'Yeah, that. And I'm sorry I've been so jealous of your job. I should have appreciated you more. I haven't been a very good brother.' He studied the rough concrete beneath their feet.

'You haven't, but I appreciate the apology and what you did, pretending you saw William beat up Anthony.'

He met her gaze. 'Thanks.'

'Did you really go out looking for me that night?'

'Yeah, I felt awful for bringing William to the house, but he didn't give me any choice. After he left, I couldn't stop worrying about what he was going to do. By the time I got home you were back. I can't tell you how relieved I was.'

She squeezed his arm. If only she'd known.

'I got my place at Le Cordon Bleu.'

Jack's eyes widened. 'You're going to Paris?'

Della nodded, struggling to contain her smile. She still couldn't believe it.

'Blimey. There's no competing with you. I may as well quit trying.' He smiled too.

A bark from next door reminded Della about her idea. 'I've still got my plait of hair from when Alice cut it. Do you reckon we could sell it and get Sam a puppy?'

'I can organise that, I know a bloke.'

She rolled her eyes — this was the old Jack. 'You always know a bloke.'

He gave her a sheepish grin. 'I'll get onto it straight away.'

* * *

After an evening of celebration in the Wilde household, Della woke to the hum of a car engine idling in the street outside before it chugged to silence. More accustomed to her sleep being disturbed by freight trains rattling through on their way to Exeter St David's station, she tugged her curtain to one side and peered out. To her shock, a car was parked immediately in front of the Wildes' terrace, its bonnet gleaming in the early morning sun. Beside it stood Mr Gillespie.

Jack burst into her room. 'Have you seen?'

Della pulled on her dressing gown. She ran past Jack, clattered down two flights of stairs and wrestled open the rusty bolt on the rarely used front door. Neighbours had been drawn from their homes by the spectacle.

'Miss Wilde.' Gillespie as formal as ever. 'If you'll permit me, I should like to drive you to London to see your portrait at the Royal Academy.'

Della pulled the door to behind her. She hadn't quite got as far as telling Ma about the portrait, Alice or her plans for the future, but here was her opportunity to go. 'I've got to get dressed.' She stated the obvious.

Gillespie nodded. 'Take as long as you need. We can breakfast on the way.'

'You'd better come in.' Della gestured for him to follow. Inside, her entire family were gathered in the narrow hall.

'What's going on?' Ma elbowed her way to the front then shrieked at the sight of Gillespie and tried to tug her dressing gown tighter over her nightie.

'You go upstairs and get ready. I'll fill everyone in,' Jack said from the back.

'Can I see the car?' Sam asked.

'Of course.' Gillespie looked relieved to have a purpose that would extract him from the house.

Without further explanation, Della raced up the stairs.

She returned ten minutes later wearing one of her best summer dresses, another folded away in her satchel which would have to serve as an overnight bag.

In the kitchen her family were gathered around a pot of tea, no sign of Mr Gillespie.

'Della Wilde.' Her mother stood and embraced her. 'I can't believe what I've been hearing. Why didn't you tell me you're in a painting that's hanging in London and that you're off to Paris soon?'

She drank in this rare moment of affection between them. 'I didn't know if any of it would come true.'

Ma released her, holding her by the shoulders. Tears pooled in her eyes. 'If your father could see you now. After all you've done for this family, I've never been prouder.'

Her own eyes grew wet. To hear those words from Ma was more than she'd ever hoped for. Jack caught her eye and winked.

'Watch yourself with that bloke. Jack says he's alright, but he's devilishly handsome. I dunno if I should be letting you go off to London with him.'

Della laughed — she wasn't about to set Ma straight.

All the Wildes assembled in the street to wave her off. Gillespie held open the car door and Della climbed in. She'd never ridden in a car before, but in that moment she felt like royalty. Judging from the adoring looks of her neighbours, they thought so too.

As Gillespie pulled away, she looked back at her imperfect family, knowing nothing would be the same again.

* * *

Six hours later, Della stood before the grand facade of the Palladian building in trembling awe. She'd determined the Ambrose could outshine the best London had to offer, but it seemed she was wrong. This incredible place was a true home for art. That a portrait of her hung within its walls was too much to comprehend.

Gillespie had left her in the courtyard, taking her satchel to the hotel and telling her Alice would be waiting inside.

Della made her way through the arched entrance and paused before a sweeping staircase framed by columns. People were everywhere, milling about in their fashionable clothes. Ladies with beautiful bias-cut dresses and matching accessories, men in tailored suits and dapper shoes. She fell into their flow and allowed them to propel her along into the first gallery, overwhelmed by the sheer volume of art in this cavernous space. Polished parquet beneath her feet, expansive walls filled to the brim with colour, panelling, frescoed ceilings with glass like a greenhouse. And light. Such exquisite light. Room opened into room through archways, the next as magnificent as the previous. Her head spun with the detail. How would she find herself in all of this and could she really be here?

'Quite remarkable, isn't it?' A gentleman in a fawn-coloured three-piece and crisp white shirt stood at her side. He was tall, taller than Alice, with sharp blue eyes behind a pair of round spectacles. She'd guess he was about her age.

'It's wonderful,' she replied, breaking his intense gaze to look at the paintings again.

He studied her openly, without embarrassment. 'I feel like I've seen you before.'

Della tried not to roll her eyes, wasn't that the oldest line in the book? She was about to reply when he gestured to the room beyond.

'It's you, the portrait in the next gallery, I'm certain. Tell me I'm right? If it's not you then someone has stolen your likeness.'

Her stomach flipped. 'Will you show me?'

'But of course.' They weaved through crowds until he came to a halt before a canvas, framed in black. It was too busy to get close, but she recognised the top of the head. 'Excuse me, excuse me, coming through.' He ushered people out of the way until a path cleared.

Della gasped at the sight as if she were seeing it for the first time. Stripped of the intimacy of the attic setting, the woman in the portrait commanded the room. Her hair was thick, the loose swirls of black curls tinted silver. Her eyes were dark, but with puddles of green light. Her lips were full, her cheeks exposed. There was something powerful, untouchable in her gaze. It was her, but also not her. She understood then, how everything they'd been through and the strength of their feelings had brought them to this moment. What a waste those weeks when Jack and William kept them apart had been. And yet, they'd prevailed. 'I need to find her.' She uttered the words out loud. 'I need to find Alice.'

'I'm here.' That voice. Della looked up into Alice's face and the crowds fell away.

THE END

ACKNOWLEDGEMENTS

Thank you to my brilliant agent Saskia Leach, whose advice, enthusiasm and belief in this novel helped shape the story. Thanks to Joffe Books and the wonderful Choc Lit team — Jasmine Callaghan, Laurel Sills, Matthew Grundy Haigh and Kate Ballard.

I'm extremely fortunate to have a lovely bunch of talented writing friends to whom I'm grateful for their insightful feedback and support: Lottie McKnight and members of the Half-baked Manuscript Club — Nick Paul, Eliza Aiken, Inge Van de Plas, Mark Dudley, Hugh Ryan and Steph Pomfrett.

In the research for this novel, my thanks to The Exeter Memories website and Facebook community, where a post about Deller's Café provided the spark of inspiration for this story.

Thanks to my readers and everyone who has supported my writing journey so far whether through purchasing my books, leaving ratings and reviews or cheerleading on social media.

A huge thank you to my family and in particular my husband Darren and son John for understanding my need to write and giving me the time and space to do so. My sister Hilary for encouragement and my cat Ditsy — still the best writing companion. Finally, special thanks to my dad, whose love and dedication in life remains an inspiration.

AUTHOR'S NOTE

In the writing of this novel, I have been inspired by or used real locations, which I have embellished to suit the story. The Ambrose is loosely based on Deller's Café and in a nod to that wonderful institution sadly destroyed in the Exeter Blitz of 1942, I named my main character Della. The Royal Clarence Hotel, which was devastated by fire in 2016, has long been a much-loved Exeter landmark. While I used the hotel as a location, I changed certain aspects. In reality there wouldn't have been a garage or back yard. Cars were more likely parked at the front of the building, but this was too open for the purposes of the story. The Royal Clarence did have a cocktail bar called the Zodiac, which opened in 1939. The name lent itself so well to the 1920s, I couldn't resist using it. I hope in some small way this story brings those wonderful lost buildings to life once more.

THE CHOC LIT STORY

Established in 2009, Choc Lit is an independent, award-winning publisher dedicated to creating a delicious selection of quality women's fiction.

We have won 18 awards, including Publisher of the Year and the Romantic Novel of the Year, and have been shortlisted for countless others. In 2023, we were shortlisted for Publisher of the Year by the Romantic Novelists' Association.

All our novels are selected by genuine readers. We are proud to publish talented first-time authors, as well as established writers whose books we love introducing to a new generation of readers.

In 2023, we became a Joffe Books company. Best known for publishing a wide range of commercial fiction, Joffe Books has its roots in women's fiction. Today it is one of the largest independent publishers in the UK.

We love to hear from you, so please email us about absolutely anything bookish at choc-lit@joffebooks.com.

If you want to receive free books every Friday and hear about all our new releases, join our mailing list here: www.joffebooks.com/freebooks.